brainy-BOOM!

By

Wally Duff

A Hamlin Park Irregulars Novel: Book 4

www.HamlinParkIrregulars.com

www.wallyduff.com

For permission requests, write to the publisher at:

Attention: Wallace Duff

c/o K, M & N Publishers, Inc.

Hamlin Park Irregulars, A Nebraska Limited Liability Co.

Suite 100, 12829 West Dodge Road

Omaha, NE 68154

Visit the author's website: www.HamlinParkIrregulars.com, www.wallyduff.com

First Edition

ISBN-13: 978-1-7324652-2-0

To Alan and Marcia: you were great friends to David and Rick and Mindy and me and many, many others. We all miss you.

Sundown is often the worst time of day for people with dementia. They can become restless and difficult.

~ Laurie Graham

Builders: their promises are as worthless as that meaningless witticism "date of completion."

~ Author Unknown

Part 1

The Loop

Chicago, Illinois

7:00 p.m.

Monday, March 4

1

"Спасибо за то, что встречаться со мной," I said, practicing the Russian sentence I'd memorized that morning.

I stood in front of the closed double doors of a top-floor corner office located in a high-rise building in the middle of the Chicago Loop business district. The Russian immigrant and ultra-wealthy money manager, Alexis Zhukov, whom I was scheduled to interview, had a reputation for hating the press. My strategy was to soften him up by thanking him in his native language for seeing me.

It was seven p.m., exactly when my appointment with him was to begin. The instructions from his PR representative were to be prompt and not to expect anyone other than Zhukov to be there.

I knocked on the double doors.

No answer.

I knocked again.

Still nothing.

Huh?

I turned the doorknob. It wasn't locked. I left the door open and walked into the reception area. It was bigger than a triple-car garage. No one was behind the modern L-shaped desk to my right. The computer sitting on the surface was turned off, but the desk lamp was on, providing enough light that I could check out the rest of the room.

Two black leather chairs and a black leather couch were on the opposite wall from the desk. The painting on the wall above the couch appeared to be an original Sarah Morris. The only noise came from the hum of the desk lamp. I sniffed and thought I detected the faint aroma of donuts.

I walked forward to another set of double doors and knocked. "Mr. Zhukov?" I asked, to the door.

There was no response. I did have an appointment, so I tried the doorknob. It wasn't locked.

What should a reporter chasing a story do?

Go in.

I gave the door on the right a gentle push. It swung open, and I stepped inside.

2

"Hello," I said.

No response.

I stood in the doorway and scanned the room. Zhukov's office was three times larger than his reception area. The illumination in the room came from Chicago's nighttime city lights filtering through the floor-to-ceiling windows on the wall in front of me and to my right.

There was an unlit stone fireplace in the middle of the wall to my left. It was a foot taller than my five eight and was at least that wide. Facing it was a long black leather couch flanked by end tables. There was a closed door to the left of the fireplace and one to the right, also closed. Once again, I thought I smelled donuts.

In front of the windows along the far wall was a conference table with several chairs. Occupying the right side of the room was a large, modern, glass and metal desk. There was a lamp on the desk but it wasn't on. A sleek chrome credenza was positioned at right angles to it. Three large computer screens sat on the credenza.

The only noise in the room came from the hum of the computer hard drives. There were two black leather chairs in front of the desk and a taller one behind it. That chair was turned toward the windows.

I squinted at it and thought I saw the top of a man's head.

Zhukov?

I cleared my throat. "*Спасибо за то, что встречаться со мной,*" I said, with greater gusto.

The man didn't turn around.

Dang it.

Maybe I wasn't saying the phrase with the proper accent. Maybe I wasn't even saying, "Thank you for meeting with me." That was the trouble with using our Russian dry cleaner as my translator. I wasn't all that sure that he even understood what I needed when I asked him for his help this morning to teach me one sentence of his native language.

Or maybe the man wasn't Zhukov.

"*Спасибо за то, что встречаться со мной,*" I said, one more time.

The man remained facing the windows. Maybe he'd been in the United States too long and no longer understood Russian.

My husband had confirmed that Zhukov had a frosty relationship with the American press, and now I appeared to be a victim of it.

I wanted to say "I think you're a pompous asshole" in Russian, but I didn't know how.

Remain positive.

I wasn't going to leave without talking to him.

As I walked into the room, my brand new, black Rolando Hidden-Platform Christian Louboutin four-inch pumps sank into the plush white wool carpet, making it difficult to move gracefully without falling on my face. Slowly stepping forward, I detected a second odor in the room. It was familiar, but I was too fixated on this interview to search the olfactory part of my brain to figure out what it was.

I stopped at the front of his desk and waited for him to turn around.

He didn't.

"Mr. Zhukov, I'm Tina Thomas. I'm with the *Chicago Tribune,* and I'm here for our scheduled interview."

I didn't exactly yell "scheduled interview," but I did increase the volume of my voice as I said it.

He didn't respond.

Before I was fired by my *Washington Post* bosses a few years ago, I was a world-class investigative reporter and didn't achieve that position by letting dickheads like this stiff me on a story. I was determined to write it, and he was going to talk to me.

I moved around the edge of his desk. "I have an appointment with you, and I am *not* leaving without an interview."

Placing my hand firmly on the top edge of his chair, I pulled. The chair slowly rotated toward me. I was face-to-face with Alexis Zhukov. He stared at me.

There was a bullet hole between his open eyes.

3

Ohmygod! Ohmygod! Ohmygod!

If the killer was still in here, I was in deep doo-doo.

Run!

My all-out sprint for the door lasted three steps before I tripped and did a face plant on the thick carpet. My four-inch high heels weren't made for running.

Leaping up, I kicked off my shoes and fled into the reception area. Going full speed, I flew out the open front door of the office into the hallway and made a hard right turn toward the exit stairs.

Or I tried to.

Whoopsie!

I wore black panty hose, making it difficult to get traction on the highly polished marble floor. To compensate, I moved my legs faster, causing me to slip and flop on my back.

My forward momentum became rotational. I whirled around three times like I was an upside down turtle before I crashed into the opposite wall and ricocheted back across the floor into the first wall.

The impact knocked the wind out of me.

Go, go, go!

I rolled onto my stomach and used my hands to help me stand up and slip and slide my way to the exit door at the far end of the hallway.

It was my friend Molly Miller's fault that I was in this mess. Earlier that afternoon, while we shopped at Neiman Marcus, she convinced me that I needed to wear the black panty hose, something I rarely do. She felt they went well with my new, classic, black Ralph Lauren power suit, which she helped me pick out. Ditto the shoes.

And worse, thanks to Molly, I didn't have my Glock 19 handgun. The tiny black Prada purse she'd loaned me was high fashion but was too small to carry anything more than my lipstick, van keys, and cell phone.

I ran down six flights of exit stairs before I stopped to catch my breath. Leaning over, I put my hands on my knees and breathed air in through my nose and out through my mouth.

The stairwell smelled dank and musty, which triggered my olfactory memory. The other odor in Zhukov's office came from the acrid stench of gunpowder. It was intense, indicating a gun had recently been fired close to his desk.

Yikes!

The shooter might be after me!

Run!

I sprinted down another flight. The cement stairs shredded the bottoms of my panty hose. I continued going down; running in bare feet gave me better traction to sprint down five more flights and outside to my van.

The gun was in my backpack, which sat on the passenger seat of my mommy van, a blue Honda Odyssey.

Get it!

My hands shook as I hit the key fob and opened the door. I slammed it shut and locked the doors. I dug out my Glock and chambered a round. I took in a deep breath. For the first time since I found Zhukov's body, I felt safe enough to reassess the situation.

How in the hell did I get into this?

Two nights before
Our Family Room
West Lakeview, Chicago, Illinois
8:00 p.m.
Saturday, March 2

4

"Are you ready to work on a story?" my husband, Carter Thomas, asked me. He is the deputy managing editor for local news at the *Chicago Tribune*.

Am I ever!

I didn't want to appear to be too excited, but I needed to write an article again, even if it was a short one. For the past sixteen months, other than daily journaling, I haven't written a simple declarative sentence that might be considered intellectually stimulating to a reader of any newspaper, even a free local publication. And I really missed the challenge of investigating stories.

But I had a reason, and I had just finished breastfeeding her when he posed the question. Seven months ago, Macy Jo Thomas was born at the MidAmerica Hospital here in Chicago. She was kind of planned, like most babies, but once I found out I was pregnant, I put a hold on all my writing activities.

When I begin chasing a story, I go all out, and sometimes that's risky, even dangerous. I've always been a sucker for a compelling tale, but I'm also an adrenaline junky.

I didn't fully acknowledge the extent of this character flaw until, after over seven years of a forced reporting layoff after being fired, I began going after stories again.

I figured it out while working on my most recent feature when, to save our lives, I shot off a couple fingers of a man who was going to shoot me and my friend Linda Misle. After the gunfire stopped, I realized how much I enjoyed the intoxicating rush of pulling the trigger and hitting my target — as long as I hadn't killed him.

Now that I think about it, I shot him in both hands, so there may be more finger parts involved; but the point is, when the gun smoke cleared, my heart wasn't even beating fast. That episode was part of the last article I had worked on with Linda and my two other close friends Cassandra (Cas) Johnson and Molly Miller. Gunfire was a prominent part of that adventure as it has been in other stories we've worked on together.

It was Molly who suggested I cut back on working on feature stories until Macy was born, and I did. She has four boys, each one year apart, so she considers herself an expert on all things having to do with birth, even though Cas was a labor and delivery nurse and clearly knows the science of pregnancy.

Even if I had wanted to pursue a story, I wouldn't have had the time or energy because I was way too busy birthing and raising Macy. Added to that, I struggled to enroll our now almost four-year-old daughter, Kerry, in preschool.

Who knew? Face-to-face interviews, an essay, and background checks for the mother and father. For God's sake, it's only preschool, but here in Chicago, that's the way it is.

And cost? Don't even bring it up. I didn't want to admit it to Carter, but any income I made from doing a feature for the *Chicago Tribune*, his employer, would go for Kerry's tuition.

For preschool.

Unbelievable.

"Honey, I would love to work on a piece again," I said. "Tell me about it."

5

Carter and I sat in the family room of our home, which is located in an upscale neighborhood in the West Lakeview area of Chicago. A satisfied Macy snoozed in my arms. Though she's still breastfeeding, we're introducing baby food, which will allow me a tiny bit of freedom to do a story for Carter and get a little much-needed sleep.

"I would like you to interview Alexis Zhukov," Carter said.

Whoa.

"The multimillionaire money manager?" I asked.

"Yes."

"I've read he hates talking to the press."

"When did that ever stop you?"

"Never, but why do a feature about him if he doesn't want to be interviewed?"

"All we know to date is that he is a Russian immigrant who made his money primarily by investing funds from other Russian immigrants to the U.S. However, a strong rumor has surfaced that his clients aren't happy with his recent returns for them."

"Thus the need for an interview so Zhukov can show his best side to me, figuring I'll write a positive article."

"Indeed. He hired a public relations firm here in Chicago to present a favorable image to the business world."

"And to his unhappy clients."

"Correct. The PR firm wants us to send a reporter for an interview, with the hope that he can begin rehabilitating his image before any negative press comes out."

"Which it will, when his bad investment returns become public."

"Again, correct. With the interview coming at their request, he will be fully accessible, and I want to take advantage of the rare opportunity for you to question the man himself."

I used to call pieces like this "executive blowjobs" and said I would never write one, but I was desperate to work on any story. However, Carter knew I would dig deeper to uncover the true facts, regardless, even if the PR firm didn't like them.

"Why me? You have reporters who would kill to do this."

"Back when we both worked for the *Post*, you wrote that three-part feature on the Russian Mafia's inroads into legitimate businesses in the United States. With that background, you are the most qualified reporter I have to do a piece on him."

Yes! I love being an investigative journalist. It's who I am.

"What's my timeline?" I asked.

"You have an appointment to interview him at his office on Monday at seven p.m. It will be one-on-one, with no pictures or recordings. He will talk to you for exactly thirty-two minutes."

"Guess I can live with that."

"You have no choice." He paused. "And, since it's a short interview, it will not be dangerous."

His comment was in reference to several features I've worked on, starting with me being fired over seven years ago as an investigative journalist for the *Post*. Then, I was blown up and almost killed chasing a story I was ordered by the FBI not to pursue. Understandably, my hubby doesn't want me to work on any risky stories. But if he's good with this, so am I.

"After I put Macy down, I'll check out Zhukov online."

And call my computer expert, Linda, for help.

6

An hour later, I was in our lower-level computer room. Our home is three floors, all above the ground, so I have two full-sized windows to gaze out of, but I'm usually busy focusing on the computer screen and rarely find a reason to open the blinds.

Since I didn't have much time, I needed to get rolling as fast as I could, and Linda was the solution. She finished her undergraduate studies at the University of Chicago with a degree in computer science and accounting. She went on to graduate from their law school and worked as an attorney until she began having babies. She is my best friend in Chicago and knows how to garner background information on people faster than anyone I know.

We met at our neighborhood's Hamlin Park, and that encounter with her, Cas, and Molly led me back to reporting after a frustrating four-year hiatus. Initially, I wrote a monthly fluff column in our free neighborhood newspaper, the *Lakeview Times*.

Why did I stoop to doing that? Simple. No one else in the industry would hire me, and it was the only writing job I could find. A year later, somewhat by accident, I began to write actual investigative stories.

Initially, my three friends began by helping me with small assignments, and then they dove in full-force. We had fun, and the experiences, especially the dangerous ones, brought us closer together as friends. One of the central characters in the first story christened the four of us the Hamlin Park Irregulars. I wouldn't consider doing another article without them.

Now that I was dusting off my investigative chops once again, I texted Linda to call me if she had time. My cell phone rang ten seconds later.

"That didn't take long," I said.

"Are you ever going to start writing again?" Linda asked. "I'm praying you have a story to work on, because there are only so many charity functions I can attend before I lose my mind."

Linda has two kids: Sandra, almost four, and Jason, sixteen months. You might think all of her time would be consumed with taking care of them, but she's a member of the lucky sperm club and her parents have banks full of money which they lavish on her. She has a full-time nanny who lives in their guest house.

"Funny you should ask," I said. "Ever hear of Alexis Zhukov?"

"I have, actually," she said. "A couple of years ago, he gave a PowerPoint presentation on his investment concepts at my parent's country club. He said it was the first time he'd solicited anyone to invest with him."

"The first time? How the heck did he get his clients before that?"

"Word of mouth from the Russian Jewish community."

"Did you put any money in with him?"

"No, and my parents didn't either, but several of the club's members did."

"Any impressions?"

"He's brilliant, assertive, and suffers fools poorly. He has bright red hair, pale skin, and is disgustingly obese." She paused. "But he does wear expensive clothes and jewelry."

Linda is also into designer everything, so she knows what she's talking about.

"How expensive?"

"He wore a bespoke Kiton slate blue windowpane suit and a pair of Louis Vuitton Manhattan Richelieu wingtips. There was a gold Rolex President on his left wrist and a large, pink diamond on his right little finger." She paused. "Considering how heavy he is, the suit fit beautifully."

Like I said, she's into expensive fashion.

She paused. "Hold on a second."

I heard clicking on her computer's keyboard. It didn't take long.

"I just sent you his bio."

My computer screen lit up.

"It was emailed to us before the meeting at my parents' country club, and I saved it," she continued. "As you can see, Zhukov is seventy-four, has a wife named Ellen, and two sons, Daniel and Ariel. They're both married and have children of their own."

"The man I'm going to interview is a grandfather?"

"He is, and in spite of his physical size, he made it clear he's into fashion."

"Meaning?"

"Dust off your power suit and high heels." She paused again. "Now that I think about it, maybe you should have Molly help you update your whole look."

"What!?"

"My impression from Zhukov's presentation is that he enjoys talking to young, fit females who are properly dressed."

"So noted."

"And, Tina?"

"Yes."

"One other thing. While I do a complete background on Zhukov, you also need to do something about your hair."

I hated to admit that she was right, but she was.

7

On Sunday, Linda emailed to me detailed background information on Zhukov. Monday morning, I made the call she'd suggested. Two hours later I was in the Creative Hair Salon in Northalsted, which is an LGBTQ section on Chicago's North Side.

David Scott, the man who was going to cut my hair, and Rick Carey, his husband who subspecializes in coloring hair, own the salon.

After helping us out on a story, David and Rick became the newest members of the Hamlin Park Irregulars. I had been in their salon to discuss stories with them but never to have my hair done. Now I was.

Their establishment's interior looks like it was decorated by a designer on hallucinogenic drugs. Picture bright orange and dark brown with canary yellow and glistening purple as the basic color scheme.

Today, the sound from the background music — which usually makes my chest vibrate and my ears ring — was more subdued, replaced by Bette Midler singing Broadway tunes.

David's hand touched my shoulder, nudging me forward toward his chair. I sat down. The aroma of his

Bvlgari's Man cologne enveloped me. He has short brown hair, which today was slicked back instead of his usual spiky 'do'. He wore a long-sleeved, salmon-colored, silk shirt with billowing yellow pants. The cuffs of the shirt were folded halfway up his forearms. The diamond earring in his right ear had been replaced by a small ruby.

"Remember, I'm all about my hair," I said.

Or I used to be before I had two kids. This was the first time a new stylist would cut my hair since I moved to Chicago over six years ago. Previously, I waited to have Tiffaney do it on my trips home to Omaha, but after Macy was born I didn't have time, and thus, my hair was a mess.

"Madam Thomas, I do," David said. "That's all you jabbered about while Christi washed your hair."

"And why did you finally decide to come in?" Rick asked, as he paused from cleaning up his station.

His hair is streaked with gray as is his carefully trimmed goatee. His eyebrows are bushy, and when they elevate, there are deep wrinkles in his forehead. He has glasses with tinted lenses and hearing aids in both ears but no earrings. Today he wore all black.

"I want to impress the man I'm going to interview tonight, so I need a great cut and style," I said.

"Who is he?" David asked. "We're dying to know."

"Alexis Zhukov," I said. "He apparently doesn't like the press, which is why I want to look my best."

"I read about him," Rick said, as he swept up the hair around his chair. "He's one of the wealthiest money managers in the world."

"He made his fortune by investing the funds from Russian immigrants who came to the U.S.," I said. "Carter said there's a rumor that his clients aren't happy with his recent returns for them."

"Oh, my," David said. "I hear that unhappy Russians are not nice people."

An elderly client sat down in Rick's chair, and he got busy snipping and styling. I shut my eyes and tried to relax.

8

It seemed like my haircut took forever before I felt David's hand on my shoulder indicating he was done. "Open, open, sweetie."

Peeking out of my right eye, I glanced in the mirror. My previously too-long, scraggly brown hair was now hanging to the top of my shoulders. The cut was perfect. The sprinkles of gray were still there, but being a breastfeeding mommy of a seven-month old, I didn't have time today to have my color done. That would have to wait until next week.

Opening my other eye, I waggled my head. The bouncy strands flipped back and forth.

"It's perfect," I said, raking my fingers through my hair and shaking my head.

"Not quite perfect," Rick added.

"The gray hair?" I asked.

"You got it," he said. "But I'll take care of that little problem next week."

He finished up with the lady in his chair. She turned and inspected me through large, round, black-rimmed glasses that magnified her black eyes.

"David did a marvelous job," she said. "I think you look wonderful, whomever you are."

"Oh, Marcia, you are too kind," David said. He stepped back and pointed at me with his manicured right index finger. "This is Tina Thomas, a fabulous investigative journalist." He turned to the woman. "Tina, this is Marcia Peebler, one of our best customers."

"Indeed she is," Rick said. "We see her every single day."

She studied me. "For whom do you write, dear?"

"Tina doesn't exactly work full time, at least not right now, what with being a mommy and all," Rick said.

"But that's only a technicality," David said. "She was also blown up a few years ago, and her husband doesn't want her to work on features he considers dangerous."

Marcia would have raised her eyebrows, but none of the muscles on her face moved. She probably had a standing appointment with her plastic surgeon too.

"I don't understand," she said.

David and Rick have no idea of the many close encounters I've had in my career — even in recent years — but they knew about me shooting the fingers off the hands of the man who tried to kill Linda and me. I glared at David but I knew it was hopeless. He loves to tell stories.

"While I worked on the last story, a man tried to kill my friend and me," I said.

"What happened?" she asked.

"I shot him."

9

Mrs. Peebler appeared to be a card-carrying member of AARP and probably had been for a long while. Her poofed-up, dyed-black helmet hairstyle was part of my grandmother's generation, which meant David or Rick had to use lung-toxic amounts of hair spray on her after they blew out her hair.

She stood up and smoothed out her dark blue Chanel skirt. She didn't weigh as much as my backpack and was barely five feet tall. Her skin was the porcelain white of a china doll, a stark contrast to her jet black hair and eyebrows.

Covering her mouth, she emitted a death rattle cough, evidence that she didn't believe the Surgeon General's warning that smoking was hazardous to her health. Her bad habit explained her gravelly voice.

"You shot someone?" she asked.

"I did, but only in the hands."

She paused as she ingested that information.

"Are you good with guns?"

"I am."

"Do you ever do work on the side?"

"I'm sorry?"

"There are several people I can think of that I would like to remove from the face of the earth. With your experience, you would be perfect for the job."

David and Rick glanced at each other but didn't say anything.

"By the way, I couldn't help but overhear you mention Alex Zhukov," she continued.

"Do you know him?" I asked.

"We've met at dinner parties. He has been to our home. My husband, Alan, is one of his investors."

Bingo.

"May I talk to him about Zhukov?" I asked.

"Alan doesn't like to talk to people."

"I promise I won't use his name as a source, but the more people I can interview about Zhukov, the more accurate and fleshed out his story will be."

David checked his appointment list on his iPad. Rick turned his back and began cleaning up his station.

"Alan is a dear friend of ours, but he stays at home most of the time," he said over his shoulder.

"That's okay," I said. "I can visit him there."

"What they're afraid to say is that Alan has mad cow disease, as he calls it when he is able to speak coherently." She coughed up a mucus plug and daintily spit it into a Kleenex. "I call what he has brainy-BOOM! and that's why I said I need to hire you. Alan needs to be put down."

10

"Marcia, please, that isn't funny," David said.

"Why shouldn't I have Tina put Alan out of his misery?" Marcia asked. "And while she's at it, we can hire her to shoot Charlie Sullivan, the worthless builder we both use. Maybe we can get a group discount."

"I have to say, your suggestion about dealing with our builder might have some merit," Rick mused.

"Anyone who has ever built a house wants to kill their builder," she reminded him. "You've said to me often enough that you want to kill Charlie Sullivan."

"Whom you suggested we hire," David reminded her.

"And I'm sorry I did," she said.

Builder?

Picking up one of the hand mirrors, I studied the back of my head in the reflection from the front mirror. "I didn't know you guys were building a home," I said.

"Not building, exactly," Rick said. "More like remodeling."

"Totally gutting would be a better description," David said.

"It's on West Henderson," Rick said.

"Close to Molly," David said.

"No kidding. Won't that be a problem?"

"A problem?" Rick asked.

"You know, like culture shock moving from where you are now?"

Their condo is in the building next to their salon.

"Dearie, we don't have to live in a gay community," David said. "We can coexist with your kind."

I felt my face flush. "I am so sorry," I said. "I didn't mean to imply that you couldn't live in our neighborhood, but you have to admit it might be a little boring."

"We want boring," David said. "It's what parents do for their children."

I whipped around to face them. "Children?"

"Yes, you know, little people," Rick said, holding his hand down to the level of his knee.

"Tiny," David said, holding his hands two feet apart.

"Guys, am I missing something?" I asked. "As I remember my biology classes, you need a boy bird and a girl bee to produce kids." I paused. "Or is it the other way around?"

"Honey, you're so yesterday," David said. "We've hired the girl bee, as you put it."

"And she is carrying our child," Rick said.

Marcia blinked and cleared the mucus from her throat again. "I need a cigarette. I'll be right back. Don't say anything important while I'm gone. I don't want to miss one word of this."

With Rick's assistance, Marcia slipped on her matching dark blue Chanel jacket over a royal blue silk blouse. She grabbed a pack of cigarettes from her blue Mahina leather Louis Vuitton purse and walked out the front door. When I saw the purse, I thought about what Linda told me about Zhukov's shoes. Marcia and my Russian interviewee had serious money.

"Guys, I would love to stay, but I have to meet Molly at Neiman's. She and Linda declared that I needed to update my look."

David glanced at Rick and nodded. "We agree. Too bad we're so busy. We would love to go along and shop with you."

"But maybe next time," Rick said.

I would have to think about that one, but I sensed a potential story. "I can't wait for Marcia, guys," I said. "Tell me what's going on with your construction business."

"It's all because of you," David said.

"And Molly and Cas and Linda," Rick added.

"The Hamlin Park Irregulars?" I asked.

"For sure," David said.

"We positively loved working on your piece about Dr. Fertig," Rick began.

"And all the Irregulars have kids, so we decided if we want to be full-time members of the group, we should have one too," David explained.

"I hope this isn't the only reason you want to raise a child," I said.

"Oh, no, no, no," Rick said. "We've always wanted to do this, but we needed a tiny shove to make us proceed."

"We're so excited, I can't begin to tell you," David said.

"We wish Sullivan would hurry up and do something soon," Rick added.

"How far along with the construction are you?" I asked.

"Think messy," Rick said.

"Not habitable," David said.

"Why is it taking so long?" I asked.

"Sullivan says his crew will be there, and then they don't show up," Rick began.

"He blames the suppliers, the weather, the city inspectors, and the construction permit people," David said. "He'd blame the manager of the Cubs if he could. The house was supposed to be completed months ago. We anticipated some delay, but this is too extreme. If he would at least show up, we wouldn't be so crazy."

"But let me tell you, he's right on time with the bills he submits," Rick said. "And he keeps trying to convince us to tack on unnecessary items to drive up the cost."

"Items I'm sure he gets cheap and then sells to us at a huge markup," David added.

There is a story here.

"After I finish with Zhukov, maybe I can look into the problems with your builder."

"That would be wonderful," Rick said. "Anything you can do to speed things along will be gratefully appreciated."

"And please call us and report in on your interview," David said. "We can't wait to hear the juicy details."

The interior of my Honda van

7:17 p.m.

Monday, March 4

11

Help!

My hands continued to shake as I dialed Janet Corritore, a detective sergeant with the Chicago Police Department. She had gotten involved in two stories with me and my friends, and I knew she was the one to call about a murder, instead of 911.

"A man has been shot!" I screamed into my phone.

"Whoa, dial it back a little," she said.

"Sorry."

"Please tell me you're not the one who did it."

"No, I didn't have my Glock."

"You got it now?"

"Yes, and I just loaded one in the chamber."

"Are you in any danger?"

"I'm not sure. As soon as I found the guy, I ran away from the crime scene to get my gun."

"You planning to go back?"

I paused. "I was kind of leaning that way. It could be a terrific story."

She knew about me being blown up and the PTSD that had followed. She also knew my almost pathologic desire to write again and that once I sniffed a feature I wouldn't stop chasing it.

"You might want to lean the other way until I get there. Give me the address and the victim's name."

I did, and she disconnected.

My gym bag was in the back seat. My running shoes were in it. A woman with a gun and comfortable shoes might want to go back to the crime scene before the police arrived.

I pulled off the rest of my shredded panty hose and put on my ASICS running shoes. I felt stupid wearing them with my black power suit, but I didn't want to go back to the scene of the crime barefooted, especially if I had to run away again.

As I slipped on my ASICS, I remembered the way-too-expensive shoes I'd left in Zhukov's office.

Gotta get those too.

This time I opted for the elevator. On the ride up I rechecked the Glock, making sure I had a bullet in the chamber and the clip was full. When the elevator doors slid open, I stepped off holding my gun two-handed in front of me.

The double doors to the front office were still open from when I'd run out a few minutes ago. Moving the gun back and forth, I stepped into the reception area. I flipped on the main light switch. The room was still empty.

The door to Zhukov's office was closed.

Uh-oh!

I was positive I'd left it open when I sprinted away.

Now what?

Go in or wait for Janet? I had a gun. Why stop now?

My heart pounded as I tested the doorknob. It wasn't locked. I nudged the door partially open and peeked in. The city lights filtered through the windows, and the screen savers on the three computers glowed. The desk lamp was still off.

Nothing has changed.

I sniffed. The irritating smell of gunpowder was faint but still present. The only noise I heard was my pulse banging in my ears and my running shoes scuffing on the thick pile of the carpet as I crept further into the room.

Once again, the chair was turned to the windows. I moved behind the desk. I pulled the top of the chair toward me.

It was empty.

Zhukov was gone.

12

There was a noise behind me. I recognized the sound. It was a gun being pulled from a holster.

The killer!

I saw the silhouette of a person crouching in the doorway. The person had a gun and swept the room with it, moving the weapon back and forth. I ducked down behind the desk.

Waiting to slow my hammering pulse, I popped my head up and rested the Glock on the top of the desk to steady my aim.

"Don't move," I said. "I have a gun. Drop your weapon."

"You don't tell the cops to do that," a female voice said. "We do that. Don't you watch TV?"

"Janet?" I asked.

"Were you expecting someone else?" Detective Sergeant Janet Corritore asked.

"No, but I was worried you might be the killer."

"If I were, you'd already be dead." She toggled the laser sight on her gun. The red dot pointed at my forehead. "I can see your head behind the desk from the lights coming in through the windows and from the computer screen. Next time you hide, think about that first."

"Good point," I said. "Hopefully I won't need to use that advice."

"You might if you keep ignoring my orders."

Janet located the wall switch and turned on the room lights. She is close to my height and has short, curly, ash-brown hair. The loose black pantsuit and black turtleneck sweater she wore couldn't hide her athletic figure.

Holding her gun down at her side, she walked toward me. "Where's the victim?"

"That's kind of a problem," I said.

"Is he still alive?"

"No, I'm sure he's dead."

"Then where is he?"

"That's the problem. I don't know."

13

"Since there's no evidence that a crime has been committed, you can stay in here with me," Janet said.

This wasn't our first rodeo together with dead bodies and crime scenes. I knew my usual place was outside the yellow crime scene tape. Until we found a victim, though, this still wasn't necessary.

And from working on previous stories with me, she knew I was competent with a gun and she trusted me with one. She'd even had her husband, Frankie, register mine for me, even though — at the time — doing it wasn't completely legal.

The detective gave the room the cop once-over. She pointed at her eyes and then at the two doors, one on each side of the fireplace on the far wall. After slipping on latex gloves, she handed a second set to me. I put them on.

Standing on the left side of one door, she pantomimed opening it and held up her hand, indicating for me to stay put. She would never let me enter a room she first hadn't cleared of anything dangerous.

She pushed the door open and entered, her gun held in front of her. I waited, holding my gun in both hands. She turned on the room's lights and waved me in. I entered a large white marble bathroom, the kind you would find in a high roller's suite in Las Vegas or Dubai.

It was empty.

We backed out and repeated the routine at the other door. It was a kitchen larger than the entire first floor of our home. The Viking appliances were big enough to service a moderate-sized restaurant. There were two windows with a spectacular view of Lake Michigan.

The room was also empty.

She holstered her gun and walked back into the office.

"Fancy," she said.

"An understatement," I said. "Especially the kitchen."

"Notice anything about the bathroom?"

"I would love to take a long hot bath in that big tub."

She shook her head. "The smell."

I walked back into the bathroom. She followed me. I sniffed several times. The irritating odor was faint but I could still smell it. "Gunpowder."

"The subject probably popped the victim and then hid in here when he heard you come in. He had the smoking gun with him."

"Good thing I ran," I said.

"Running is always good when there's a shooter with a loaded weapon in the room next to you, especially when you don't have your gun."

14

Janet walked to Zhukov's desk. I followed. She stopped. So did I.

"Speak to me," she said.

"When I came into this room, the desk chair was turned away from me, and all I could see was the top of his head," I said.

"Zhukov?" she asked.

"Yes, and I forgot to tell you he's a Russian native."

"I already knew that. Driving here, I ran his name on the computer. Lots of people seem to be unhappy with him. Is that why you're doing the story?"

"It is."

"You sure it was him?"

"According to my research, Zhukov has bright red hair. It was dark, but when I turned the man around, I'm sure his hair was that color." I paused. "And I've never met him, but he looked like the pictures I'd seen of him."

"One difference."

"The bullet hole."

"You got it."

She walked behind the desk and swiveled the chair around to face away from us. Using a small flashlight, she focused the beam on the back of the chair. She bent down and studied the leather.

"I don't see anything," she said.

"Hopefully the lab guys will find something," I said.

"If I call them."

I could feel heat begin to rise up in my neck.

"I know what I saw. Zhukov sat right here with a bullet hole right between his eyes. The shot was up close and personal."

"Then where is he?" she asked. "It's hard to picture him walking out, him being dead and all."

"I do have one clue. I know how to identify the killer."

She raised her eyebrows. "Oh?"

"He wears a size eight shoe."

"And how would you know this?"

"The killer stole my brand new black Rolando Hidden-Platform Christian Louboutin pumps."

She nodded. "Dude has good taste."

15

"It's always nice to have a dead body," Janet continued. "It gives me a reason to call in our CSI guys."

"What about the gunpowder smell?" I asked.

"It helps, and it's one reason I believe you."

"And the other?"

"You know what a dead body looks like. You want to write a story, and you wouldn't make this up." She glanced around the room. "A big operation here."

"He ran a large investment firm."

"Guys like that have high-priced lawyers. I doubt they'll be happy having fingerprint powder and such all over this nice office."

"What do we do?"

"The suspect who did this is probably a pro. I doubt there'll be much in the way of useful evidence in here."

"But he had to get the body out somehow."

"It sounds like we need a detective."

She got down on her hands and knees and rubbed her hand across the pile of the carpet.

"Are you detecting?" I asked.

"I am."

She shined her small flashlight on the pile of the carpet.

"Something?" I asked.

"Thick. Is this why you took off your shoes?"

"I did a face plant first and then kicked them off."

"Which the suspect then took."

"Someone swiped them. I'm sure it wasn't Zhukov."

"I wonder if the suspect can trace who you are through the shoes."

"Why would he do that?"

"You're the only witness. If the suspect is a Russian, that might be a problem. Those guys don't play fair. They'll kill anyone who gets in their way, including your husband and kids."

16

Forty minutes later, I walked in our front door.

"How did the interview go?" Carter called out from the family room.

"Not too well," I said.

I joined him. He worked on his laptop editing his reporters' stories. The girls were already in bed. There was a glass of red wine on the table next to him.

Kicking off my running shoes, I padded over and gave him a kiss. He closed his laptop and leaned back.

"Zhukov has always been a notoriously difficult person to interview," he said.

"I wouldn't know," I said, as I took a small sip of his wine. "This is good."

"It's a Grenache from Mila. They are relatively new to the game, but I agree, it's a compelling wine."

I sat down next to him on the couch. He took the glass from me and put it down. He began massaging my tight neck muscles. I shut my eyes as the tension in my body slowly dissipated.

"What went wrong?" he asked, when he heard me sigh.

"There was not a living soul in his office when I arrived."

This was not exactly a lie, since the killer probably was in the bathroom when I walked in, but no need to trouble Carter with minor details like that.

"I can understand your disappointment, especially since you dressed so beautifully for the occasion," he said.

"I didn't think you noticed," I said, as I raked my fingers through my new haircut and then shook my head.

"I always notice you."

I turned my head right and then left to give him a better view of my hair. "But what do you like the most?"

"Honestly?"

Raising my eyebrows, I leaned toward him awaiting his answer.

"Those new heels you had on. They were stunning."

Telling him the killer stole my shoes might not be smart if I wanted to keep working on the story.

I leaned back. "Not my hair?"

He motioned that silly notion away with a wave of his hand. "Your hair is always terrific. No, it was the heels. They made your legs look fabulous."

"Don't my legs always look great?"

His blue eyes widened, and he knew he was in trouble. I had gained a few pounds when I was pregnant with Macy, and I was struggling to lose them. The weight was bugging me, and he knew it.

He cleared his throat. "You are the most amazing woman I have ever seen."

"Even if I've gained a couple of pounds?"

He picked up his glass of wine and took a long drink. I was sure he didn't know what to say next.

"You won't mind if I keep working on this?" I asked, before he could reply.

His face softened, relieved that I had changed the subject. "Of course not. Why would you even ask that?"

"You keep saying that you don't want me to do any stories that might be risky."

"And I don't, but what could possibly be dangerous about interviewing a Russian money manager at his request?"

"Can't think of a thing."

Unless that Russian money manager had been murdered and the killer knew who I was.

17

Tuesday morning, I sent a group text to the Hamlin Park Irregulars detailing what happened to me at Zhukov's office and the possibility that we might have a great story to work on. I told them I would have more information for them soon.

Twenty minutes later, I met with Janet Corritore.

"Carter said I could keep working on Zhukov's story," I said.

Janet stared at me. "That's hard to believe, him wanting you not to work on anything dangerous."

We sat in our neighborhood Starbuck's, which is across the street from Dinkel's Bakery, a Hamlin Park Irregulars favorite eating and gathering place. Macy was asleep in the stroller. Kerry was in preschool.

We were there instead of Dinkel's because the unsweetened iced green tea in front of me had significantly fewer calories than anything I would be tempted to eat from Dinkel's.

"He said, and I quote, 'Of course not. Why would you even ask that?' " I said.

"This before or after you told him about the bullet hole in Zhukov's forehead?"

"I didn't exactly mention that part."

"What did you mention, exactly?"

"That I didn't see a living soul in the office."

"Clever."

"Thanks."

"You'd make a good lawyer."

"I'll leave that to Linda. Did you check the recordings from the building's security cameras?"

"I did. The head of security is a retired Chicago cop. He let me watch them." She took a small spiral notebook out of her jacket pocket and flipped it open. "On Monday, at 1330, the security cameras in the outside hall recorded Zhukov entering his office."

"Coming back from lunch?"

"Yep, and it looked like he enjoyed eating."

"He was reported to be a little over six feet tall and weighed about two hundred thirty pounds, including the red hair."

"You might need to check that weight. This guy was way fatter than that."

"Cameras add ten pounds, or so."

"So do donuts. He had a box of them when he went into his office."

Explains what I smelled.

"Are you sure it was Zhukov?"

"Fat guy with red hair. Expensive suit. Gold Rolex watch on his left wrist. Big diamond pinky ring on his right hand."

"Which describes what I've heard from Linda about him, but that night I was too scared to see any jewelry."

"You didn't stay around all that long."

"With good reason."

She flipped a page. "No one else came in the rest of the afternoon. At 1702, the cameras in the outside hall show a female leaving his office. We identified her as his secretary." She turned a page. "At 1900, another female entered the office. Left the door open."

"Me."

"It was."

"At 1911, you ran out the open front door. No shoes on. Started to run and fell on your ass. Began doing an imitation of a pinball being played in a machine."

"Not easy to run on a polished marble floor in panty hose."

"Never tried it."

"Don't. It doesn't work."

"You sprinted out the back stairs exit and disappeared. You came back on the elevator at 1932. You held a gun in front of you when you walked into his office. The door was still open. At 1936, I arrived."

"And?"

"Nothing until this morning. At 0900, a secretary came in."

"How did the killer get in?"

"And how did he carry the body out?"

18

"You're missing something," Janet said.

"Obviously," I said.

I assumed she meant Zhukov's body.

"In his office," she prompted.

I pictured the room in my mind. Zhukov had a lamp on his desk, three computer screens on the credenza, and one large picture on the wall to the right of the desk and credenza.

"Was it that big picture on the wall?" I asked.

"Yes. It's a map of Cold War Leningrad." She checked her notes. "It's now called St. Petersburg, and it's his birthplace."

"I remember reading about that from the background information Linda sent to me on Sunday night."

Janet continued to read from her notes. "The map was made by CIA cartographers. It showed the city's labyrinthine streets, canals, and alleyways in painstaking detail."

"Linda's research said Zhukov was proud of it."

"He was. Did you notice anything else in the room?"

"No."

"What about the framed paper money hung on the wall next to the picture?"

"I missed that."

"The face of Nicholas II, the last czar who was executed after the revolution, was printed on it," she paused, "and it's the solution to what happened to Zhukov."

"I don't understand."

"It covered the release latch to a door hidden behind the picture."

Huh?

"Did the Leningrad picture conceal a staircase?"

"No, an elevator that went down to his private garage."

"Were there any security cameras in there?"

"None. When I didn't see the suspect carrying out the body on the security recordings, I asked the security guy what I was missing."

"Did he know about the secret elevator?"

"Yep, and he was the only one in the building other than Zhukov who did. He said Zhukov used the elevator to sneak female visitors into his office."

"A convenient way to keep his wife — or anyone else — from finding out."

"It would be."

"The killer might have known about the elevator."

"I agree. The security guy said she might have been a working woman who could have brought her pimp up there with her and he shot Zhukov."

"Or she was alone."

"Possible. Female shooters are becoming more popular."

"Interesting. She comes to service her client, but the pimp shoots him instead. They wait for me to leave and then drag him over to the elevator and disappear."

"Good thing she had a man with her. She would have to be super strong to drag a dead weight that heavy without help."

"Did you go back and inspect the carpet in front of the picture? They must have left some deep tracks struggling to tug his fat body onto the elevator, maybe even left some blood spatter."

"I wanted to, but I ran into a snag. The security chief called Zhukov's secretary to let me into the office, and she informed him that her boss was out of the country."

"Zhukov? Out of the country? That's impossible. He's dead."

"According to the note he left on an email from his computer to her computer, he flew to Brunei. It came in to her computer at 1923 last night. It was time stamped. She forwarded a copy of it to the head of security's computer. He sent it on to me."

"That was after I left the first time and before I came back."

"It was."

"The killer sent it."

"A possibility."

"Why Brunei?"

"The secretary told the security chief that the sultan is one of Zhukov's clients. Her boss cashed him in before the fund tanked. The sultan was the only client who didn't lose any money."

"Convenient."

"It is, if that's a place where you want to hide out."

"This should be easy enough to check."

"I'm working on it."

"Until then?"

"You better find the suspect before he finds you. If you're the only witness and you disappear, there won't be a crime if the cops can't find Zhukov's body."

"And without me as a witness, the killer will be in the clear."

Part 2

19

Tuesday afternoon, I sent out another group text to the Irregulars with my game plan for the story. That night, Molly Miller and I stood in the alley outside of what I hoped was the entrance to Zhukov's private garage. Carter babysat the girls. I told him I was going to work on Zhukov's story.

"Tell me again why we're doing this," Molly said.

Her attention span is short. We'd talked about this on the drive there.

"We need to search Zhukov's office before the cleaning crew ruins the crime scene and destroys any remaining evidence."

"Why don't we call the CSI guys? That's what they do on TV."

"I suggested that to Janet, but she can't do it until she has evidence that a crime has been committed."

"How about the dead guy's body?"

"Works for me, but I kind of lost it."

"How do you lose a body?"

She would have wrinkled her forehead trying to figure that one out, but, like Marcia Peebler, her recent Botox injections eliminated that possibility.

"It isn't easy, which is why we're here. I need to prove the body was removed."

"Why didn't you ask Cas or Linda to come along instead of me?"

"The killer might be a woman. If she is, I think she's a hooker, and neither one of them can imitate a prostitute."

She flung her coat open and thrust out her spectacular chest. "But I sure can."

Amen.

If any man with a functioning penis were to amble down the alley while we were breaking in, Molly would be the perfect cover. Tonight, she wore a micro-mini black skirt, black fishnet hose with thigh-high black leather boots, and a black lace bustier that made her 875 cc breast implants seem to defy gravity. If she sneezed, she was going to give herself a pair of black eyes. It was cold, so she also had on a long black leather coat which she could throw open if someone came along.

I wanted to appear to be Molly's pimp coming along to protect her during her visit with Zhukov, so I was dressed like a man, with no makeup and my newly cut hair tucked up in a bun under a black stocking cap. A black peacoat, black pants, and black, low-heeled ankle boots completed my disguise. I also had my usual equipment, including my Glock, in my backpack.

"After I talked to Janet this morning, I went online when I returned home and accessed the plans for Zhukov's building," I continued. "There's a garage for the tenants, which has a door at street level. There was no indication of any other garage, so before Kerry got out of preschool, I drove down here with Macy and circled the perimeter of the building. I found this." I pointed to a single garage door and a regular door to the right of it.

"Where do those doors go?" Molly asked.

"Hopefully down to his private garage."

"Do you think the missing body is down there?"

"Probably not. I think the killer shoved Zhukov's body on the elevator and then carried it away in a vehicle. I hope to find some blood spatter that will prove that's what happened."

"Way cool. How do we do that?"

"Janet gave me a bottle of luminol."

"I've seen that on the *CSI* shows. They sprayed it on stuff and turned out the lights. If there was any blood, it glowed. They swabbed it and ran it for DNA. In a couple of minutes, they had the picture of the killer and his address." She paused. "It's kind of weird, but the bad guy was always home when they got to his house."

"I don't think this is going to be that easy."

"How are we going to get in?" she asked.

I reached into my purse and pulled out my lock pick gun and torque wrench. "With this," I said.

Both pieces of equipment had been held by the police as part of the crime scene in the last story we worked on. Right before

Macy was born, Janet brought them back to me after that case file was closed.

"Does that work on keypads too?" she asked.

20

Dang it!

When I chased major stories before I had two kids, I would never have made a rookie mistake like this. I'd driven by both doors but hadn't spotted that there were no locks on either of them.

Maybe I should just stay home and make more babies.

"Now what?" Molly asked.

"I assumed Zhukov had a garage door opener so he could go in and out. I also figured he gave the women a key so they could come in this door and then use the elevator."

"But there's no lock, so why would they need a key?"

"I guess we either figure out the combination or we go home."

"It's 10-13-69."

"And how would you be knowing this?"

"The farmers taught me."

Molly traveled the world as a supermodel before she married her husband, Greg. He introduced her to his friends at one of our embassies overseas. They recognized Molly's many talents, so they hired her to do jobs for them. She originally told us they were farmers but later admitted that, even though they were listed as agricultural attachés, they were CIA agents.

"What did they teach you?" I asked.

"Where to hunt for combinations," she said.

"Why would you ever need information like that?"

"Well, duh? For when they wanted me to break into places. They said most people can't remember their passwords to computers or combinations to locks so they always write them down somewhere. I'm thinking that this Russian guy told the women the combination, but most of them are probably like me so they forgot it."

"And they wrote it down somewhere. Smart thinking. Where did you find it?"

"Where I would put it."

She fluffed her hair and shifted her weight.

"Molly?"

"What?"

"The combination. Where did you find it?"

"Sorry, I get distracted. These boots are new and they're starting to hurt."

"But they look great."

She smiled and struck a model's pose.

I stared at her and shrugged.

"Oh, right," she said. "The combination. Like I said, they told me to always check in the place where I would write it."

"And where would that be?"

"Right up there," she said, pointing up at the lintel of the doorjamb above us. "Most of us wear super high heels so we can reach up that far."

10-13-69 was written on the lintel. I put on a pair of latex gloves and punched in the code. The locked clicked, and we were in.

21

The door opened into a windowless, cement staircase that plunged down into total darkness. Suddenly a light went on, illuminating the stairway.

"That's pretty cool," Molly said. "It's automatic."

"My guess is it's connected to a warning system so Zhukov would know his visitor was on the way."

The echo of Molly's heels clickety-clacking on the stone steps was the only sound as we descended two floors, entering into a dark, low-ceilinged, cement room. When we arrived there, the stairway lights went off, and the lights in the garage came on.

It was big enough for at least four vehicles. I sniffed several times, but except for a dank, musty smell, I didn't detect any lingering exhaust fumes. No cars had been running in there recently.

The garage wasn't heated, and it was cold enough that we could see our breath. Molly tugged her long coat around her. I stomped my feet and blew on my latex-gloved hands as I studied the room.

"Over there," I said, pointing at the only other door in the garage. It was on the far wall, and it had a keypad too. I strode over and punched in 10-13-69. Nothing happened.

"01-23-71," Molly said, pointing up at the lintel of the doorjamb.

I punched in that combination and opened the door. A pinewood-paneled elevator big enough for four people stood empty in front of us.

I held up my hand. "Wait a sec'."

Reaching into my backpack, I pulled out the spray bottle of luminol Janet had given me. Legally, she would never be able to use any evidence of blood spatter I discovered, but if the tests were positive, she would have proof that a murder had been committed.

I left Molly in the garage and closed the door. I sprayed the walls and the industrial brown carpet covering the floor of the elevator to check for traces of blood. I turned out the lights. A faint blue glow appeared on the carpet near the front of the elevator.

I swabbed the area with two Q-tips and put them in a baggy. The killer had dragged Zhukov's body into the elevator, probably by pulling on his feet. This would position his head near the front where I found the bloodstains.

I turned the elevator's lights back on and opened the door. Molly faced me. Her eyes were wide open, her lips forming a nearly perfect oval.

Before I could say anything, I heard the reason for the terrified look on her face. The clickety-clack of high heels echoed on the cement steps behind us. The lights on the stairway had come on.

Uh-oh!

22

Before Molly could speak, I grabbed her arm and yanked her into the elevator. The garage room's automatic lights went off as I pulled the outside elevator door shut.

On the elevator wall to my right were two unmarked buttons, one on top of the other. I jabbed at the upper one several times and waited as the elevator door slowly closed.

Hurry up!

The elevator jerked a couple of times and finally ascended.

"Whadda we do?" Molly whispered.

"We hide somewhere," I whispered back.

"Where?"

"It can't be in the bathroom."

"He has a bathroom in his office?"

"A big one, but that's where the killer hid when I came in the first time. If she's here to see if she left any evidence behind, that'll be the first place she might check."

"The killer's a woman?"

"I'm not sure. It's possible the woman had her pimp with her and he was the shooter."

"It sounded like a woman's high heels. I didn't hear any other footsteps. Maybe she came back by herself."

"Or she acted alone and she's the killer."

The elevator jerked to a stop, and the door slid open. We faced a second door with a waist-high button in the middle. I pushed it, and a door opened into Zhukov's office.

The last time I was here, the room was dark except for the light from the three computer screens and the windows. It was again. I took out a small flashlight from my backpack and turned it on. Molly followed me into the shadowy room.

Reaching back into the elevator, I punched the down button and stepped back. The door slid closed, and I heard the elevator descend. The large picture of Leningrad covered the other side of the hidden elevator door. I pushed it closed.

Using the flashlight to guide us, I sprinted toward the kitchen. Opening the door, I looked over my shoulder, expecting to find Molly close behind me. She wasn't. She stood by Zhukov's desk, staring at the screen savers on his computers.

"Molly, what are you doing?" I said, waving at her. "Get in here."

"But I've seen these pictures before."

"Which isn't going to help us right now. If the lady coming up in the elevator has a weapon with her, you're going to be stuck in the middle of a gunfight."

"Oh, right."

She ran toward me and made six steps before she did a "Tina," catching her high heels in the carpet and doing a full face plant. She shook her head and tried to stand up. I heard the elevator begin to ascend.

Adrenaline surged through my system. I ran back, put the flashlight between my teeth, grabbed her arms, and dragged her toward the kitchen. As we reached it, the elevator stopped.

I heard a click.

The intruder had arrived.

23

I glanced over my shoulder and saw the picture of Leningrad opening toward us.

Hurry up!

Dragging Molly into the kitchen, I quickly closed the door and spit out my flashlight. She sat up and opened her mouth to speak, but I put my right hand over her lips to stop her.

"Do not say anything," I whispered. "Someone is in the next room. Do you understand?"

She nodded.

I removed my hand.

"But..." she began.

I whipped my hand back over her mouth and frantically shook my head back and forth.

"Quiet," I whispered.

"Oh, right," she mumbled through my fingers.

I helped her up and grabbed my flashlight. I turned it off and put it back into my backpack. I walked to the door to listen. I heard the clicking of a computer keyboard.

What is going on in there?

I reached out to open the kitchen door enough to see what was happening. Before I could do it, a light unexpectedly came on behind me. I whirled around. Molly stood in front of one of the two Viking refrigerators. She held the door open. I snapped my fingers at her. She turned to me and shrugged her shoulders. I pantomimed shutting the door. She did and the light went out.

I turned back to the kitchen door and could still hear the clicking of the computer board keys. I opened the door a sliver, enough to see that the intruder was a woman. She was alone and had flipped on the desk lamp.

She was small and slender, almost petite. She had thick, long black hair. Large designer sunglasses had to make it hard for her to see in the dim room light, but they also hid her eyes and masked much of her face. Her face was white, possibly from makeup, and she wore bright red lipstick.

She had on latex gloves and worked at the middle computer. I watched as she inserted a flash drive and began downloading the contents from the hard drive. While she waited, she opened up the other two computers. She scanned the screens but didn't put a flash drive in either one of those machines.

While the middle computer continued to download the contents of its hard drive, she picked up a large handbag and walked to the bathroom to the left of the fireplace. She took out a bottle and rags from the bag.

I closed the door, pulled the Glock out of my backpack, and turned back to Molly. I pointed with the gun to my right to indicate that the intruder was in the room to our right. If she was the killer and came into the kitchen, my only option was to try and stop her before she shot us.

I opened the door and peeked out. The sound of running water meant only one thing. She was cleaning the bathroom to destroy any evidence that she had previously been in there.

24

When the woman finished cleaning the bathroom, she walked back to Zhukov's desk. She removed the flash drive and shut down all three computers. She picked up a different bottle from her purse and sprayed the chair and desk.

She did the same thing to the carpet that led from Zhukov's chair to the elevator. She shut off the desk lamp. A faint blue glow appeared on the carpet in front of the elevator. She turned on the lamp and cleaned that area and then the desk and chair.

I thought I saw her begin to turn toward me, so I closed the door and waited with my ear to the wood and the Glock in my hand. The only sound I heard was my rapidly increasing pulse pounding in my ears.

I heard a click and peeked out. I watched her pull back the Leningrad picture/door, step back, shut off the lamp, and step onto the elevator.

With the computers and desk lamp shut off, the room was totally dark, but I was able to get a good look at her from the lights in the elevator. For the first time, I observed her muscular legs, which were made more impressive by the heels she wore.

They were mine.

"Gosh, check that out," Molly said. She stood behind me looking over the top of my head.

"Check what out?"

"Her shoes. They're like the ones I helped you pick out."

"They *are* the ones you helped me pick out."

The woman closed the Leningrad picture/door. I heard the noise of the elevator door closing. The sound of the elevator moving indicated she was leaving.

Finally.

I turned on my flashlight and used it as we walked into the dark main office. I snapped on the desk lamp and turned off my flashlight.

"How did she get your shoes?" Molly asked.

"After I found Zhukov's body, I tried to get out of here, but I did a faceplant on the carpet just like you did. I couldn't run in those stupid high heels, so I left them."

"And she stole them."

"Obviously."

"Why would she wear them here?"

"If she leaves any imprints on the thick carpet from the shoes, or any trace particles from the soles, it will come from my shoes and not hers."

"Then the CSI guys will hunt for you and not her."

"That's probably her plan." I handed Molly a pair of latex gloves. "Put these on."

"Don't think so."

"Why not?"

"They don't go with my outfit."

"Humor me. This is a potential crime scene. We don't want to leave our fingerprints." I took several Handi Wipes out of my backpack. "Wipe down anything you touched in the kitchen."

While she did her assignment, I went into the bathroom. The odor of industrial strength cleaning solution made my eyes water and my nose sting. I was glad the odors no longer triggered one of my PTSD attacks, something that had plagued me since I was blown up chasing a story in Arlington, Virginia.

Any evidence that had been in the bathroom was gone. I opened the bathroom cabinets, hoping she had missed something, but I stopped when I heard a noise that sounded like the squeaking of metal springs. This was followed by a loud thump on the floor in the office.

Now what's going on?

25

Molly stood next to the couch in front of the fireplace. She had thrown the cushions on the carpet and opened a foldout bed. The sheets were wrinkled.

"How did you find this?" I asked, pointing at the bed.

"Well, see, if I came up here to have sex with the Russian guy, where would we do it?"

Good question.

"I don't know." I looked around. "Maybe on the desk?"

"Looks good in a movie, but it kills your back."

"The carpet?"

"No way. I hate having rug burns on my butt and back. And my knees? Forget it."

"He had to have a bed."

"For sure, and here it is." She paused. "He was a little kinky."

"And how do you know this?"

She pointed at the ceiling. I glanced up and saw my reflection in a large recessed mirror I hadn't noticed before. Molly stared in the mirror and then ran her fingers through her hair and shook her head. She reached into her purse and put on fresh lipstick. Greg said she never passed up a chance to check herself out in a mirror, and he was right, even if it was on the ceiling.

"Greg doesn't like our ceiling mirror," she continued.

"I can't imagine why."

"He says I spend too much time watching myself while we're doing it and I don't concentrate."

"I can see where that might be a problem."

"Only for him, honey."

She opened my backpack and took out the bottle of luminol.

"Now what are you doing?" I asked.

"Gosh, don't you ever watch *CSI*?" she asked.

"We don't watch much TV."

She sprayed the sheets. "I'm hunting for pecker tracks."

"I'm sorry?"

"Pecker tracks. Guys don't care what happens after they come. They fire away without thinking about what a mess they're making. We can get DNA from this."

"I guess I missed the pecker track episode."

"It's a good thing you brought me and not Cas or Linda. I don't think they know much about this kind of stuff."

"You're right about that."

I turned out the room lights. The sheets lit up like the Las Vegas strip.

"He was a horny dude," she said.

"Obviously."

"Let's strip the bed," she said. "We can take these sheets with us and run the DNA through a cool machine with blinking lights and get the killer's name and address."

She pulled the sheets off the mattress. I went into the bathroom and found fresh ones in the linen closet. We put the sheets on and wrinkled them up enough to make them appear to have been used.

"The woman didn't seem to be in much of a hurry when she was here," I said. "If she took her time making sure she didn't leave any evidence behind, why didn't she take the sheets?"

Molly stared at them. "Maybe she wasn't in this bed last night."

"Or maybe her DNA isn't in a database and she doesn't care if it's found on the sheets."

"Isn't everyone's DNA in a file somewhere? It sure is on all the cop shows."

"Hers would be, too, if she's been arrested in the United States."

"But you don't think it is."

"Maybe they imported her from Russia specifically for this job."

I folded Zhukov's sheets and stuffed them into my backpack. We closed up the bed and replaced the cushions.

26

Preparing to leave, we stood in front of the Leningrad picture. I levered the money display switch. The door opened. I pushed the button to bring the elevator back up to us.

I glanced at the computers to my left.

Huh?

"What did you tell me about finding the combination for the keypad to the door?" I asked.

"I said the farmers told me most people can't remember their computer passwords or combinations to locks, so they always write them down somewhere."

My heart did a somersault against my sternum. The killer just came into Zhukov's office, and the first thing she did was download everything from his computer before she cleaned up any evidence.

"Where would you hide the password for these computers?" I asked.

She sat down behind Zhukov's desk and swiveled back and forth in his chair as she inspected the area. She didn't touch anything. She then swirled the chair around to face the windows. She pointed at the windowsill. "I would put it right there."

MW9151660D was printed on the windowsill.

I sat down in front of the middle computer preparing to enter the password. The screen saver was a color family portrait picture of Zhukov, his wife Ellen, and two sons, Daniel and Ariel.

"He's kinda' strange looking," Molly said.

"You mean the red hair?" I asked.

"The red hair, the white skin, the pudgy body. No wonder he was paying for sex."

"This picture is an old one. His sons are married and have children of their own."

"He was a grandpa?"

"Yep. He was seventy-four."

"No wonder he was kinky."

"Does being that age make you kinky?"

"No, see, what I'm saying is that old guys aren't usually into regular sex. They need something special to rev them up."

"Should I ask how you would know this?"

"Before I met Greg, an older guy I hung out with when I was modeling told me a man can only have ten-thousand ejaculations in his lifetime. He said he regretted wasting so many of them when he wacked off as a teenager. He was down to his last couple of hundred and he didn't want any mercy sex from his wife. He wanted something special."

"That sounds like a line to me."

"I kind of thought so, too, but he gave me expensive presents so I didn't say anything." She paused. "Plus, his wife weighed more than his Bentley, so I couldn't blame him for fooling around. He loved to watch himself doing it, so he put a camera behind his ceiling mirror and made a videotape recording whenever he had sex. Old guys can't do it that often, so maybe the only way he could get it up was with kinky sex."

"Good to know, but I'm not sure how I'll use that in this story."

I punched in the password Molly had discovered and hit enter. From what I could see flashing on the screen, this was his business computer.

"What about the other two computers?" she asked.

"Good question. The killer only copied this one."

The screen saver on the computer to my left was a fancy sports car. That computer also had the same password, so I opened the files. I found exotic car information and sections on watches and art.

Shutting it down, I turned to the computer on my right. This screen saver was a brick mansion. I turned to Molly and shrugged.

"I saw that picture in the Robb Report," she said. "It's La Grand Reve in Winnetka. You can buy it for twenty-eight million."

I opened that computer and scrolled through the first few files. I found information about ultra-expensive homes around the world. I shut it down and sat back.

"This would fit with the background on Zhukov," I said. "He grew up poor in Russia and always had pictures on his desk of expensive items he wanted."

"I wonder if he was going to buy one of them?"

"Good question. I'll check into that. Maybe that's where some of his investor's money went."

"What's next?"

"We need to download the details from these computers."

"Do you have one of those little things you can stick into the computer to copy stuff?"

"A flash drive?"

"Yeah."

"I didn't know I would need it, so I don't have one with me."

"What are you going to do?"

"Come back tomorrow night."

27

On Wednesday afternoon, my mommy assignment was to fill out Carter's list of ingredients for him to prepare dinner when he came home from work.

I took the girls to the Paulina Market on the corner of Cornelia and North Lincoln. It's an old world meat market with new age offerings. Most of the time I stop at Whole Foods, which is closer to our front door, but Kerry loves to pull the "take a number" out of the large pink plastic pig's head which stands inside the front door at Paulina's.

It was sleeting, so I drove the van and then pushed the girls in their tandem stroller into the store. I found a surprise in the line when I entered. I tapped him on the shoulder.

Detective Tony Infantino turned around to face me. "How could you lose a freaking body?"

Sixteen years ago, he was the first real love of my life. He is a movie-star-handsome, third generation, Italian Chicago cop, the first one of his family of cops to make detective. He still isn't married, but he doesn't lack for female companionship.

"You've been talking to Janet," I said.

Tony pulled his number out of the pig's mouth and then inched forward in the long line. He wore a double-breasted camel hair topcoat with a dark brown cashmere scarf around his neck. The bright lights in the market glittered off his highly polished, brown, Italian leather boots.

"She's my partner," he said. "Hard not to talk about stuff like that when you're riding around together."

Macy was asleep in the stroller. I pulled Kerry out of it and lifted her up to the pig's mouth.

"Okay, Kerry, it's your turn," I said. "Pull hard."

"Yes, Mother," she said.

A term she picked up at preschool.

She grabbed the ticket and pulled as hard as she could. When I tried to help, she pushed my hand away. She succeeded and turned to me. "We have number twenty-eight, Mother."

More knowledge from her expensive preschool.

I put her down, and she ran directly up to one of the meat counters. She turned around and impatiently stared at me. "Come on, Mother. We need to order."

"Not your turn yet, kid," Tony said.

"She thinks that when she pulls the ticket out that means we're next."

"Whatever. All's I know is I'm in front of you guys."

I took Kerry by the hand and pushed Macy in the stroller as we toured the store while we waited for our number to be called. Tony followed us.

"I haven't had a chance to call Janet yet, but I know how the killer got rid of his body," I said.

"You know where the stiff is?" he asked.

"No, but at least I know how it was removed from the building."

"You still don't have it."

"*Yes*, Tony, I still don't know where the body is, but I do know Zhukov was murdered. I saw the bullet hole in his forehead and there was blood on the carpet of his elevator."

"Somebody's blood, but doubt it was his."

"It was his."

"Then how'd the dude fly to Brunei the day after you claim he was murdered?"

What?

28

"And how would you know this?" I asked.

"Janet had one of Frankie's boys access United's computer records," Tony said.

Frankie is Janet's husband. We don't know exactly what he does, but he can get things done, a great perk when we need help with our stories.

"His guy says the flight records show that yesterday, Alexis Zhukov boarded a United flight at 10:50 a.m. from O'Hare going to Shanghai," he continued as he as he looked at his watch. "That means dude landed in Brunei a couple of hours ago."

"Did United check his passport too?"

"According to the computer check Frankie's guy ran, they did."

"What about the security camera recordings from the airport? Did he check those?"

"His guy is working on that."

"But you'll have it."

"Maybe, but not sure we need it."

"You're convinced that Zhukov flew to Brunei."

"Yep." He paused. "Until you come up with something new, we're not gonna work this anymore."

"Maybe I can convince you to reconsider if you have your lab guys analyze something for me."

He held up his hands. "Not again. You asked me to do this before, and I got in trouble for doing it."

"But you became a media star because of it."

For the first story I worked on with the Hamlin Park Irregulars, I'd begged him to analyze a trash sample for me. The results led to him being hailed in the press as a hero when he gunned down a bad guy at O'Hare.

It wasn't the last time I'd made a request of him like that. Without his help accessing the Chicago PD lab, I wouldn't have been able to write any of our other stories.

He sighed. "Okay, what do you want analyzed?" he asked.

"Bed sheets for DNA," I said. "I have them in the van. I'll give them to you when we leave."

"Done, but one other thing."

I waited.

"Be careful with these Russian guys."

"Why?"

"Russians make the Italian Mafia look like the cast of *La Cage Aux Folles*. Don't screw with the Russians, understand me?"

I ran my fingers through Kerry's hair and patted her head. I was going to have to be careful if I decided to pursue this story.

29

On Wednesday night, after we had a family dinner, I told Carter that Cas and I were going to XSport Fitness for a yoga seminar after I cleaned up the dishes. He did his daddy part and put the girls to bed.

Instead of going to the seminar, I went back to Zhukov's office building. I knew the system, so entering was fast even though I had a new accomplice. Cas Johnson walked in beside me.

She is about six inches shorter than me and muscular, with a square jaw, olive skin, and dark brown eyes. She wears her black hair either in a ponytail, or tight bun. Today, she was bun girl. She is married to Joe and they have two kids; Luis, seven, and Angelique, six.

Cas was trained as an RN but now works part-time as an exercise instructor at XSport Fitness, our neighborhood exercise facility where the Irregulars go to work out. My choice of her was easy. She is fit and tough and isn't afraid of anything. She carries a Taser and her version of pepper spray, a can of Raid Wasp and Hornet aerosol. If we got into a mess, she would have my back — as she's done before.

We put on latex gloves as we rode up in the elevator to Zhukov's office. The room was dark, and since it was cloudy, there wasn't any light coming through the windows. I turned on the flashlight from my backpack and used it as I walked to the middle of the three computers. After I entered the password, I slipped in the flash drive.

While the files were being downloaded, I showed Cas what I'd discovered the first two times I'd been there. She was impressed with the kitchen and bathroom, but she was stunned by the couch/bed and mirror above it. The polar opposite of Molly and her husband, Greg, Cas would never have considered having a mirror over her bed. Neither would her husband.

She stared at the ceiling. "You want to know what's strange?"

The computer continued to make soft downloading noises.

"On the drive down here, you told me how Molly discovered the bed and that the old guy she hung out with was kind of kinky," she continued.

The visual of Molly and an elderly man having sex would be forever burned into my brain. "The one who gave her gifts," I added.

"Yes. Molly told you he had a mirror like this, but also that he had a camera behind it."

"She said he got off by watching them have sex."

The computer clicked off. I removed the flash drive and shut down the computer. When I glanced up, she was gone. "Cas? Where are you? It's time to go."

"I'm in the bathroom."

"You can go later. Let's get out of here."

"I don't have to go. I'm hunting for something."

I joined her in the bathroom. She had already turned on the lights.

"What?"

"The recording machine for the camera."

30

"What are you talking about?" I asked.

"The last time you were here, did you check in the bathroom for a recording system?" Cas asked.

"I did search, but only for clean sheets. I didn't look for a recording system."

"If what Molly told you about old guys is correct, there has to be one in here."

Whoa.

"You might be right."

I pointed my flashlight out of the bathroom door toward the bed/couch and the ceiling mirror. Then I opened the door to the toilet room, which was separated from the main bathroom, and stepped in. There was no cabinet where Zhukov could have hidden recording equipment, but I heard a noise and watched as the toilet seat rose up.

"I've never had a toilet lid greet me before," I said. "That's cool."

"Toto," Cas said.

"I hope that's the brand name and not something that has to do with sex with old guys."

"The toilet's from Japan. Feel the seat."

"I don't think so."

"Do it. It's heated."

"You're kidding."

"Trust me."

I felt the seat. It was heated.

There was a horizontal row of buttons in a frame beside the toilet.

"Okay, toilet expert," I said. "What are all these buttons for?"

Cas began pointing. "This one cleans your front with warm water. This cleans the back. This is for drying." She paused. "You ought to try it."

She walked out and shut the door. When I turned around to sit down, I saw myself in a mirror on the opposite wall.

"Cas, come back in here a sec'. Have you ever seen anything like this?" I asked, pointing at the mirror.

"Molly said old guys are kinky."

She left. I sat down on the warm seat.

It was heaven.

31

After I finished using the toilet, I decided to try the "front cleaning" button. A gurgling sound was followed by a gentle flush of warm water, which cleaned the just-used area of my body. I discovered an "oscillate" button so I pushed it. The gentle stream of water began to slowly move back and forth. I shut my eyes and began to plan how I was going to con Carter into buying a toilet like this.

I pushed the "dry" button, and a whisper of warm air began to dry the same area. There was one other button, but it was unmarked. I pushed it. There was a soft hum as the mirror I was facing slid into the wall, exposing a TV.

Aha. There you are. Thank you, Molly.

The screen flickered on. I saw a man wearing a suit staring up at me.

Jumping off the toilet seat, I instinctively covered up my private parts.

"Check this," the man said, pointing my way.

He looked into what I knew was the mirror on the ceiling in Zhukov's office, but it felt like he could see me and was talking to me. The room lights were on.

Uh-oh!

I pulled up my pants, but my hands trembled and it was hard to do. A taller man, also wearing a dark suit, joined the first. He, too, seemed to stare directly at me. "I heard Zhukov was a little bent," he said. "Guess this is part of it. I wonder if there's a camera behind the mirror."

"If there is, we might want to find it in case there are any recordings of his activities," the first man said.

This should have been a quick visit so I'd left my backpack and gun in the van. I had to warn Cas so we could find a place to hide.

As I opened the door from the toilet room, I heard a third man speak but I couldn't see him on the TV screen.

"I think you better wait until Zhukov's company lawyer arrives," he said. "I called him when you guys showed up."

"Before you became head of security, you were with the Chicago PD, right?" the shorter man asked, as he glanced over his shoulder.

"I was, so you probably know that none of us like the FBI."

The two men moved away from the bed/couch, so they were no longer visible on the screen.

I need to see what's going on.

"We get that a lot, but you have in your hand a legal warrant to remove the items indicated."

"The hard drive from his computer."

"Exactly."

"And any records in his office."

"Why don't you stop being an obstructionist, and let us do our job so we can go home to our families?"

"I didn't think anyone in the FBI had a family. I presumed you spent all of your time screwing the local police out of cases."

I tiptoed into the main bathroom. Cas turned around and shrugged her shoulders. I put my index finger to my lips.

"Do not say anything," I whispered in her ear. "There are men out there," I jerked my head toward the office, "from the FBI."

Her eyes widened.

"Wait in the room with the toilet. You can hear what's going on in there."

She went in. I stayed in the main bathroom area and opened the door into the office a crack so I could see what was going on. The two men in suits stood by Zhukov's desk. A third man dressed in a blue shirt and work pants was in front of the three computers. The security guard was out of my line of vision to my right, so I couldn't see what he was doing.

I fingered the flash drive in my pocket and said a prayer of thanks that I'd already removed it and shut down the computer.

The two men went through Zhukov's desk. The third man worked on the computer's hard drive. The shorter agent slammed a drawer shut and stood up.

"What's in there?" he asked, pointing at the door I was hiding behind. That question made it difficult for me to breathe.

"It's the can," the unseen voice on my right said.

"And over there," the agent said, pointing to the other door.

"The kitchen."

"If he has a camera hidden behind that mirror, it's probably in one of those two rooms."

The agent walked toward me. My heart began racing at a lethal level as I tried to think of something I could say that would keep us from getting arrested.

32

"Don't even think about it," the unseen voice said. "Your warrant is good for this office and this office only. It does not mention any other rooms. If you want to go in there, get another warrant."

I exhaled the breath I was holding in. I couldn't see the man but he was my new best friend.

The agent turned around to the computer worker. "You done, Steve?"

The man pulled the hard drive up and placed it on the desk. "Ready to roll."

"We'll be back," the second agent said. "Don't touch anything in those two rooms. I'm going to seal his office. No one is to enter until we come back, got it?"

"Oh, I got it, pal. Why don't you guys get the hell out of here?"

The door slammed. I heard a click as room lights were shut off and a snap as the office door was locked from the outside. I peeked out. The room was dark and empty. I heard strange noises from the toilet room. I went in. Cas sat on the toilet watching the TV.

"I found them," she said.

I studied the screen. Two people were engaged in a sex act. I quickly turned my eyes away. "I guess you did," I said.

"There's a whole bunch of DVDs here. Should we take all of them with us?"

"Definitely, but why don't we let Molly be in charge of this part of the investigation? She's had a lot of experience in this area."

33

We left via the secret elevator. Cas waited in the mommy van while I made a stop that might save me from a future FBI visit. I walked in the main entrance of the building where Zhukov's office was located. A male security guard sat at the front desk.

"I'm sorry to bother you, but is your boss still around?" I asked.

He eyed me for a few seconds. "How do you know he's even here?"

A reasonable question for which I had no reasonable answer. In the old days, I never would have made a blunder like this.

"I mean that if he's on site, I need to speak to him. I think he'll recognize my face."

"It's your butt I remember," a man's voice behind me said. "I've never seen anyone spin around like that on a marble floor."

A medium-height, physically fit man in his mid-forties stood in a hallway to my left. He was dressed like the security guard at the desk with a blue blazer, gray slacks, blue shirt, and dark blue tie.

He walked up to me. "Pat Adley," he said, extending his hand.

We shook, but I didn't give him my name.

"I wondered when you would drop by," he said. "I assume you already know that Detective Corritore was here to watch the recordings from that night."

"That's exactly why I'm here," I said. "I don't want," I nodded at the other security guard, "other people to see them."

He raised his eyebrows. "Let's go into my office."

I followed him down the hall into a brightly lit room with a bank of TV monitors.

His face was grim. "What 'other people' are you talking about?"

"The FBI," I said.

"How do you know the FBI is involved in this?"

Another good question. He wasn't going to like the answer.

"I was in Zhukov's office tonight when they visited," I said.

He sat down and stared at me. "Should I ask how you got in there?" He paused. "And why the hell you were in there?"

"You have the right to do that since you are head of security, and I would like to answer, but that might get us both in trouble if the FBI begins asking you questions about me."

"I hate the FBI. I don't have a problem with screwing with them, but I don't want you to jerk me around. My job could be at risk. What the hell is going on?"

I told him.

34

"Obviously, Corritore didn't tell me those details," Adley said, when I finished. "She said you were here and found Zhukov's body and then lost it."

"I didn't lose it," I said. "The killer removed it."

He smiled. "I know. He pulled the body onto the elevator."

"Luminol?"

He nodded. "I used it after Corritore left. I wanted to know what happened up there. I found the blood spatter on the carpet in front of the elevator. That was good enough for me."

"She must be strong to pull a dead weight like that," I said.

"She?"

"I guess I forgot to mention that. The killer is a woman."

"How do you know that?"

"I saw her the last time I was here."

He glared at me. "You were here one other time?"

"I was. Last night, I came here to see if I could figure out what happened to the body. I used luminol on the carpet in the elevator. While I was here, a woman arrived on the secret elevator. I hid in the kitchen."

"How do you know she's the killer?"

"She downloaded the contents from his hard drive and then used luminol to find any blood traces, which she cleaned up."

"That doesn't make her the killer."

"She also wore the shoes I left behind Monday night."

He rubbed his lips with his index finger. "The only footprints she left were from your shoes. Seems like she wants to frame you for Zhukov's murder," he paused, "if anyone finds out he was killed."

"You're right." My stomach began to feel funny. "Right now your recordings show I was the only person here that night." I hesitated before I spoke any further.

Ask him!

"I don't suppose you would consider destroying them, would you?"

"Not a chance of that, lady, but I'll make you a deal," he said. "You tell me everything that's going on — and I mean everything — and I'll keep these recordings out of the FBI's hands."

"What if the feds find out what you're doing?"

"They won't think about it. Nothing much in the way of criminal activity ever happens here."

"Except Zhukov's murder."

"Might want to call it an 'alleged murder' since we don't have a body."

"Any ideas about that?"

"A good bet it's either in a landfill or at the bottom of Lake Michigan."

35

Mid-morning on Thursday, Linda Misle and I were in the lower level of our home. We sat next to each other in front of my computer screen.

Earlier that morning, I'd texted her about the events of yesterday involving Tony, Cas, and Pat Adley, the head of security at Zhukov's building. She'd texted back that we needed to meet.

Linda and her husband, Howard, have a daughter, Sandra, who is almost four, and a son, Jason, who is close to toddler age. Kerry and Sandra were at preschool together. Jason was home with his nanny. I'd breast-fed Macy, and she was asleep in my arms.

Linda is my height of five eight. We used to be in the same one hundred thirty pound weight range, but not any longer. I'm closer to being back to that weight. She still has a way to go to join me.

She took out a ballpoint pen and yellow legal pad. Writing on it is her preferred way to take notes. She had questions already listed on the first page. I felt like I was in a deposition.

"Let me be clear about the timeline," she began.

"Great."

"On Saturday, you texted me that you were going to write an article for Carter about Alexis Zhukov, a Russian investor who had a lot of unhappy clients, and you asked me to begin a background check on him."

"I did."

She checked the first question.

"I told you I'd seen him at my parent's country club where he gave a solicitation talk to invest in his fund."

"You did."

A check mark on question number two.

"On Tuesday morning, you texted the Irregulars that he was dead when you arrived in his office."

"I did, and he was."

Number three checked off.

"After you allegedly found his body, you ran away to get help."

"Not allegedly. I did find his body. He had a bullet hole between his eyes."

She ignored my response. "And when you returned to his office, he was gone."

"His body was gone, yes."

She hesitated and then checked off the question.

"About that. In your text to me this morning, you indicated that, yesterday, Tony told you United Airlines computer records show Alexis Zhukov boarded a plane and flew to Brunei through Shanghai the morning after you thought you saw him dead in his office."

"I say again, I found him dead in his office."

"What about his passport? Did the records indicate Zhukov used it along with his ticket?"

"That's what Tony told me."

Another check. "What about the security camera recordings at the airports?"

"Tony said Frankie's guy is working on that."

She put her pen down. "Now what?"

"That's why you're here. You're a lawyer. You used to prosecute white-collar crime before you went into private practice. You're the perfect one to figure this out."

"That's the problem I'm having here. Figure out what?"

"All the background material you sent me on Zhukov showed that he was in deep doo-doo with his investors. He'd lost millions of their dollars. I think he embezzled the rest of their money and he had an escape plan."

"And?"

"The killer put a bullet in Zhukov's brain to stop that from happening. She then removed his body and activated his escape plan before she left his office."

She wrote that down and then looked up.

"This makes no sense. How could she know about his plan?"

I began to rock Macy back and forth in my arms. "I saw Zhukov's body for a few seconds, but the one thing I remember is that he appeared so calm, like he sat in his chair and let someone blow his brains out."

"Why would he do that?"

"I think the killer came to his office and made him an offer he couldn't refuse. Give her the password to his computer and tell her the truth about what he was planning to do and she would let his family live."

She wrote that down. "What does his family have to do with this?"

"Historically, if you screw the Russian Mafia, they torture and kill your entire family, including the grandchildren. This time, the killer gave him an out. Give them what they wanted, and they would let his family live."

"And then he sat there while she shot him."

"It's the only thing that makes sense."

"But you arrived and changed the killer's plans."

"She had to assume I would bring the police back, which I did. All she had time to do was send an email from his computer to his secretary's, and then she left with the body."

"And came back the next night, after the secretary had gone home, to steal what she came for in the first place — the contents of his computer's hard drive."

"The perfect plan. Zhukov appears to leave for Brunei, taking any remaining money with him."

"But the Russian mob searches through his files before the FBI does and finds out where he hid the money. They take it all back before the feds can find the money."

"And I'm left without a story unless you can help me." I handed the flash drive to her. "Now you have the same contents from his files the Russians do. If you can help me figure this out, we'll have a compelling tale to write."

"I'll check the files, but aren't you forgetting something?"

"Ignoring would be a better word. I know the killer saw me the first night."

She re-read her notes and then tapped the pad with her pen. "You're potentially the only flaw in their plan. If they think you have figured this out, they won't hesitate to kill you. Maybe you should work on another story."

"I might have one. David and Rick recently purchased a home a couple of blocks from here. They're redoing it and said it's taking forever for the builder to complete the project. It's also gone way over their budget."

"Let me guess, they hate their builder."

"That's exactly what they said to me."

"The same thing happened to Howard and me with our home." She put down her pen. "That would be a great article."

"And it would be a whole lot safer."

36

I went upstairs, put Macy down for her nap, and turned on the Nanit. When I returned to the computer room, Linda had already inserted the flash drive I had used to copy Zhukov's computer files and had the material on the screen. I watched as she scrolled through page after page of financial data.

"This is giving me a headache," I said, after fifteen minutes of watching.

"Exactly how his investors must have felt," Linda said. "This was an extremely sophisticated Ponzi scheme."

"Like Bernie Madoff."

"Yes, but Zhukov was better. Initially, he paid high returns to the first clients from the money given to him by the next group of investors. But all of them were wiped out when the scheme fell apart."

"Wow."

"And from the last names, most of the investors appear to be Jews."

"Russian?"

"That would be my guess."

I pointed at the screen. "What about the Sturgeon Corporation? It looks like it took a massive hit."

"That might be the key to all of this. I think the Sturgeon Corporation is a Russian Mafia front to launder their illegal monies."

"Why would you say that?"

"When I prosecuted white-collar crime, money laundering was a common occurrence. It's easy for criminals to make money illegally, but it's very difficult to get it back into circulation to spend it without sending up red flags to each governmental agency in the world."

"And you think that's what happened?"

"The Sturgeon Corporation is a privately owned company in Russia, but," she pointed at the screen, "check its holdings here in the U.S. They own fur, jewelry, and art shops in places like Aspen and Vail, along with dry cleaners, laundromats, and car washes in big cities."

"So what?"

"These are well-known fronts for laundering illegal money."

"How do they do it?"

"It's actually pretty simple. The funds these businesses generate from legal sales are mixed with larger amounts of the Russian Mafia's illegal money. The books are then cooked to show the businesses produce only legal profits, which then go back to the Sturgeon Corporation, which appears on paper to be a legitimate business."

"Which the Russian Mafia owns."

"That would be my guess. All the businesses owned by the Sturgeon Corporation pay rent, employee salaries, FICA, and — most importantly — their local, state, and federal taxes."

"The IRS has to love that."

"Which is one major reason they ignore this business practice. Our economy needs the revenue."

"Even though most of the money is illegally generated."

"Yes, but there are also legal profits produced, and it's better to be able to collect the larger combined taxes than those that would come from the much smaller legal profits."

"I must be dense, but why go through all this? It seems like a lot of taxes are being paid. Why would the Russian Mafia essentially lose that money?"

"They are willing to give away a small amount of tax money to get more illegal money back into circulation without the government finding out."

"These crooks were paying taxes on their illegal money."

"You got it, but it gets better. The Sturgeon Corporation's board of directors took that laundered money, which was now legally in circulation, and invested it with Zhukov because of his fabulous returns. He paid them a thirty percent return each year, and since that money was legal, they paid taxes on that too."

"What did Zhukov get out of this?"

"He charged one point five percent to manage the fund and received twenty percent of the generated profits from his fund."

"No wonder he was rich."

"Really rich," she continued. "But it wasn't enough. This is where Zhukov topped Madoff. Zhukov figured out how to hack into the funds in the Sturgeon Corporation's bank account. When his scheme began to unravel, he embezzled their money to keep his returns up." He paid that embezzled money back to the clients, including the Sturgeon Corporation, as a dividend."

"Wow. He returned a dividend to them with their own money. That took real guts."

"But he had to steal more and more cash as his investments continued to crash until the Sturgeon owners found out and wanted their money back. His only option was to escape with all the money. He emptied out what was left of his other clients' money, wiping them out. He also took all the money he could from the Sturgeon Corporation."

"How much?"

"Over one hundred million dollars from the Sturgeon Corporation alone. It might be as high as one hundred fifty million."

"They found out he was planning to escape with all their money and killed him — but only after he gave them the password to his files so they could find their money."

"And the money from the other investors. Do we even care where the money is now?"

"Not if it means pissing off the Russians, but it sucks not to know for sure what happened to Zhukov. Rick and David's builder story is looking better and safer."

Part 3

37

Friday morning, I dropped Kerry off at preschool and then left Macy with our across-the-street neighbor, Alicia Sanchez, who is our go-to babysitter.

Turning left onto West Roscoe, I pulled up in front of Cas Johnson's home. Like the rest of the houses in our neighborhood, it's a brick, three-story, all-floors-above-the-ground style, but her husband, Joe, is frugal, and they have the bare basics for decorating inside and out — the polar opposite of Linda's fabulous home, which could easily be featured in *Architectural Digest*.

I honked and she came running out. I needed someone to cover my back in case we had an unanticipated problem where I intended to go: David and Rick's home.

Cas hopped into the passenger side of the van. "I thought we were working on that Russian guy's murder."

"We are, but I'm backing off for now until I figure out if doing an article involving pissed off Russians is worth it."

"What's this one about?"

"David and Rick's builder is working at a snail's pace, and they're about ready to kill him."

"What else is new? Our builder took forever to finish our home, and he charged us thousands more than the original quote. Joe and I wanted to strangle him."

From North Paulina to North Ravenswood there's a tree-lined median on West Henderson, the cross street. The median divides the street into two one-way streets, one east-to-west and the other west-to-east. David and Rick's home is halfway down the east-to-west side. It's a three-story, reclaimed brick structure built over fifty years ago.

I parked the van on the west-to-east side of West Henderson. We jogged over the median and crossed the street. David and Rick's front stoop was gone, replaced by two long boards going from the dirt to the front door.

There were a few loose boards and chunks of cement scattered randomly in the frozen dirt front yard. A wheelbarrow was turned upside down to the left of the front door.

Cas studied the mess in front of us. "Now I totally get why David and Rick are upset."

I fished around in my backpack for my cell phone. Charlie Sullivan Homes was the name listed as the builder on the big sign prominently displayed in the front yard. I took a picture of the contact information.

Cas pointed at the lock box on the front door. "How are we going to get in? Did they give you a key?"

"I have something better."

Reaching into my backpack, I pulled out my lock pick gun and torque wrench.

"I forgot you had that," she said.

"I never leave home without it," I replied.

38

We walked up one of the wooden planks to the front door. Using my equipment, I had the lock box open in ten seconds. We stepped inside and closed the door.

Cas looked around. "Jeez, it looks like a bomb went off in here."

The ceiling had been removed from the original entryway, which was now two stories tall. There was no staircase to the second floor. The stairs had been replaced by a ladder covered with various colored paint stains.

It was difficult to tell whether the wall studs were being knocked down or hammered into place. Drywall had been removed in many places, but some of it remained. Wires hung from the ceiling and stuck out of what was left of the remaining walls.

To my left was one intact wall with a door. I opened it and stared down into a black abyss.

Basement?

The stairway was missing. There wasn't even a ladder to gain access to the lower level space. Cement and musty dirt fumes drifted up and began to irritate my nose.

I took out the flashlight from my backpack and scanned the dark void below me. Part of the floor was gone, and all I could see were chunks of concrete and piles of dirt. The drywall had been ripped out, and only the cement block walls remained.

Cas followed me as I stepped over loose boards and nails and walked to the back of the house. We entered into what appeared to be a vaulted-ceiling great room. There were two sawhorses supporting a piece of old plywood, which functioned as the builder's desk, but there were no plans on it.

There were a couple of empty soda cans and a wadded up sack from Taco Bell on the floor. I sniffed but didn't smell freshly sawed wood, glue, or paint.

Not much happening here.

To my right was a room that could have been the kitchen, but it was hard to tell. To my left was a tangled mess of walls and electrical wires. I had no clue what was going on in there.

Outside, excavation for a room addition had begun, but it had a long way to go since only the dirt had been turned. To the left of this, a worker had dug down about three feet for frost footings.

A veranda?

We walked back down the plank leading from the front door to the frozen ground and returned to the van. Did all people want to kill their builder? Who could blame David and Rick? This place was not even close to being ready to be lived in.

"What do you think?" Cas asked.

"There might be a story here," I said. "Most people would relate to it."

"I agree."

"But I won't consider working on it without discussing it with all of you guys first."

39

I dropped off Cas, picked up Macy from Alicia's, and went home. While I breast-fed my daughter, I texted the rest of the Irregulars, including our newest members, David and Rick, about needing to meet to discuss the Zhukov and home builder stories. David called me when he received it.

"Sweetie, let's do it at our condo," he said.

"Great, if it's not too much trouble," I said.

"For you ladies, it never is. And there have been some recent developments, so we have a lot to discuss. I'll text the rest of the girls. See you around seven."

Carter had stories to edit, so he was happy to stay home with our daughters. At six thirty, I picked up Molly, Linda, and Cas and drove to David and Rick's condo in Northalsted.

Their unit is on the top floor of a three-story, modernistic, white brick building in the middle of the block. There are no retail stores in their building.

On the first floor of the three-story building on the left is an Oriental restaurant, a dry cleaners, and a pizza joint. The upper two floors contain condos. The entire first floor of the building to the right houses their salon, and the upper two floors have more condos.

Across the street is a four-story open garage sandwiched between two four-story office buildings.

Their condo is a little cluttered, but somehow it all flows together. There is no central decorating scheme or color. It's almost too much to absorb. Each time I come in I see something that I haven't seen before.

We sat in their family room. I stood up to tell the group what had happened with Zhukov, but David waved me back into my chair. He wore his deerstalker hat. He loves playing Sherlock Holmes to Rick's Dr. Watson.

"We have to go first," David said.

"Definitely," Rick said.

"It happened this morning," David said. "It could be tragic."

"Terrible," Rick added.

David smiled. "As you know, our clients tell us everything."

"Most of which we don't need to know," Rick said.

"But you absolutely must hear this," David said.

Rick pointed at me. "Especially you, Tina."

David frowned. "It's that awful Diane Warren."

"She is such a bitch," Rick agreed.

"You won't get any argument from me," Cas said.

As a nursing student, Cas had an intense affair with Diane Warren's then-future husband, Dr. Peter Warren. Diane and Cas hated each other because of this. It didn't stop when he killed himself over a year ago by driving into a cement bridge abutment. Diane wasn't exactly the reason he did this but was a major donor — at least that was Cas's assessment.

"I think we all agree Diane isn't the sweetest person in the universe, but what else is new?" I asked.

"This morning, Leslie Van Horn at The Factory called," David continued. "Since Diane fired us for not allowing her to bring Bear, her monster dog, into our salon, Leslie's stuck trying to make her awful hair presentable."

"She told him that MidAmerica Hospital is in severe financial trouble since Dr. Fertig died," Rick said. "And as you know, she owns the hospital."

"And Leslie says she blames the Hamlin Park Irregulars for this," David added.

What?!

"Have you ever heard of any hospital in this area losing money?" I asked.

David pondered that. "Now that you mention it, no."

"If what Diane told Leslie is factual, MidAmerica is the only one in Chicago that is," Rick said.

"How is that possible?" Linda asked.

"In one word, Dr. Randall Fertig," David said.

"Honey, that's three words, but who's counting?" Rick asked.

40

Dr. J. Randall Fertig was a breast cancer surgeon who claimed his surgery cured one hundred percent of the patients he operated on. From the beginning, I was skeptical of that claim.

Fertig was the head of surgery at MidAmerica Hospital and produced over seventy-eight percent of their total revenue. I thought the story was great and worked hard on it until he ended his career by flying his plane into the ground from twenty thousand feet.

"Diane told Leslie that if you hadn't pursued the story on Fertig, he wouldn't have killed himself," David said.

Cas jumped up. "That is total bullshit, and we all know it! Fertig had incurable AIDS. He killed himself to keep the world from finding out about it."

"That is not her version of the events," Rick said. "Leslie said she is positive you did this to get back at her due to your relationship with her late husband."

"Guys, Diane has more family money than she can count," Molly reminded us. "Why doesn't she close the hospital and go on a world cruise or something?"

"Her gigantic ego is the reason," David said.

"Apparently Diane has pushed all her chips into the pot to save her hospital," Rick said. "She wants to prove Fertig wasn't the reason for the hospital's financial success — it was her management skills that were."

Might need to look into that.

"If it goes under, she'll be down to her last few million dollars, poor dear," David said.

"She is bellowing to the world that the Irregulars harassing ways were the cause of her husband Peter's death," Rick added.

"Because of all of this, Leslie said she is out to get you," David warned.

"Then we should have Tina shoot her before she does something to us," Molly said. "That's what the farmers taught me."

"Not funny, Molly," I said, "but that reminds me of something that happened the night the guy who worked for Diane attacked us in the garage at MidAmerica Hospital and I shot off his fingers. Linda, do you remember how he knew where we were?"

"He said he put a GPS transponder under your fender," she said. "I found it."

"I wonder if Diane had one of her employees do it again," I said.

"Gosh, if she did, this would be the perfect time to do something to us," Molly said. "We're all together, and we don't have our kids with us."

My hands began to sweat. "Cas, do you have your Taser and Raid Wasp and Hornet spray with you?" I asked.

"Always," she answered.

"If there is more than one of them and they start shooting at us, those won't do much good," Linda said. "Do you have your gun, Tina?"

"It's in my backpack."

"Then there you have it," Molly said.

"Have what?" Linda asked.

"If they start shooting at us, Tina can take care of them. Simple."

"I would prefer not to be involved with any more gun play," Linda said. "I don't want to see any more fingers shot off."

"We should call the police," Cas said.

"And what would they do?" David asked. "As a former lawyer, I can assure you that until a crime is committed the police will not assist us." He turned to Linda. "Don't you agree?"

"I do, but maybe we're worrying for nothing and no one is outside."

"Are you willing to bet on that?" I asked.

No one spoke.

"There's only one solution," I said. "I'll call Frankie."

41

Whatever it is that Janet Corritore's husband, Frankie, does, he always has at least two bodyguards with him. He is the perfect friend to have in a situation like this.

I called him. "We might need your help," I said.

"Already on it," Frankie said.

"On what?" I asked.

"Me and the boys are outside."

"Outside... here? I don't understand."

"It's the way we roll when the boss gives us an assignment."

"Janet?"

"Yeah. After you found the Russian stiff, she called me. She was worried about you. One of us has been on you ever since." He paused. "Russians are tough dudes. They aren't the kind of guys you want to fool around with."

"You sound like you're afraid of them."

"Just being realistic. They're good at what they do."

"Which is?"

"Killing people they don't like."

My heart began to thump against my sternum. I left the family room and walked into the dining room, which faced the street where we had parked our cars. I walked over to the window and peeked out. "I don't see you."

"Enzo is on your left at the end of your side of the block. He's in a Ford Taurus. Luca is on your right in a Chevy truck at the other end of the block."

Checking both ways, I saw the two vehicles. The windows of the vehicles were tinted, making it difficult to see if anyone was inside.

"Where are you?" I asked.

"Watching."

"Watching what?"

"The guy who showed up the same time you all arrived at David and Rick's condo. Enzo's been with you all day. This is the first time he's seen anyone following you. He texted me. Luca and I hustled over here."

I peeked out the windows again and scanned the street below me. "I don't see anyone."

"He's in the parking garage across the street, third level, behind the second cement pillar. He's using night vision goggles. Good stuff too. Expensive."

"It's nice to know he's well-equipped. Where are you?"

"The roof."

"Which one?"

"The building to your right, same side of the street as you. Watch."

I glanced in that direction and saw a quick red flash coming from the roof of the three-story building next door.

"A laser sight?" I asked.

"Yeah, I have it on my sniper rifle if he decides to make his move tonight."

"Who is he?"

"Not sure. He's driving a black Ford van with stolen plates. He parked it on the far side of the same floor of the garage he's on. I can't see his face clearly enough to get a picture so Janet can make an ID."

"What's the plan?"

"When he leaves, we follow him to where he lives and have a serious talk with him," he said. "Hold on. Enzo is calling me."

I waited.

He came back on the line. "The guy's on the move."

"Where's he going?"

"Not sure. This roof is higher than you are and my vision of the third floor is partially blocked by the fourth floor of the garage. You got eyes on him?"

Since I was on the third floor, the man was directly across from me. I could make out a figure walking toward a black van parked at the far end of the garage.

"Got him," I said.

"What's he doing?"

"Opening the back of the van and pulling out a crate."

"A crate?"

"Yeah, a wooden box about three or four feet long. He's opening the box and taking out a black tube with a strap attached. It's about three feet long."

"Fuck," he muttered to himself.

"What's wrong?"

"Sounds like it might be an RPG."

"What's an RPG?"

"A rocket. He's gonna blow you guys up."

42

All I could think about were my two kids and loving husband, who would kill me if he knew what was going on. Unless the man across the street did first.

"Where's he now?" Frankie asked.

"Still standing by the van," I said.

"Hold on. I'll call the boys and send them up there."

"Tell them to hurry. He shoved something into the black tube and now he's slung the strap of the tube over his shoulder."

The driver's doors of the two vehicles on each end of the street flew open. Enzo and Luca exited so fast they left the car doors open. They sprinted toward the entrance of the parking garage.

Frankie came back on the line. "I don't want to scare you, but I can't see him well enough to have a shot. If the boys don't get there in time, you gotta put him down."

"Frankie, I'm a mommy! I can't do this!"

"Man up, babe. You got no options."

Running back into the family room, I yanked the Glock out of my backpack. The Irregulars were beginning to eat the snacks that David had put out.

"Guys, I don't want to scare you or anything, but you might want to leave," I said.

"Why?" Cas asked.

"There's a man across the street and he might have some kind of rocket thingy in his hands."

"Is it an RPG?" Rick asked.

"I think that's what Frankie called it," I said.

Rick's voice was instantly hard. "David, get everyone out of here right now. Go to the basement and hurry." He turned to me. "Show me."

David opened the front door of the condo, and the Irregulars scrambled out after him. Rick followed me back into the dining room.

"Where is he?" he asked.

I pointed at the garage. "Right there, behind the second pillar from the street."

The man's right leg and shoulder were all we could see. He seemed to be fumbling with the tube. Rick opened the window in front of us. There was no screen. Street noises intruded into the room. I smelled pizza being cooked in the restaurant across the street.

"He has to step out to fire," Rick said. "When he does, that's when you shoot."

I jacked a round into the chamber. "And how would you know how to do any of this?"

"Sweetie, I told you I was a medic in the first Iraq war, but I was also a sniper. I used to do stuff like this a lot."

I turned the gun around to hand it to him. "I'm a mommy. I don't do stuff like this."

He put up his hands. "I haven't fired your Glock, and I don't know how it's going to react. You have, and you can do it."

My hands began to shake. "Please, Rick, I can't."

"You want to tuck your daughters in tonight?"

"Of course I do."

"Then suck it up, buttercup. When he steps out, you aim for his center mass and give him a double tap."

"But what if I miss?"

"Probably not good to think about that right now. Try to shoot in between your heartbeats."

That wasn't going to be easy since my heart was racing from the surge of adrenaline rushing through my system. My father taught me how to shoot in Nebraska from the time I was a little girl, so I know my way around guns.

But what if I miss?

The man stepped out from behind the pillar and raised the tube. Assuming a shooter's stance, I concentrated on the middle of his chest and relaxed my shaking right hand. The man seemed to be fumbling with the controls as he aimed the tube at us.

Pray for mommy, kids.

Taking a deep breath to slow my heart rate, I fired two rounds at the center mass of his chest.

43

The impact of the two bullets blew the man backward. The rocket tube flew out of his hands as he landed on the garage floor. The roar of the Glock being fired in the small dining room was deafening. The odor of gun powder surrounded us. I saw a couple of people run out from one of the shops in the building next to the one we were in, but when they didn't see anything, they went back inside.

Rick said something to me, but my ears were ringing and I couldn't understand him.

"What?" I asked.

"Great shot," he said. "Right in the O-ring."

I started to sob. Rick put his arms around me and gave me a hug. "You didn't have an option. If you hadn't done it, we would all be dead."

"But…" I whined.

"No buts. It's over. Your kids still have a mommy and your husband a wife."

Enzo and Luca exited the stairs and ran into the garage with their guns in front of them. When they got to the man, Luca kicked the tube further away and then knelt down and put his hand on the man's neck. He turned to us and gave me a "thumbs up."

They put their guns down as Frankie ran out of the same garage door toward them. He said something to them. Luca nodded. He handed his weapon, a lupara, to Frankie and stepped back.

Frankie took the sawed-off shotgun and, at point blank range, fired both barrels into the man's chest. He handed the smoking gun back to Luca. Strangely, I didn't hear any sound from those shots.

I was still crying as I turned to Rick. I had to clear my throat to speak. "What the heck is going on? Isn't the guy dead?"

"Oh, I'm sure he's dead. I think Frankie is cleaning things up a bit." He paused. "Speaking of which…"

He picked up the two hot bullet casings from the dining room carpet and put them in his pocket. "Old habit. I never left any evidence behind. If anyone ever finds the body, they won't be able to tell that you shot him since there isn't much left of his chest."

I kept crying. Rick handed me a tissue. I dabbed my eyes and blew my nose. "I want to go over there."

"Are you sure? After what Frankie did, it might be a trifle messy."

"I just murdered a man. I have to."

And this is a big part of my story.

He closed the window. "I'll make sure David and the girls are okay, and then I'll walk over there with you."

44

As soon as Rick and I entered the third floor of the parking garage, the acrid stench of gunpowder drifted toward us in the cool March night air. Rick took out a handkerchief and covered his mouth and nose.

"I hate that smell," he said through the cloth.

We walked toward the body. "That's a strange comment coming from a sniper," I said.

"Sweetie, I might have been a sniper, but I am a *tres* sensitive person."

"How many gay snipers did they have in Iraq?"

"Don't ask, don't tell, and believe me, when you're as good a shot as I was, no one ever asked."

Frankie put up his hands to stop us when we were about twelve feet from the body. Frankie's face is square, and his olive skin bears small scars from adolescent acne. A narrow soul patch runs from the edge of his lower lip to the deep cleft in his chin.

Like Enzo and Luca, who are younger than Frankie, he is blocky but not fat. It looks like they all work out together, and from the size of Frankie's biceps, it looks like he could more than hold his own lifting heavy weights with his youthful companions.

The aroma of the fresh blood and body fluids oozing from the body onto the cement floor of the garage now overwhelmed the gunpowder smell.

Frankie moved to block my view of the corpse. "Not a good idea for you to check this mess."

I felt like I wanted to cry again. "I need to see him," I said softly.

Rick stepped around me and removed the handkerchief from his face. He man-hugged Frankie.

"Dude," he said.

"What up, bro?" Frankie asked.

"You guys know each other?" I said.

"He cuts my hair," Frankie said.

"And we ride motorcycles together," Rick said. "We have for a long time."

Didn't see that coming.

Rick walked over to the body.

Frankie turned back to me. "Bro has serious ink," he said, nodding toward Rick.

"I guess I shouldn't be surprised. At least one of my friends does too," I said, as I remembered a tattoo I'd inadvertently seen on Linda's lower back when she was in the hospital. "I need to see the body."

Frankie didn't move, but peeking over his shoulder, I could see Rick lean down.

"Uh-oh," Rick said to himself.

"Uh-oh, what?" I said.

He stood up holding the tube. "This RPG is a Tavolga."

"That sounds like something from an opera," I said.

"Nothing musical about this. It has a thermobaric warhead. Way more than enough to blow away our condo." He paused. "It's Russian-made."

Bile bubbled up into the back of my throat.

45

Elbowing my way around Frankie, I walked up to the body. Luca held the lupara shotgun in his arms. Enzo had an Uzi at his side. They stepped back.

"Yikes," I said, when I saw the corpse.

Rick stood up. "A bit untidy I'm afraid."

I tried to speak, but my breath caught in my throat.

What have I done?

Over a year and a half ago, while working on another story, I accidentally shot my terrorist neighbor while defending myself in my kitchen. We had struggled for his gun. It went off and hit him in the chest. The wound bled profusely, and after he died, he pooped and peed all over my kitchen floor. But that was nothing compared to this.

The entire front of the victim's chest was a mangled mess of bone, skin, muscle, cartilage, heart and lung tissue, and other body parts I couldn't identify. The twin blasts from the sawed-off shotgun had destroyed any physical evidence that I had shot him first.

Rick squatted down and pried open the victim's mouth.

I swallowed and cleared my throat again. "Are you a dentist too?" I asked.

"I'm sorry?" he asked, glancing over his shoulder at me.

"Why are you checking his mouth?"

"Russians have shoddy dental care. The RPG was Russian. I thought that was interesting."

I opened my mouth to asked him how he knew this, but he held up his hand and I stopped.

"On a couple of secret missions, I saw a few Russian bodies, and all of them had stainless steel fillings in their teeth." He held the victim's mouth open. "I don't see any. His teeth appear to be normal."

"Maybe the Russians are getting better at dental care."

His voice was hard. "And maybe he's not a Russian and he bought the RPG on the black market."

He pulled up the man's right sleeve, exposing his upper arm. He looked at a large tattoo of a weird-looking fork. "Interesting."

Frankie walked over and looked at it. "Bro."

"I know," Rick said.

"What are you guys talking about?" I asked.

"Rick, show her."

He pulled up his own right sleeve. He had a similar tattoo.

"It's a Seal trident," Rick said.

My heart felt like it skipped a beat. "Does that mean…"

"I was a Seal. He was too."

No!

I'd killed one of our military men.

Rick looked up at me. "Don't feel bad. Not all of our men work for the good guys when they get out. Guys like him drift to the dark side and do wet work for money."

He picked up the victim's right hand and then his left. "Huh?"

"Huh, what?" I said.

"Small wonder that he fumbled with the RPG. He's missing a few fingers."

Uh-oh!

46

The tension that had been escalating in my neck now blasted into my temples. It felt like a belt was being tightened around my head. I massaged my neck with my left hand.

For the first time, I studied the man's face. "I know him," I said, as I continued to rub my neck, "and you're right, he's not a Russian."

Rick stood up and brushed off his hands. Enzo stared at me. Luca did too.

"This the guy Janet told me about?" Frankie asked. "The one you plugged in the garage at MidAmerica Hospital?"

I stared at the corpse's face. He was someone who blended into the background, a man you would see and not remember five minutes later. He seemed average when I first encountered him, and he still did — with the exception of the gaping hole in his chest.

And I killed him.

"Yeah, it is."

"Who is he?" Rick asked.

"He accosted me in the parking lot at Costco and told me to stop working on the Fertig story. I took out my

Glock and told him to leave us alone. He verbally threatened me, but he left. Then he attacked Linda and me in the garage at MidAmerica hospital and tried to shoot us. I fired first and shot off a finger or two on his right hand." I paused, remembering that event. "He laughed at me. When he reached for his gun a second time, I had no option but to fire again to protect Linda and me, and I shot off part of his left hand."

"It would appear that laughing at you isn't exactly a healthy thing to do if you value your fingers," Rick said.

"Especially if it's a man who is laughing," I said. "That does upset me."

47

Frankie walked over to Enzo and Luca. He lowered his head and spoke to them in Italian. They nodded and walked over toward the victim's truck. Frankie rejoined us.

"Don't you think we should call Janet?" I asked.

"I'm thinking that's a definite negatory," Frankie said.

"This guy tried to kill us," I said. "I shot him. He's dead. We have to call the police."

Frankie glanced at Rick before he replied. "It might be a problem if we call the cops."

"I have to agree," Rick said. "We should keep this in house, so to speak."

"Guys, we have to call the cops," I said.

"And say what?" Frankie asked.

"A man has been shot and killed," I said.

"And who was the shooter?" Rick asked.

"I was."

"You shot and killed a man you already shot twice before," Frankie said. "And you called Janet the last time, so the police have a record of it."

I am so screwed!

"This doesn't look so good for me. What do we do?"

"We need to change things a little bit," Frankie said.

"There are no security cameras in the garage or on this street, something we as shop owners constantly complain about," Rick said.

"Unless someone was watching out a window, no one saw what happened," I said. "What about the noise from the lupara?"

"Did you hear anything from the condo?" Frankie asked.

"No."

"It's been tricked up a little bit so it doesn't sound like a shotgun, but the boys still need to remove the evidence."

"The body?"

"The body, the van, and the body fluids evidence on the garage floor."

"Where will you take them?" I asked.

"It's harder to get rid of a vic's body than you would think," he said. "Best place is in new construction before they pour the cement."

"Isn't that what happened to Jimmy Hoffa?" I asked.

"I'm sayin' this method has been used for years by my countrymen, and it works," he said. "Now all we have to do is find a construction site."

"I have one," Rick said. "We're remodeling a house on West Henderson in Lakeview. The basement will be the perfect place. We weren't ready to pour cement for the floor, but now we can be."

"What about the van?" I asked.

"The boys'll leave it on the South Side with the keys in it," Frankie said. "Won't last long before it's stolen and disappears in some neighborhood chop shop."

Enzo drove the van up beside the body and stopped. Luca was in the passenger seat. Frankie walked over to tell them the plan. They got out and quickly moved the body and the RPG into the van.

"Rick, isn't it going to be a little weird having a dead body buried underneath your home?" I asked.

"Personally, I think it's kind of kinky, but then I've always been slightly bent."

"What about David?" I asked.

Rick made a motion with his hand to zip his mouth shut. "Best not say anything, at least not yet. He doesn't do well with blood, and I mean to tell you, a dead body buried under the washer and dryer in our basement would totally freak him out. I'll tell him that part later, like a striptease, with a slow reveal."

48

Rick called David on his cell phone and put him on speaker. We listened as he told David what happened. Rick didn't mention specific details or what was going to happen to the body, but he told David to keep the girls way from the windows facing the parking garage.

David and the rest of the Irregulars sat in the family room when Rick and I returned to their condo. No one was talking or eating the food that had been prepared. The questions began before we could sit down to tell them what happened. I was afraid I was going to cry, but I didn't have a chance.

"Do you think Diane Warren sent the guy?" Cas asked.

"That is a patently stupid question," Linda said. "Obviously, she did. She hates you and Tina."

"Gosh, I'm not so sure," Molly said. "The guy was mad at Tina for shooting off his fingers, so maybe he did this on his own."

"Then why didn't he attack her at her home?" Linda asked. "Why did he include us in this rocket bomb fiasco? We could have been blown to bits."

"Tina, you are kind of a bomb magnet," Cas said, referring to the time I'd been blown up before.

I held my hands up. "Stop. This is not my fault."

"Then whose fault it is?" Linda said. "It most certainly isn't mine."

"Ladies, please," Rick said. "You were not 'almost killed.' Tina did a masterful job in handling this minor problem."

"Thank you, Rick," I said.

"You're welcome," he said.

"What exactly did happen over there?" Linda asked.

I opened my mouth to tell them, but Rick beat me to it. "Initially, we assumed the man had a rocket launcher of some type, but it proved to be a large telescope with a camera attached. By the time we arrived, Frankie and his crew had convinced the man to leave us alone forever."

"And Tina didn't shoot him again?" Linda asked.

"Do you see any evidence of that?" Rick asked. "Like shell casings for instance." He stood up and waved his arms around the room. "Anywhere? Or the sound of a gunshot?"

"No, I don't, but we were in the basement so we couldn't hear anything," she said. "And I thought I smelled gunpowder when we walked past the dining room."

Rick peeked at David and raised his eyebrows. "Right," David said. "That is the new furniture polish I found at Costco. Rick loathes it."

"I do, indeed," Rick said. "If Tina shot him, where is his body? Except for Zhukov, dead people don't get up and walk away."

"And you can call Frankie and ask him," I said. "He'll tell you exactly the same thing."

Linda glanced down at her hands. "I'm sorry. Guns scare me, and I don't even have words to describe how much a rocket would terrify me."

"If I'd known the guy was going to be taking pictures of us, I would've worn something hot," Molly said. "Do you think he'll tell us next time so I can be prepared?"

"Honey, that's one thing I can assure you of," Rick said. "For him, Frankie told us there won't be a next time."

"I think we need to address this problem with Diane Warren," I said. "We have to assume the guy worked for her."

"Worked?" Linda asked.

This was the problem with having a smart lawyer for a friend. She didn't miss a thing.

"Who cares?" I retorted. "He was here and now he's gone, but she isn't going anywhere, at least not that I know of. And we're all safe."

"I agree with Tina," David said. "From what Diane's hairstylist, Leslie, said, I feel certain that her dislike for all of you is genuine, and the sooner we do something to stop her, the better."

The room was silent. Linda stood up and began pacing back and forth. "Diane Warren owns MidAmerica Hospital. Fertig, her major moneymaker, died. Now she's having financial problems, which she blames on us. I think we need to investigate the severity of these problems and see what she's doing to solve them."

"And why she's even bothering to do it," Cas added.

"Do you think it's something illegal?" Molly asked.

"She's capable of it," Cas said. "She won't let breaking a few little laws stop her."

"We need to research her hospital's present cash flow and see where it's coming from," I said. "Any ideas where we begin?"

"How about visiting MidAmerica Hospital?" Linda asked. "Let's go directly to the source."

"Linda's right," Cas said. "Employees and nurses love to gossip."

"Then we need to be there to listen," I said.

49

Saturday morning, Linda and I stood in front of the double doors of the Medical ICU at MidAmerica Hospital. We were dressed as members of the janitorial company that serviced the hospital and the building where the Warren Law Offices, Peter's family's firm, were located. The office was attached to the MidAmerica Hospital.

Frankie's friend owns the cleaning firm. The man had previously helped Linda and me do this before when we broke into those same offices while working on another story, so we already had picture IDs to open all the hospital's locked doors. All we needed this time were the clean green uniforms which we now wore.

"Why do I always have to be a janitor?" Linda asked. "Why can't I be nurse or, better, a doctor?"

"You've had experience at being a janitor," I said.

"Doesn't this company have any other color uniforms?" she continued. "Forest green isn't good for me." She held up her ID badge. "And I want a new picture. This one makes me look fat."

"Do you always have to complain when we do something like this?"

"I'm good at it. That's why I became a lawyer." She paused. "By the way, you look tired."

Almost being blown up and then killing the man who tried to do it didn't do anything to help me sleep last night. When I arrived home from the David and Rick's, all I wanted to do was hug my two girls. Carter noticed but, thankfully, didn't ask me what was wrong. But I had to leave them again on Saturday morning because Diane's story — and our safety — demanded it.

Working on stories and daily journaling had been my way to push through tough times before. I was doing the "work" part now. The journaling would come tonight after my family was asleep.

We pushed through the double doors and entered the ICU. Medicinal odors immediately attacked my previously injured PTSD brain. I had to stop and close my eyes as the memories of being blown up and near death in an ICU like this washed over me. Other scents, like gunpowder, I can handle, but hospital smells still bother me.

"Are you okay?" Linda whispered.

"Give me a second," I said. "I don't do well in an ICU."

"I guess almost getting killed while chasing a story will do that to you."

"Tell me." I took in a deep breath and opened my eyes. "I'll take the nurse's station. Where are you going?"

"Not the bathroom. I don't do bathrooms." She turned her cart around. "I'm thinking the break room. The nurses will be relaxed and be more likely to talk."

"And there might be some free snacks from drug companies."

"There is that, but I'm back on my diet, so that's not a problem."

I began emptying wastebaskets at the nurse's station. A doctor stood at the nurse's desk.

"I'm sorry, Doctor," one of the nurses sitting down behind the counter said. "Would you repeat that?"

He mumbled something, but she didn't react. They stared at each other until he moved to one of the computer terminals and typed in what he needed.

His orders flashed up on her screen. "Right away, Doctor," she said.

When she stood up, I caught her eye and nodded toward the man's back as he walked away. "They're hard to understand," I said. "A lot of them seem to have accents."

"Almost all of the FMGs are like that."

"What's that?"

"Foreign Medical Graduates. Makes for long days for the nursing staff, especially with all the low sick patients we've been seeing lately."

"Aren't they all sick in here?" I asked.

She took a sip from a can of Coke. "They are, but recently there have been all kinds of weird autoimmune admits. It would be easier on all of us if these doctors could at least communicate with us in English."

"Where's he from?"

"Who knows? India, Pakistan, Russia — some place he didn't learn our language." She went to the medicine cabinet and unlocked it. "It's not like the old days."

"I've only been here a month. What happened to the doctors who speak English?"

"No one will say, but I heard they got fired."

There was a commotion in the hallway. I turned around to see what was going on. Two security guards walked out of the break room. Linda was between them.

Each guard held one of her elbows as they pushed her toward the elevators. My gun was jammed underneath the trash in my cart. Pushing my cart in front of me, I quickly followed, trying to catch them while at the same time rummaging around in the trash hunting for my gun.

They stepped on the elevator and the door slid shut before I could get there. I stood in front of the closed doors pounding on the down button.

"Finally," a nurse said, who'd walked up next to me.

"Excuse me?" I asked.

"They caught the person who's been stealing our free snacks."

50

The elevator doors opened, and I shoved the cart on. The nurse entered behind me and pushed the button for the main floor.

"Where's the security office?" I asked.

She stared me. "Don't you know where it is?"

"I'm new here. The lady they busted was showing me around."

"Was she teaching you how to steal our food too?"

"No way. Did you see how big her butt is? I was the one doing all the work while she ate."

"Security's on the ground floor, near the pharmacy."

She pushed "G" for me and then exited on the first floor. I pushed my cart off on the ground floor and parked it in front of the first women's bathroom I came to. I dug the gun out of the trash, put it in the back of my pants, and pulled my top down to cover it up. Then I entered the bathroom and speed-dialed Frankie on my cell phone.

"We're in trouble," I said. "The security guards at the hospital made us."

"How?" Frankie asked.

"Linda ate some food that was intended for the nursing staff. I think they saw her do it by using a surveillance camera hidden in the break room."

"Better ditch the janitor outfit."

"I can't. I dressed at home and don't have any other clothes."

"Got your gun?"

"I do."

"Maybe you can shoot your way out."

"I have a better idea, but your guy needs to shut down the security cameras."

"I'll call him, pronto, but you gotta give me five."

"Better make it three."

51

I had to do something in a big hurry.

Fertig.

When I worked on his story, I accessed the male doctor's locker room using the same picture ID card Frankie's guy had made for me that I was now wearing again. This time, the female locker room was my answer.

My heart pounded against my sternum as I rushed toward that door. I prayed the security cameras had been disabled as I ran my ID card over the lock. The green light flashed on. There was a click, and I pulled open the door.

Several nurses and a couple of female doctors were in there changing clothes, but I wore my janitor's outfit and no one looked up when I walked in.

I took a blue scrub suit into the bathroom and changed as quickly as I could, transferring the Glock into the back of my pants and again covering it with my top. I walked out wearing my scrub suit and left the janitor's suit in a laundry basket.

By the exit door into the OR, I found paper scrub hats in a box on a shelf along with the paper surgical masks and paper booties. I slid on the paper booties over my ASICs. I put on the hat which covered my hair, but even better, except for my eyes, the mask hid the rest of my face.

I saw a long white lab coat hanging on a hook. There was a stethoscope in the pocket of the coat. I put it on and hung the scope around my neck. I grabbed a pair of disposable protective plastic eyeglasses and slipped them on too.

When I stepped back into the main hallway, two security men ran past me. They pulled out their guns when they saw my janitor's cart in front of the bathroom.

One of them yanked out a handheld radio. "We found her cart in front of the women's bathroom on the ground floor," he said. "What do you want us to do?"

"Go in and get her," the voice said over the radio.

With their guns held in front of them, they slammed the bathroom door open and barged in. The noise of them banging the stall doors open echoed out into the hallway, followed by a "She's not here…" call on the radio.

The guards came out and checked up and down the hallway. When they saw me staring their direction, they sprinted toward me. The white coat made it impossible to reach my Glock, effectively eliminating it as a choice if I needed it to defend myself. I had nowhere to go.

"Dr. Lee?" the guard said, glancing down at the nametag on my white coat.

"Yes?" I said, trying to keep my voice from quivering.

"Did you see a female janitor come by here? She's wearing a green jumpsuit."

I slid the plastic glasses on top of my head and undid the ties to the top of my scrub mask, causing it to slip down partway off my face but not enough so they would recognize me.

"As a matter of fact I did. It was weird that she was running. None of them ever move that fast. But anyway, she came flying out of that bathroom and ran toward the emergency room."

He yelled into his phone. "We got her! She's headed toward the ER. Get everyone down there!"

They sped off. I pulled up my scrub mask and went the opposite direction toward the security office.

I called Frankie. "I'm going to the security office to see if I can find Linda. I might need some help."

"Already rollin'," he said.

52

Several more security guards ran past me toward the ER. With my head down, I walked in the opposite direction toward the security office. When I opened the door into the office, I saw one guard monitoring a bank of security TV screens. He had his back to me and fiddled with the dials, but all he had on the screens were wiggling lines. Frankie's guy had come through.

"Jack, do you have anything on the screens?" a voice asked over the speakers.

"Not yet," he said. "I have to reboot the system. Give me a couple of minutes."

"Better hurry. We can't find Thomas, and the boss lady is pissed."

Pulling the surgery mask down, I walked up behind him.

"Jack," I said, as I pressed the Glock into his right ear, "I think it would be a good idea if you leave the security system alone."

I saw the muscles in his shoulders tense up.

"Not a good idea, Jack," I said. "Put your hands on the table in front of you."

He begin to lean back against me.

"You probably think you can move before I decide if I want to use this gun or not, but that would be wrong. Ask the guy who is missing several of his fingers."

He moved forward, preparing to jump up. I stepped to his side and pointed the Glock at his crotch. "I can shoot off other things than fingers. I told you to put your hands on the table in front of you."

This time he complied. I moved the Glock back toward his chest.

"You'll never get out of here," he said.

"Oh, I think I will, but I'm curious. How did you make us?"

He hesitated. I pointed the Glock back toward his crotch.

"We have facial recognition software on our security cameras. The one in the breakroom identified Misle. We lost you when you got to the ground floor, and then the cameras went down." He studied the screens, which now were back to normal. "How did you do that?"

"Do what?"

"Screw up the security cameras."

"Must be a computer error. I didn't do anything to your precious system." I waved the gun at him. "Where is Linda?"

He hesitated again. I was running out of time. I fired the Glock into his chair about two inches in front of his crotch.

He lurched backwards and fell out of his chair onto his side. The noise from the gun blast was deafening in the small room.

When he turned back toward me, I was pleased to see that he had peed in his pants.

"Where is Linda Misle?" I asked again.

He stared at me. I pointed the Glock back down at his crotch. He curled into the fetal position and put his hands in front of his private parts.

"Ease off, lady. She's in the back room."

"Show me, and move slowly or else you'll be singing soprano in the church choir for the rest of your life."

53

The guard rolled onto his stomach and pushed himself up on all fours. Standing up, he walked to a closed door at the end of the hallway. I followed.

I raised the Glock and got into a shooter's stance in case it was a trap. "Open it."

He used his ID card to unlock it and pulled open the door. Linda sat in a chair in the center of a small, windowless room. She jumped up when she saw me.

"Tina, thank God you're here!" she exclaimed.

I shoved the gun in his back. "Get in there."

Jack complied. I took his ID card and the radio from his belt.

"Linda, wait for me in the hall," I said. "I have to do something."

She walked out. I shut the door and raised the gun. Jack's face blanched as he held up his hands. "Lady, I did what you wanted. Give me a break here."

"Only if you answer a question for me."

"Anything. But please don't shoot me."

I lowered my gun slightly. "The guy with missing fingers tried to blow us up with an RPG. Was he following orders, or was he working on his own?"

"He told us he was leaving town, but before he left, he said he was going to settle a score with you bitches."

I raised the gun. "Bitches?"

"His word, not mine."

"Diane Warren didn't order the visit?"

"Not so far as I know."

I backed up toward the open door.

"I gotta question," he said.

I waited.

"What happened to Bobby?" he asked.

"Bobby?"

"The guy with the missing fingers."

"He told you he was leaving town, right?"

"Yeah, he did," he said.

"He told you the truth," I said. "He's gone and won't be coming back."

I locked the door and left.

Frankie and Enzo stood outside of the security office when we came out. Linda was with them.

"Before Linda came out, I heard a gunshot," Frankie said. "Got another body to get rid of?"

We began speed-walking toward the exit.

"No," I said. "The guy needed some encouragement to tell me where to find Linda."

"A finger?"

I pointed at his crotch. "Something more valuable to him. A guy has ten fingers but only one set of those."

"I can see why he talked."

I turned left to go to the garage. Linda followed me. Frankie and Enzo went to the right.

"Guys, my van is in the garage," I said.

"It was," Frankie said. "I figured the security guys might be waiting for you down there. Luca and a couple of my boys are there to discourage them from doing that."

"How are we getting home?" I asked.

"With me. Luca will bring your van."

"He doesn't have a key."

Frankie peered at me over the top of his designer sunglasses. "Luca has unique skills. Boosting cars is one of them. He won't even leave a scratch."

54

In the hospital's outdoor parking lot, Frankie opened the driver's rear door to his black Mercedes AMG GT. Enzo did the same on the passenger side. Linda and I climbed into the back seat. Enzo and Frankie climbed in the front. Frankie was at the wheel and called Luca on his car's Bluetooth as we drove away. He spoke to him in Italian. I talked to Linda.

"Are you okay?" I asked, patting her hand.

"I'm not too bad," she said.

What!?

"You have got to be kidding. You're not mad at me?"

"Not at all. This was exciting."

"The first time something like this happened, when I shot the man's hands, you wouldn't speak to me for weeks." I paused. "And do I need to remind you about what happened last night at David and Rick's condo?"

"No, but when I went to bed after that was over, I realized that, even though I was scared to death both times, I enjoyed the experience. Kind of like being on stage playing the piano or giving an opening argument in the courtroom. I miss that adrenaline rush."

"This was a little more rush than I needed. I was terrified I wouldn't be able to save you."

"I had complete confidence in you."

"More than I had in myself, but I guess it worked out okay."

"Did that security guard really urinate in his pants?"

"He did. Having me shoot a bullet close to his private parts might have had something to do with that."

Frankie disconnected and pulled onto the Kennedy Freeway.

"How did they know we were there?" Linda asked.

"They made us with facial recognition software," I said.

"Good to know," Frankie said. "I'll talk to my guy about that. If you do this again, it shouldn't be a problem next time."

"I hope we're done with this," Linda said.

I'm not sure about that until this story is finished.

"What did you guys figure out?" he asked.

"Before the security guards arrived, the nurses in the break room talked about how hard they were working," Linda said.

"I heard the same thing," I said. "Something about autoimmune diseases."

"Sounds like you need a doctor to help you figure this out," Frankie said.

I had one in mind.

Eddie.

Frankie drove me home first before he dropped off Linda. An hour later, Luca parked my mommy van in our garage. Carter had already put Macy down for her nap. He was in the family room helping Kerry with her preschool homework.

I went down to the lower level and sat in front of my computer with the Nanit beside me on the tabletop. I had three potential stories to work on. Zhukov stealing his client's funds, which was followed by his murder and the disappearance of his body. Diane Warren's financial problems and the possibility that she wanted to harm the Irregulars because she blamed us for it. And Charlie Sullivan, the unreliable builder whom David and Rick wanted to kill.

I began a file on each one of them.

The immediate danger the vindictive Mrs. Warren presented to our group put her at the top of the list. If we were going to stop her, we needed to see if she was doing anything illegal to make more money at the MidAmerica Hospital.

And if she was, why? I had an idea. I called an old journalism friend.

"Jeff, this is Tina Thomas."

Jeff Taylor is a topflight reporter for Bloomberg. He might know about Diane's hospital business. I told him what I needed.

"And you would be spot on," Jeff said, when I finished. "We were going to do a major feature on her as the CEO and owner of the most profitable hospital in the world."

"But...?"

"I researched her financials. Since Dr. Fertig died, she has been propping up her hospital's income with her own money. If I wrote the story, she would have been exposed. Since our original story was, therefore, changed completely, we elected not to do it without being able to investigate more thoroughly."

There it was. Diane's ego was driving her to do anything she could to save her hospital. A shiver ran down my spine. We needed to be careful. We are moms with little kids and no superhero skills. She has money and the ability to hire killers.

Hold it.

There was a MidAmerica Hospital Foundation, and Fertig's patients contributed over one hundred million dollars to the fund. Diane and Fertig were the directors. Fertig was dead. Diane had access to those funds in addition to her family money.

Big bucks.

If she was illegally using the foundation's money to keep her hospital solvent, she was breaking too many local, state, and federal laws to count. This might be the real story.

I thought of Dr. Edward Wallace, an ENT doctor in Omaha. Next to my husband, Carter, and my brother, Jimmy Edwards, Eddie is my closest male friend.

I called Eddie and explained to him my concerns about Diane Warren.

"Is this is about the doctor who cured all of his breast cancer patients?" Eddie asked.

"It is," I said.

"You said he brought in three quarters of the total revenue to his hospital."

"A little more than that, but yes, that's correct."

"With him gone, she has a massive hole in her income stream."

"No kidding. I need to know more about hospital financing."

"Are the Irregulars involved in this?"

"They are."

"How about this? I'll fly to Chicago and discuss it with you."

"Done."

"Set it up and let me know when you want me there."

55

I spent all day Sunday being a mommy and wife while I processed all that had happened since Friday night. I had to remember my family came first above any story. All I wanted to do was cuddle Kerry and Macy and hug Carter.

By Monday morning, I had my emotions mostly back together, but I didn't recognize my van when I opened the door. It was spotless and smelled like a new car, not dirty diapers, spilled food and drink, and baby spit-up.

I called Frankie as I drove to my hair appointment with Rick to have him color my hair. Kerry was in preschool, and Macy was with Alicia.

"What did Luca do to my van?" I asked.

"Got it detailed," Frankie said. "Said it was so dirty inside there was no reason to ever lock it. No carjacker would ever steal a van that smelled like that."

I disconnected, parked, and walked into Creative Hair. This hair color appointment was a new experience for me. I'd never needed to have any color done, but now my mother's gray hair genes were cropping up.

Mom was my age when she began to turn gray, and she never did anything about it. By the time I was in junior high, she was almost completely gray. When I graduated from Indiana, the gray had been replaced by white. It looks great on her now, at age sixty-eight, but I wasn't going to let that happen to me. At least not yet.

I sat down in Rick's chair. He didn't say anything as he walked around me. He crossed his right arm in front of his chest, rested his left elbow on his right palm, and tapped his lips with his left index finger. He then slid his finger to his left cheek and sighed.

"Jack Benny," I said.

"Who, sweetie?" he asked.

"My parents had black and white DVDs of Jack Benny's TV shows. We used to watch them on Sunday nights when I was a kid. He used to stand like that after he told a joke."

"And?"

"Is my hair color a joke?"

"Oh, my, no, but it does need a lot of work." He fingered my hair. "A whole lot of work."

"Then let's get to it. Macy is with Alicia, and I promised her this wouldn't take too long."

"You might want to rethink that. Better text her so she doesn't worry."

I did, as he began mixing up his magic ingredients. Marcia Peebler sat down in David's chair. Her abnormally black hair was wet. She wore a black and white tweed Escada suit with black, sling-back, patent leather pumps.

David was at another station finishing up a woman with red hair.

Marcia turned to me. "Shot anyone recently, honey?"

My heart began racing. "I... ah... no, not exactly. Why, have you heard anything?"

She nodded toward David. "He knows I adore gossip."

"He told you?"

"He did. What's it feel like, killing someone?"

Rick stepped into the back for more potions and couldn't hear our discussion.

I felt tears well up in my eyes. "Can you keep this between us?"

"I most certainly can. God knows I've been through enough family issues which I don't want anyone to know about. My lips are sealed."

The tears started to flow. "Honestly, even though it was in self-defense, it sucks. I'm having nightmares about it."

"I can understand that, especially if it's someone you know."

She had a point. I still had bad dreams about the few previous shootings I'd been involved in even though they, too, were in self-defense.

I wiped my nose. "How much did David tell you?" I asked.

"As much as he knew, but obviously he wasn't in the room where it happened, so the juicy details are missing. Anything you would care to share, you know, between us girls?"

"The man was going to blow us up."

"Oh, really? Tell me more."

I thought about Carter. "Promise you won't tell anyone. I don't want my husband to find out."

She zipped her right hand over her lips.

When I finished telling her about the events, I felt better. She stared at me through her large glasses, which magnified her black eyes. "And there's nothing else I need to know?" she asked, after coughing into her hand.

I continued to worry about these stories becoming more dangerous to me and my friends. I needed all the help I could get. "There is one thing. Your friend Alex Zhukov seems to have disappeared."

She leaned forward. "He will never be my friend. As I told you before, he handles Alan's money, if you can call it that. I know him socially." She sat back. "But you say he has disappeared? And how would you know this?"

"I'm the one who lost him."

56

Rick returned with his hands full of bottles and jars. He began working on my hair. It took fifteen minutes to tell Marcia the story about my first visit with Zhukov. I didn't mention the next one to his office with Molly or the last one with Cas. I could have done it faster, but Rick and then David, who began to work on Marcia, kept interrupting with questions.

"Is this what you wanted to discuss with the Irregulars Friday night before we were interrupted?" Rick asked, when I finally finished.

"Irregulars?" Marcia said. "Who are they? I thought we were discussing Zhukov."

"Marcia, sweetie, the Hamlin Park Irregulars are a group of stay-at-home moms who help Tina research and write stories. We are now part of the group."

She covered her mouth and tried to stifle her recurring smoker's cough. "Is this why you two want to have a kid?" she asked, after she'd cleared her throat.

"It is one reason," David said.

"But only a minor one," Rick said.

David began to trim Marcia's hair. Rick continued to slop chemicals on my head.

"It's too bad Alan's brain blew up," she said. "He might be able to help you with Zhukov's story."

"Does Alan ever have lucid intervals?" I asked. "If he does, maybe I'll be lucky and he can tell me something."

"He has his moments. Even if he can't remember anything, he is always a perfect gentleman, and he can be extremely charming."

"I would love to meet him. This might be a terrific story even though it might be a little dangerous."

"How so?" David asked

I told them about the Russian Mafia connection.

"I remember Alan talking about them," Marcia said. "Disgusting people, according to him."

"Did I miss something?" I asked. "How does your husband know so much about the Russian Mafia?"

"At one time Alan knew a lot about many things, dear. He was a genius."

"Dr. Peebler was once one of the top medical diagnosticians in the country," Rick said.

"Patients came from all over the world to be examined by him," David added.

"I didn't realize your husband is a physician," I said.

"Was. He no longer practices, at least not in the conventional sense."

"Does he still see patients?"

"In a manner of speaking he does. I know this is a bit confusing. You will understand it better after you talk to him."

57

David began to blow-dry Marcia's hair.

When he finished, she turned to me. "If I help you with this story, may I become a member of the Hanscom Park Irregulars?" she asked.

"Hamlin, Marcia dear," David said. "Not Hanscom."

She glared at him, and it sounded like she growled. David jumped back and put his hands up in front of his face. Making her hand into a fist, she drew her right arm back.

"Marcia," I said, trying to stop her before she slugged him.

She unclenched her fist and smiled sweetly. "Yes, dear."

"We would love for you to become part of our group."

"Splendid," she said, David's sin having been forgotten. "We must have a dinner party to celebrate."

"You don't have to do that," I said.

This time I was positive I heard her growl. Rick saved me.

"A marvelous idea, Marcia," he said. "Marcia and Alan, when he attends, give smashing dinner parties."

Marcia sat forward in the chair. "How many will there be?"

I counted on my fingers. "There are four Irregulars and their husbands, so that would be eight."

"And us," Rick said. "Ten total."

"What about Frankie and Janet?" David asked.

"And who might they be?" Marcia asked.

"Janet is a Chicago police detective," Rick said.

"And Frankie is, ah, how do I describe Frankie?" David asked.

"Frankie is Frankie," Rick said. "A guy with a soul patch and a Glock, who rides motorcycles and loves clothes and interior design."

"What about that other detective?" David asked. "The Italian Stallion."

"Tony Infantino?" I asked.

"We must invite him," Rick said. "He is positively yummy."

"I'm sure he'll be thrilled that you two are such admirers," I said. "But he'll probably bring a date."

"Such a pity, but if he must," David said.

"And Eddie," I continued.

"He is…?"

"Eddie Wallace is an ENT doctor friend of mine from my hometown of Omaha."

"David, write this down," Marcia said. "We must begin with a theme."

"A theme?" I asked. "For a dinner party?"

She peered over the top of her large glasses. "Young lady, I would never give a dinner party without a theme. How would I select the flower arrangements and the colors of the tablecloths and napkins, let alone which china and silver to use?" She raised her voice. "My God, if I am to be an Irregular, we must have standards." She turned to David. "We need addresses for the invitations. Call Larry Carlson and have him select a theme and appropriate color scheme."

David began scribbling on a pad.

"Whom do you usually employ for a caterer, Tina?" she asked.

"A man named David John used to cook for our group, but he kind of disappeared."

"I totally understand. Hired help can be so unreliable, especially builders, but caterers aren't far behind."

"He wasn't hired. He was one of the Irregulars, and he didn't disappear exactly. He ran away after he did a couple of things."

"Things?"

"He blew up abortion clinics and then killed a couple of people."

"And he was one of the Irregulars?"

"He was," I said. "Several years ago he blew up an abortion clinic in Arlington. I was pursuing a story about that and was wounded in the blast, but, in a bizarre twist, we became friends here in Chicago and he saved my life when another man tried to murder me while I was in the hospital."

I was able to tell her this calmly because I'd done it before, but way deep in my PTSD-addled brain I was still unnerved by remembering those events.

"Why were you in the hospital?"

I took in a deep breath to center myself. "That's complicated. Essentially, David John hit me in the abdomen with a rifle. Scar tissue ruptured and began hemorrhaging. I went to the hospital and, while I was there, another man tried to kill me."

"But this David John person, who had already tried to kill you two times, saved you?"

"I told you it's kind of complicated."

She coughed violently and then cleared her throat. "I need a cigarette. Joining the Irregulars might be the most exciting thing I've done since I divorced my last husband."

58

Rick finished my hair. "Gone, gone, gone," he said as he circled me one more time. "No more of those sneaky little gray things."

David came over for a closer examination. "Rick, you are an artist. Tina looks terrific."

Marcia returned from having her cigarette, her Escada suit reeking of tobacco smoke. "I agree."

Standing up, I leaned closer to the mirror in front of me. I pulled the strands of my hair apart in several places but didn't find any gray. Rick had also done some highlights and lowlights. From a distance it didn't seem like he'd done anything, but I appeared to be a couple of years younger.

"Wow," I said. "Am I glad I found you."

"I know you are, sweetie, but don't get any ideas," David said. "He's all mine."

"While I was outside I called my secretary, Amanda, and checked on dates," Marcia said. "How does next Saturday night sound?"

"Let me check our schedule," Rick said, scanning his iPhone.

"I'm sure that will be okay with all of us," I said. "As a group we don't go out too often because we all have young kids."

"I never had that issue with my boys," Marcia said. "We had a nanny or two when they were growing up, and I was always busy with other things."

"You have children?" I asked.

"Two sons. Ted is the older one. He's married and has one grown child. John is divorced, but he fathered one son and a daughter that we know of. We're not sure if there might be some others out there somewhere."

"Are they physicians too?"

David laughed. "Hardly. The boys don't work. As Marcia's sons, they live off of her money."

Marcia coughed again. "They are twits, but they are my sons and I indulge their opulent life style."

"You said they're your sons," I said. "Does that mean Alan isn't their father?"

She stared at me before she replied. "You're smarter than you look to pick up on that, but you're correct. The boys' father was Joe Williams, a worthless sot, but he was better than Bob."

"Bob?"

"Manchester, my first official husband. All he did was fool around on me." She paused. "But, then, so did Joe."

"Rumor has it that those two bad boys shared one intriguing trait," David said.

Rick held his hands about twelve inches apart. "We hear they both were, shall we say, well endowed."

The three jeweled bracelets on Marcia's right wrist clattered as she dismissed that statement with a wave of her hand. "Old news." She coughed again. "Since your friend David isn't available to cater the evening, whom would you suggest? I have no idea what type of food your group likes."

"Frankie would be my choice, and I'm positive he would like to do it," I said.

"Isn't he the detective's husband?" she asked. "I thought you didn't know what he does for employment."

"We don't, but Janet says he loves to cook. So does Carter, but he's way too busy at the newspaper."

"I can't wait to meet the Irregulars," she said. "They sound like an interesting group."

"You have no idea," I said.

"You have to come by the house as soon as you are finished here. When I left, Alan was having a good day. You need to talk to him while it lasts."

59

Marcia and Alan's home is located among the other mansions on Chicago's Gold Coast. Or maybe it's two homes. When I drove into the circular driveway, it looked like two massive houses of a subtly different style and age had been joined together by a two-story brick structure.

There were builder's tools and equipment scattered around the side yard of the house on my right. The landscaping was in total disarray, a mess of dirt and chunks of cement, reminding me of David and Rick's building project.

I parked my van by the front door of the other home. A woman wearing a maid's uniform opened the home's tall double front door. The smell of cigarette smoke enveloped her and wafted over me.

"Tina?" she said. "I'm Amber. Please come in."

The hallway resembled the entrance to the Metropolitan Museum of Art in New York, complete with tall Greek statues on either side of me. Facing me from twenty feet away was a two-story, curving staircase with a landing one story up.

"Marcia is in the garden room," Amber said.

She led me down a long, dark hallway into a sunny, circular room full of white rattan furniture with cushions in various hues of yellow and green. There were fresh flowers in vases, which, unfortunately, couldn't mask the odor of cigarette smoke.

Marcia sat at a partner's desk. A dark-haired woman about Marcia's size sat opposite her. They glanced up when we came in, and both stubbed out their cigarettes. Marcia waved her hand in front of her in a futile effort to whisk away the smoke.

"A disgusting habit," Marcia said, as she stood up. "But it's the only sin I have left since I gave up drinking."

She had changed into a long-sleeved, beige silk blouse and pants with a Judith Leiber belt. Beige hose and classic beige and black-toed Chanel sling-back pumps completed her at-home leisure outfit.

She nodded toward the woman across from her. "This is Amanda, my secretary. She smokes more than I do, which is why I keep her around."

Amanda wore a black power suit, black hose, low-heeled pumps, and an off-white silk blouse. Thank God I had cleaned up for my hair appointment, but I was still way underdressed decked out in black slacks, a black turtleneck sweater, and my black North Face jacket. Marcia eyed me up and down but didn't comment on my attire.

"I'll be right back," Marcia said to Amanda. "I made an appointment for Tina with Alan."

"That will be interesting," Amanda said.

"Will it ever," Marcia said under her breath.

60

I followed Marcia down the hallway, across the entry, through a dining room with three circular tables each set for twelve, through two doors, and finally into another larger room. She is short, but she moved quickly in her Chanel heels, almost too fast for me to keep up.

"Marcia?" I said, hoping to slow her down.

She wheeled around to face me. "Yes, dear?"

"This room. This art. It's amazing."

"Have you ever been to the Frick in New York City?"

"I have."

"Then you should recognize this room. It's an exact replica of the West Gallery. It was Alan's favorite place in New York City. This room is ninety-six feet long and thirty-three feet wide. The height of the ceiling is a little lower than in New York because of some stupid Chicago building code, but we were able to reproduce the skylights." She pointed to the end of the room. "This is where Alan initially became upset with Charlie Sullivan, our builder. He simply could not seem to get the arched portals exactly right. That was the first time Alan wanted to kill him."

I walked over to a large Rembrandt. "This is amazing."

"Frick's art collection puts mine to shame, but I do have some nice pieces."

If having a Rembrandt, a Van Dyck, two Goyas and four Picassos is "nice," then her collection qualified.

"As a physician, Alan knew what to expect when he found out he had Alzheimer's," she said. "I would never let him waste away in some grimy nursing home, so I bought the house next to us and joined the two houses together. I hoped it would help his memory if he sat in a room that he remembered from all our previous visits. He helped design the room when he still had all his marbles."

"Does Alan live with you?" I asked.

"In a manner of speaking he does. He resides in his house most of the time. The doors are always locked so he doesn't wander off and become lost." She paused. "To be honest, I worry about his safety, and this was the best way to protect him from the outside world."

"He must enjoy this furniture," I said, as I ran my hand over a table to my left. "It's stunning."

"A funny story about that. These pieces are of the Italian Renaissance style. Even I couldn't afford some of the items Alan wanted, but I presumed at some point he wouldn't know that they were reproductions." She stifled a cough. "And that proved to be correct. Alan loves to sit in that chair over there and stare at the Rembrandt."

"And the chair is a reproduction?"

"It is, but he doesn't know it, poor old fool."

61

We reached a single door under a smaller, arched portal on the far wall. The door had a combination lock. She punched in the combination and opened the door.

"We leave it locked at all times," Marcia said.

"Is someone with Alan constantly?" I asked.

"Not yet. He is locked in, and so far there haven't been any problems. Lori, his nurse, lays out his clothes in the morning. We eat most of our meals together in the big house. She leaves at five o'clock. When he tires, I walk back here with him, and he goes to bed."

"Sad."

"It is, but we are making the best of it." She ushered me in. "It can be maddening talking to Alan. As I told you, this morning he was sharp as a tack, but then something happens in his head and the lights go out. Watch his eyes. That's the clue." She paused. "Sometimes changing subjects helps bring him back. He might not be cogent for long but while he is, pay close attention. He can come up with some brilliant observations."

"Good to know."

"You must check in with Lori, who is also his receptionist. She will escort you into his office. When you are finished, she will let you out."

"Receptionist?"

"It's a doctor's office. What did you expect?"

"I thought Alan has some sort of dementia."

"He does."

"How can he still see patients?"

"He doesn't, at least not in the conventional sense. Medicine was his life, and when he began to deteriorate mentally, he became understandably depressed, so I came up with a solution. I had his medical office reproduced in the new house. It even has his old desk. When someone comes to visit, they sit in there and he talks to them like he used to do with real patients. It gives him something to do, and it seems to make him happy."

"What does he do the rest of the time?"

"He exercises."

"You mean like using a treadmill or something?"

"Oh, no, it's far more physical than that. Alan has a personal trainer and has had forever. For the past few years, it's been a young man named Rod Falter. Ever since Alan's brain blew up, Rod has been a lifesaver for me. They spend at least four hours a day together."

"Alan can work out that long?"

"He jumps rope, lifts weights, and does yoga. He also plays tennis, both indoors and out, runs, bikes, and rollerblades for miles and miles, but always with Rod so he doesn't get lost."

"Don't his mental problems impact his ability to work out?"

"No. Sadly, his physical status is that of a man several years his junior. I wish I could say the same thing about his brain power."

"Personal trainers are expensive."

"They most certainly are, but I want Alan to be content with the time he has left, and I don't care what it costs." Tears glistened in her eyes. She blinked them away and beckoned for me to go into the room. "Hurry up. You'll miss your appointment."

62

Marcia left. I heard the lock click as she closed the door behind her. I entered into a small waiting room. There were two patterned wingback chairs on either side of a French antique table. An Oriental carpet covered most of the dark wood floor. Four large oil paintings hung from two of the cherry wood walls. The third wall was covered with Dr. Peebler's framed medical diplomas and awards. The only smell came from furniture polish. In the background, I heard Chopin being played on a piano.

On the fourth wall was an open sliding glass window. A woman wearing a white nurse's uniform stared at me. She looked enough like Marcia that she could have been her daughter.

"Mrs. Thomas?" she asked.

I walked up to the window. "That would be me, but please call me Tina."

"I'm sorry, but Doctor Peebler would never allow me to do that," she said. "I am Lori Elliot, his nurse and receptionist. I have some papers for you to fill out."

"Oh, see, there's been a mistake," I said. "I'm here to interview Dr. Peebler, not be seen as a patient."

I winked at her so she would know that I was in on the charade.

She handed me a clipboard with a small stack of papers on it. "Dr. Peebler will not see you unless these papers are completely filled out."

She didn't wink back.

I sat down in the nearest chair. "Got it."

While I filled out the papers, I had a moment where I wondered if giving my private medical information to him was safe. It seemed like this playacting was stretching things a bit. I wasn't sure why a doctor with Alzheimer's needed this much detail about my complete medical history, but if this was what it took to question him about Zhukov, I would do it.

It took me fifteen minutes to fill out the forms. I walked to the window and handed the papers back to Lori. While she carefully reviewed them, I moved to the wall which displayed Peebler's diplomas. He was a graduate of Harvard Medical School. He had taken his internal medicine residency at Massachusetts General Hospital. He had one other advanced degree in neurophysiology from Johns Hopkins.

Awards from all over the world covered the rest of the wall. They had to do with the outstanding medical care he had given to his patients. The last one was dated three years ago, but after reading about his training, I felt my information was secure — even if his brain had blown up.

Lori finished with my papers and glanced up at me. "I'll be right back."

She left the room with the papers in her hands. The piano music suddenly stopped. I continued to study the wall with Peebler's memorabilia.

"That's impressive," I said, when she returned. I nodded toward the wall.

"Dr. Peebler has amazing credentials," she said. "It's tragic that he can no longer use them on a daily basis, but the damage to your head will interest him."

"I try to not think about it."

"Getting blown up must have been frightful."

I remembered waking up in the ICU in D.C. after suffering an epidural hematoma, a ruptured bladder and diaphragm, a collapsed lung, and lacerated liver.

I fingered the semicircular scar on the right side of my head compliments of the neurosurgeon who had saved my life. "It sure ruined a great haircut."

63

Lori ushered me into a combination doctor's office and examination room. It was decorated like the reception area, with the same cherry wood walls and a smaller Oriental carpet. Two oil paintings hung from the walls. On the right, totally out of character with the rest of the room, was a generic, gray metal desk with a computer. There were two metal chairs in front of it and one black leather chair behind it.

To my left was an examining table covered by white butcher's paper. On the wall behind it was a blood pressure cuff and machine. Next to it were four white cabinets. Below them were a brown Formica countertop with a sink in the middle and four more white cabinets. A box of disposable latex gloves were positioned on the countertop edge closest to the examining table. A green wastebasket sat on the floor below the box of gloves.

"Please sit down in one of the chairs," a male voice behind me said.

I complied and then turned around to find the source of the command. It came from a man doing a yoga headstand in the corner. He appeared to be about Marcia's size. He had short salt and pepper hair. His face reminded me of a rodent with wrinkly skin and a pointy nose. It looked like he might have had a nose job.

He wore a double-breasted blue blazer with gold buttons and a white pocket square. There was a red rose in his lapel. His wrinkled, beige cargo pants and white tennis shoes were a jarring contrast to his heavily starched white shirt and small black bowtie.

He read my medical history while he was still upside down.

"A significant blow to the head, yes, Mrs. Thomas?" he asked, as he turned the pages.

"Call me Tina, please," I said. "I was in a coma for a few days."

"Any residual neurological deficit?"

"I don't think so. At least no one has said anything."

"If there is, at least you'll still be smart enough to be an orthopedic surgeon."

I didn't respond.

"That was a joke," he said. "I am accustomed to people laughing when I say something funny."

"I'm sorry. I didn't realize that, but now that you mention it, some of the orthopods I've met aren't too bright."

He smiled, or at least it looked like he did. It was hard to tell with him being upside down.

"Quite so. The lowest quarter of any medical school class is populated by future orthopods and psychiatrists."

He closed my chart and performed a graceful dismount from his headstand.

He removed his rimless, half-reading glasses and tugged his blazer into place. His eyes were dark brown, almost black. He appeared to be fit, with almost no body fat. At five eight, I felt like I towered over him. He was an inch or two taller than the diminutive Marcia.

He extended his hand. "I am Doctor Alan Peebler."

We shook. His grip was firm. He went behind his desk and unbuttoned his coat. He had a full roll of toilet paper on his belt.

64

Peebler sat down behind the desk. He pulled off one piece of toilet paper from the roll and wiped his nose. He wadded up the toilet paper and shot it into the wastebasket. He made it.

He looked up and stared at me. I stared back and couldn't help but notice that his bowtie appeared to be a small black bat.

He didn't say anything.

Sitting quietly, I put my hands in my lap and continued to stare back. After an uncomfortable five minutes of silence, I couldn't take the pressure any longer.

"Dr. Peebler?" I said.

His dark brown eyes were vacant. "Yes?"

"I'm Tina Thomas," I said, trying to get the conversation started.

He put his reading glasses back on and studied my chart. I saw his eyes flicker. "Thomas? Right, Thomas. Let's see, the last time I saw you it was to assess your head trauma, isn't that correct?"

"I, ah, yes."

"Do you think you have any residual neurological deficit?"

"No."

"If there is, at least you'll still be smart enough to be an orthopedic surgeon."

I didn't respond.

"That was a joke," he said. "I am accustomed to people laughing when I say something funny."

"I'm sorry, I didn't realize that."

"The lowest quarter of any medical school class is populated by future orthopods and psychiatrists."

He closed the chart.

"Now, let's have a look at you."

I considered running out the door, but I remembered a story my friend Eddie told me and opted for a different solution.

Eddie had a scrub nurse who had delivered twelve children and had an additional three miscarriages. Knowing that she was a good Catholic, he asked her how she stopped becoming pregnant. She said her husband was an alcoholic and used to come home in a drunken stupor on Friday nights. He would pass out and then wake up and want to have sex. She would give in, leading to the fifteen pregnancies.

One Friday night, she decided she'd had enough children. He woke up and made his usual sexual advance.

"You want to do it again?" she asked, knowing that he hadn't done it the first time.

"What?" he asked, his whisky-soaked breath blowing in her face.

"When you came home, we had sex," she said. "You were great. I can't believe you want to do it again."

"Huh?" he said as he rolled over and passed out.

She never became pregnant again.

"Doctor, you just examined me," I said. "Do you need to do it again?"

He took off his glasses. His eyes were dull. "No, your neurological exam is well within normal limits. As I told you before, NSAIDs should take care of the headache that's been troubling you."

He closed the chart and stared at me.

65

"Doctor, I understand that you know Alex Zhukov," I said.

He blinked, and his focus seemed to return. "And why would you be interested in him?" Peebler asked.

"I was doing a story on him, but I seem to have lost his body."

"Explain, please."

I told him about the first visit to Zhukov's office. His eyes brightened as he listened.

"A bullet hole, you say," he said, using another piece of toilet paper to wipe his nose.

"Between his eyes."

He shot another basket with the toilet paper and then stroked his chin. "A bullet in the anterior midline would traverse the skull and cause considerable damage to the brainstem. Phylogenetically, the brainstem is the oldest part of the brain and controls all basic body functions like pulse and respiration. With these areas severely damaged, I assure you that he could not walk away."

He was still paying attention.

Push him a little.

"He left a message on his computer that he had left for Brunei," I said.

"Which you obviously do not believe."

"I do not, but without a body, I can't call the police."

"Then find the body."

"I don't know where to look, and that's why I need your help. I'm sure Zhukov is dead, and if I can find his body, I'll have a story to write. Any background information you can provide might give me a clue as to where his body might be."

He twirled his reading glasses around in his fingers. "I have known him for a long time. As a young man, he was a dentist in Russia, but he could not pass the certification test to practice in the United States. A shame, but he threw his energies into investing and, I'm told, became extremely successful."

"I was under the impression that you had invested money with him."

The lights went out in his eyes. "With whom?"

"Alex Zhukov."

"I have known him a long time. As a young man he was a dentist in Russia but he could not pass the certification test to practice in the United States. A shame, but he threw his energies into investing and, I'm told, became extremely successful."

I took Marcia's advice and changed the subject hoping to get his brain back on line. There was another, more pressing, story that I needed help with.

"Do you know Diane Warren?" I asked.

66

Peebler's head snapped up and his eyes shone. They seemed to change color from dark brown to coal black. "Diane Warren is a vile human being. She ruined several of my colleagues."

"How so?" I asked.

"She bought their practices for inflated prices. In this medical climate of decreasing revenues, they greedily took her money without considering the consequences."

"Which were?"

"They signed three-year employment contracts. When the time was up, she offered them a new contract for one half of the previous amount. To a man, the doctors wanted to resign, but she owned their practices, which included their equipment and all of their patient charts. In spite of that, the doctors quit and were left with nothing. To replace them, she hired FMGs for a much lower salary."

"I heard that term recently. FMG means a foreign medical graduate."

"Correct. A few are well-trained. Most are not, in my opinion, since their medical schools are not up to par with those in the United States or England. But to stay in the U.S. they will work long hours for low wages. She charges the patients exorbitant prices for their slipshod care so she makes more money. Highly unethical."

"But legal."

"Sadly, yes, but that's what greed does, both to the doctors who sold their practices and to her." He tore off another piece of toilet paper and wiped his nose. Another basket. "Vasomotor rhinitis. A consequence of my mad cow disease. That and anosmia. Extremely troublesome."

"I wondered about the toilet paper."

"It keeps me from having to find a Kleenex box all the time."

"Problem solving."

He wiped his nose again. "Why are you interested in Diane Warren?"

"One of her employees recently tried to kill my friends and me."

He wiped his nose again. "Please tell me what happened."

I did.

67

Peebler took notes on my chart. "You shot the man in the chest?" he asked.

"I did," I said. "A double tap in the O-ring."

"Ah. Two shots in the center of the target. Well done."

I was shocked that he knew what I was talking about. He glanced up. His eyes were still bright and still looked black. "Don't be so surprised. My knowledge is limitless." He paused and glanced down at what he had written. His face drooped. "Or at least it used to be before the mad cow disease. I still have my moments."

I wanted to ask if that bothered him, but from the sagging corners of his mouth, I was positive I knew what his answer would be.

"What did you do with the body?" he asked.

I hesitated. Should I tell him? I decided to, hoping it might encourage him to provide some helpful details and counting on the progression of his mad cow disease to ensure he would forget everything shortly after I confessed it to him.

"I didn't do anything with it. Frankie's boys took care of it."

"Frankie? I don't remember you mentioning him."

"I didn't. He's a friend of mine."

"Is he in the body disposal business?"

"No. It needed to be done, so he did it."

"What does he do for a living?"

"I'm not sure, but I think some of it might be considered to be illegal by most people, especially his wife Janet."

"Is she a lawyer?"

"No, she's a Chicago police detective."

"An interesting couple. Doesn't she object to this type of behavior?"

"Not if she doesn't know about it. Frankie is good that way."

"Where did they take the body?"

"His guys buried it in the basement of a house that is being rebuilt."

He raised his eyebrows. "Did you select random construction?"

"Not exactly. One of the Irregulars suggested we use his home."

He wrote that down, and then it appeared he added a large question mark. "Irregulars?"

"It started as a group of bored stay-at-home moms who wanted something more stimulating to do, so they began helping me try to write compelling stories to revive my journalism career. We now have two male members too."

"Would Frankie be one?"

"Not exactly. He's more like a consultant. The men are David Scott and Rick Carey."

"Marcia's and my hairstylists?"

"They are. It was Rick who suggested that Frankie put the body in the basement of the home they are remodeling. The builder's subcontractor hasn't poured the concrete yet, so Frankie's boys buried the body in David and Rick's basement. The sub is supposed to pour the concrete tomorrow."

He wrote that down. "Good luck with that. They hired Charles Sullivan, the same worthless builder we employed, and his cement subcontractor never showed up when he said he was going to be here."

"I saw the chunks in your yard."

"He still hasn't picked them up. A worthless sot. If I took care of my patients with slipshod behavior like that, they would all have died." He raised his voice. "I cannot and will not tolerate incompetence, and Sullivan and his crew are at the top of the list!"

He really doesn't like Sullivan.

"By the time the inside construction was nearly completed here, Marcia and I wanted to kill Sullivan and most of his worthless subcontractors. They always lied about when they would be here. It drove us crazy!" He yelled the last part.

"A lot of people seem to want to do that."

He slammed his hand on the table top. "Clearly it would be justifiable homicide!"

68

"Will you tell me something about autoimmune diseases?" I asked. "I went online but what I read was confusing."

Peebler's eyes narrowed. "How would you even know a term like that?"

"My friend Linda and I did some spying in the ICU at MidAmerica Hospital. The nurses were complaining about the sudden increase in admissions of those types of cases."

"Was this in conjunction with your investigation of Diane Warren?"

"It was."

He stared at me for several seconds. I thought I'd lost him, but then he nodded to himself and smiled. He also wiped his nose again.

"Autoimmune diseases are heterogeneous disorders that share certain common features, including inflammation of skin, joints, and other structures rich in connective tissue, as well as altered patterns of immunoregulation including production of autoantibodies and abnormalities of cell-mediated immunity." He closed his eyes. It seemed like he was reading behind the lids.

"While distinct clinical entities can be defined, manifestations may vary considerably from one patient to the next, and overlap of clinical features between and among specific diseases can occur."

He opened his eyes and realized I was staring at him. "You can shut your mouth now," he said.

I reached up to my lips, not realizing my mouth had dropped open while I listened to this amazing recitation.

"I wrote the chapter about this subject for *Harrison's Manual of Medicine*," he said.

"That was amazing, but I'm not sure I understood what you said."

The muscles in his face drooped, and his eyes dulled.

Picking up my chart, he stood up and glanced around — almost as if he was confused by his surroundings. He shuffled away from his desk, and a frightened look came into his eyes.

"Dr. Peebler?" I said. "Are you okay?"

He turned completely around. "I'm late. I have to make rounds at the hospital. I have patients waiting there for me. I can't seem to find my car. I know I parked it here somewhere."

He didn't seem to be aware that I was in the room with him.

"I enjoyed our visit," I said. "May I come back and see you again?"

"Don't bother me. I have to find my car. My patients need me."

He kept turning around in circles. I ran back into the outer office. Lori worked on her computer.

"You need to do something. Dr. Peebler is hunting for his car."

Her shoulders sagged. "He does that when he becomes agitated. You should probably leave now."

"He was doing so well. Was it something I said?"

"No. This is happening with increasing frequency these days. He can seem totally normal and then he begins to act like this. Was he speaking English?"

"Doesn't he always?"

"Oh, my, no. He is fluent in several languages. When the mad cow disease takes control, he reverts back to the language of his youth. It's maddening, because I only speak English."

"How old is Dr. Peebler?"

"He's in his late sixties. Why do you ask?"

"From the dates on his medical diplomas I guessed he would be younger, but it's not important. There are several things I would like to discuss with him. May I come back?"

"Let's see how upset he is. He likes visitors and seems to enjoy the mental stimulation, or at least he does for as long as he can assimilate what's being said." She gave me a card. "Call me. Maybe you can have lunch in the gallery with him next week. I know he would like that."

69

It was midmorning Tuesday. Alicia watched Macy so I could make a detour before I worked out at XSport Fitness. I'd had another sleepless night thinking about the man I'd shot, and I had to keep working to not become any more depressed about what I had done to him.

I turned left onto the east-to-west part of West Henderson Street. Two cement trucks were parked in front of David and Rick's home. I found a parking place behind them. Several Hispanic men pushed wheelbarrows of cement inside the house. A tall man stood in the front doorway. He rolled a steaming Venti Starbucks cup back and forth in his gloved hands.

I walked up to him. "Are you Charlie Sullivan, the builder?"

His graying, curly hair was sticking out from beneath a Chicago Bears stocking cap. His cheeks were bright red from the biting March Chicago wind howling in from the north.

He took off his glove and extended his hand. "I am. Do I know you?"

"No," I said, as we shook, "but several of my friends want to kill you."

He laughed, and his breath came out in clouds. "Let's see. That could be about any of my clients. We have six major projects going right now, and all of the owners want their home finished first. Hard to do with one crew." He took a long pull on his coffee. "Which ones do you know?"

"David and Rick, and Dr. and Mrs. Peebler."

He laughed again. "Wow, you do know the ones who want to kill me. Rick had a hissy fit yesterday and absolutely insisted this be done today."

"Are you usually on site when cement is poured?"

"Never, but when the sub who does it didn't show up, his crew called me to supervise."

"Does that happen often?"

"You mean subs not showing up?"

I nodded.

"It should never happen if they want to keep working for me, but it does. Like today. Saul is usually reliable, but he's not even answering his cell phone."

It was my turn to laugh. "Maybe somebody killed him."

"More than likely it has to do with his papers."

"Is he an illegal?"

He waved his arms around. "Ma'am, most of them are illegal. I wouldn't be in business without them."

The wooden planks leading from the yard into the front door sagged under the weight of the wheelbarrows full of wet cement being pushed into the house.

"Your crew is working hard," I said.

"Harder than they need to," he said. "Rick wanted the floor four inches thicker than the normal pour. Hard to figure, but it's his money."

I know why.

Rick wanted to be certain the body of the man with the missing fingers would never be found. So did I.

"Mind if I go in and see what they're doing?" I asked.

"Not at all, but they're only pouring cement. It's not all that interesting."

"Trust me, I love to see cement being properly poured."

"Follow me."

70

I followed Sullivan up the planks into the entry hall. The inside of the house was almost as cold as the outside, but at least the painful north wind wasn't blowing in our faces.

There was another set of wooden planks going into the basement. Next to them were temporary wooden stairs. We walked down the stairs as one of his men pushed a load of cement down the planks into the basement.

The room was large, at least three thousand square feet. The floor that was not covered by fresh cement was dirt. Portable gas heaters in the corners of the room made the air hot and dry. The area smelled like sweat and dust, with a touch of mold.

"It's warm down here," I said.

"It has to be or the cement won't set up properly," Sullivan said.

"Why is the floor dirt? Isn't that unusual for an older home like this?"

"The house had several cracked sewer pipes," he said. "Rick and David didn't know about it when they bought the place. We had to break up the floor to find the problem. I told them we could fix the broken pipes and leave the room with a dirt floor, and that was the plan until Rick called and said they had changed their minds and wanted the corner of the floor where we placed the new pipes covered with cement, so I pulled the men off another job and here we are."

"What about the rest of the dirt floor?"

"At this point, Rick said they might not cover it."

I guessed Rick didn't want it cemented now in case more bodies needed a resting place. I wanted to make sure Sullivan hadn't picked up on Rick's unusual request.

"That's going to look kind of strange, isn't it?" I asked.

"Ma'am, they're the owners. I do what they pay me for. No more, no less."

In the north corner was a patch of freshly turned earth covered by rebar. Sullivan saw me stare at it, but before he could say anything else, the workers poured two loads of wet concrete over that spot and began smoothing it around.

Hopefully my RPG man was now gone forever.

71

As I walked toward my van, a freezing drizzle began pelting me. I pulled my red Indiana Hoosier stocking cap out of my pocket and tugged in on my head. I snuggled up the collar of my North Face parka and hunched my shoulders against the screaming north wind. My face began to sting as the drizzle intensified.

My ski gloves kept my hands warm but didn't help my manual dexterity, resulting in me dropping my van keys on the slushy street. Cursing to myself, I bent down to pick them up. When I stood up, I saw to my right a large black SUV at the end of the block near Paulina Street. The engine was running. The SUV hadn't been there when I first drove up.

I climbed into my van and turned on the engine and the heater full blast. The windows were iced over, and I had to wait until the defrosters kicked in to see well enough to drive. While I waited, I wiped the driver's window and adjusted the rearview and outside mirrors. I wanted to see the car behind me.

It appeared to be a Chevy Suburban SUV, but my outside mirror was also frosted over and it was hard to tell.

The storm made it hard to see through my van's back windows, but it looked like there were two people in the front seat.

An unexpected tap on my passenger window made me jump in my seat. I could see the form of a person standing outside the window, but the heavy ice on the window precluded me from seeing who it was. The person tugged at the locked door handle.

I ripped off my thick gloves and yanked the Glock out of my backpack. Jacking a round into the chamber, I threw my door open and jumped out of the van. I leveled the gun across the roof at the man who was trying to open the passenger door.

It was Detective Tony Infantino.

72

"Tony, you scared the crap out of me!" I yelled, as the drizzle turned to snow.

"Sorry, sweets, but I was freezin' my ass off and wanted to get in out of this freakin' terrible weather," Tony said. "Unlock this damn door."

I climbed back into the van and unlocked the passenger door for him. He climbed in and slammed the van door.

Even covered with snow and ice from the worsening blizzard, his appearance was nearly perfect. He wore an Indiana Jones brown fedora, wraparound mirrored Oakley sunglasses, a brown cashmere topcoat, and an off-white cashmere scarf. He still had his ever-present tan.

I pointed at his feet. "I don't believe what I'm seeing. Tony Infantino in rain boots."

He leaned back and I could see them better. "Hunter. Only way to go. Thick socks are the secret. Got tired of ruinin' my Italian leather shoes."

"Aren't the boots a problem since they go over your calf?"

"Problem?"

"With your ankle gun and holster."

"Got it covered." He reached down into the top of his right boot and pulled out a tiny gun. "American derringer LM5, 15 ounces, .32 with four shots."

"It's cute."

He glared at me. "Sweets, I don't do cute guns." He pointed at David and Rick's house. "Anything you need to tell me?"

"Nope."

"You sure?"

"Absolutely, why would you even ask?"

"Rumor has it that there might be a 'Jimmy Hoffa' goin' on in the basement. Guessin' you might know about it."

"What did your partner say?"

"Might have mentioned some wet work Frankie and his boys are involved in. Didn't want to check it out, for obvious reasons. Here to make sure it's all being handled."

It took a few seconds for me to understand what he meant. Janet was using Tony to make sure the body was totally covered so Frankie, his boys, and I didn't have any risk of getting caught. "Got it. Janet covering all her bases."

"What a woman does for the man she loves. Think I need to go in there?"

"The builder's guys are covering the basement floor with a thick layer of cement," I paused, "especially the area where some dirt seems to have been recently turned over to fix some broken pipes."

"Broken pipes? From what I heard, a lot more than pipes are buried there."

"A shotgun blast to the chest can necessitate that."

"Double tap from a Glock'll do that too. Good thing I taught you how to shoot."

My father was my first and only shooting instructor. Later, Tony shot on the range with me, and because of that, he always took credit for any of my recent shooting successes.

I turned on the rear windshield wipers and checked the rearview mirror. "Did you spot that SUV behind me when you drove up?" I asked.

"Yeah, you been pissing off the feds again?"

My hands began to sweat even though the interior of the van was still cold. "Why would you ask that?"

"Chevy Suburban. Two passengers. Man driving. Woman in the passenger seat. Both watching you. Might as well have FBI painted on the side of the truck."

73

Tony climbed out of my van and went inside David and
Rick's house. Through the open front door, I saw him walk up to
Sullivan. He didn't badge him, so my guess was Tony had probably
identified himself as a neighbor and not a cop. He laughed it up
with Sullivan, but I was certain he was going to double check the
cement work in the basement.

I reached down to put the van in gear, but a knock on the
driver's side window stopped me. I powered it down and saw a man
and a woman standing in the street staring down at me. I
remembered the man from Zhukov's office. The woman I'd
encountered during another story, but I didn't know her name.

"Mrs. Thomas," the female said, "I'm FBI Special Agent
Michelle Jana. It's been a while."

Her hair was tucked under a black stocking cap. She wore a
buttoned-up, long, black wool overcoat and black slacks.

"It hasn't been that long, Agent Jana," I said. "I think the
last time was when the president came here to speak."

She didn't respond.

"Is that what this is about?" I continued. "David John? I
can save you a lot of time. I haven't seen or heard from him, and I
don't know where he is."

I started to power up my window, but the man put his hand on top of the window to stop me.

"We would like to find Mr. John, but another man also seems to be missing," he said.

Wonder who?

"Do you know what happened to Alexis Zhukov?" he asked.

I began sweating under my winter coat. I was afraid that Adley, the head of security in Zhukov's building, had given them the security recordings from Monday night which showed me running out of the office and then returning with a gun.

The agents stood huddled together in the freezing drizzle and blowing snow waiting for me to respond. I should have taken pity on them.

But I didn't.

"I'm sorry," I said to the man, "do I know you?"

"I'm Special Agent Patrick Gillman," he said.

"Really? It's hard to be certain since I haven't seen your credentials." I nodded at her. "And now that I think about it, Agent Jana, I haven't seen yours either."

They fumbled in their jackets for their wallets. Finally, they had to take off their gloves so they could produce their FBI credentials. I gave each one a protracted examination.

"Good to know you are who you say you are," I said. "Now, what was the question, Agent Gillman?"

"According to Alexis Zhukov's secretary, Heidi Rae, you had an appointment for an interview with him," he said. "He hasn't been seen since that night. What happened to him?"

"He wasn't in there when I arrived. I waited in his office for about fifteen minutes and then left. Later, I was told that Zhukov sent Heidi Rae an email and informed her that he was flying out of Chicago and leaving the country."

"There's a problem with that," Jana said. "The airport security recordings prove Zhukov was never there and never got on the plane."

"Maybe he took a different flight. Happens all the time at O'Hare."

"I'm sure you'll alert us if you hear from him," Gillman said.

"If I know you guys, you're trampling on my civil rights with a phone tap, or something equally as devious, so you'll know the same time I do."

Jana's lips compressed into a thin line. "Rest assured we will be watching you."

74

Due to the spring blizzard that was still bombarding our area, there was no school on Wednesday, so the Irregulars had play day at Cas's home. The older children hung out in the family room. Molly's were the loudest, but they always are. The raucous, often destructive behavior of her four sons has made me appreciate Kerry's girly-girl demeanor. I hope Macy will take after her big sister.

We needed to talk about our stories, but we had a snack first. David and Rick were working. I would fill them in later about what we discussed.

Linda threw down her half-eaten sandwich. "Are you sure David John isn't hiding out in Chicago somewhere? I miss his food."

He used to prepare scrumptious lunches for the Irregulars, but after he disappeared, it was now up to us to provide our own lunches. Since Molly's husband owns several different fast food chains, finding food isn't much of a problem. Food that we like is another matter.

"Gosh, guys, I don't know why you always complain so much about Greg's food," Molly said. "The kids and I have it all the time."

"It's not exactly that we don't like these sandwiches, but how old are they?" Cas asked.

"Don't have a clue," she said. "Greg hates to let anything go to waste, so they might be left over from yesterday."

"Or the day before," Linda said.

I held up my hands. "Stop complaining. We have a lot to discuss." I turned to Linda. "Do you want to tell them or should I?"

She took a swallow of her iced tea. "After what happened to Tina and me at the hospital, Diane Warren has, in effect, declared war on us."

"What are you talking about?" Cas asked.

No one spoke after Linda finished talking about our recent visit to MidAmerica Hospital.

"Any ideas, Cas?" I asked. "Molly?"

"Maybe we should try and contact David John," Molly said. "He's good at making bombs. He could blow up Diane's hospital and cook another meal for us before he left town again."

"Or, better, blow up Diane," Cas said. "That woman pisses me off."

"Guys, we still don't know if the guy with the missing fingers was working on his own or for her," I said.

"What difference does it make?" Linda asked. "Those security guards weren't just going to throw us out of the place. They were going to kill us."

"That's a little dramatic," Cas said. "Are you sure?"

"You weren't there," Linda said. "I'm positive they were going to murder me."

"What about you, Tina?" Cas asked. "Were they going to kill you too?"

"I'm not sure, but it was scary," I said.

"Terrifying enough for us to come up with a plan," Linda said.

"We need to set Diane Warren up to take a fall," Molly suggested.

"I don't even know what that means," Cas said.

Molly began scrolling though Facebook on her phone.

"Molly?" I said. "What do you mean?"

"About what?"

Talking with Molly is always fun.

"Setting Diane up to take a fall," I continued.

"Oh, right. The farmers taught me that. She's greedy so she's probably willing to do something crooked — especially if she's short of money."

"Or she might already be using other money illegally," I said.

I told them about Diane's access to the MidAmerica Hospital Foundation's one hundred million dollars and how she might be illegally using that money to keep her hospital solvent.

"We need to bait a trap to catch her," Molly said.

"Bait a trap?" Cas asked.

"We could have someone present an illegal financial opportunity to her that would cover her tracks," Linda said.

"When she goes for it, Janet arrests her," Molly said.

"All we need is the bait," I said.

75

Before Carter came home from work, I called Rick
to tell him about our meeting.

"We can hear all about it at Marcia's dinner party,"
Rick said. "We have more pressing matters to discuss."

He was on speaker with David.

"We're on our way to our construction project,"
David said. "Meet us there in ten."

"But..." I protested. They had already hung up.

When their baby was born, they would learn parents
can't always drop everything for spur-of-the-moment
meetings. Fortunately, Alicia's daughter Liv was home from
school and could watch both girls.

David and Rick were outside of their house when I
drove up. The sun had come out but the temperature was
still in the low thirties. They stood on one of the wooden
planks to keep their boots out of the slush.

I walked up and stood on a plank facing them.
"Guys, what's wrong?" I asked.

"We keep losing subcontractors," David said.

"Not losing, David," Rick reminded him. "They
keep disappearing."

"I can relate, having lost a body myself," I said. "What happened?"

"Three days ago we scheduled a meeting with the plumbing person," David began. "We have very specific ideas about our master bathroom."

"Which will require innovative plumbing," Rick added.

"Well, honey, he didn't show up," David said. "Completely blew us off."

"David didn't complain," Rick said. "He's such a softy, but I completely blew my stack and went to the man's home. That's when the trouble began."

"Trouble?"

"It seems he has disappeared," David said.

"Vanished," Rick added.

"Guys, Sullivan told me this happens a lot, especially if the subs are illegals," I said.

"You're not hearing us," David said. "According to his wife, he left to meet with us and he disappeared instead. She hasn't heard from him since he left their house."

"Did she call the police?"

"Not yet," Rick said. "She doesn't have her papers, meaning she's afraid of the cops."

"Should we check into it?" I asked.

"We better do something, or we'll never finish this house," David said.

76

"There have to be other plumbers Sullivan can hire," I suggested.

"There are, but that's not the only problem," Rick said.

"It's also the framer," David said. "If we ever find another plumber, we can't proceed until the framer finishes his work."

"Let me guess," I said. "He's gone too."

"Positively evaporated," Rick said. "Right from here, according to the two men who worked for him."

"He was here, and then he disappeared?" I asked.

"The men had finished for the day and their boss, the sub, was putting away his tools as they drove off," David said.

"They came here the next day, and he didn't show up," Rick said. "His tools were still lying on the floor, and they said he would never leave them overnight unless something had happened to him."

"Did you go to his home?"

"We did," Rick said. "Spanish language newspapers are piling up in his driveway."

"And the mail is overflowing in his mailbox," David said.

"Maybe we need to check inside his home," I said.

David glanced at Rick. Rick nodded back at him.

"We already did that," David said.

"I learned how to pick locks in the service," Rick admitted.

"What's Sullivan say about all this?" I asked.

"The poor man is pulling out his luscious hair," Rick said. "It's naturally curly, you know."

"A fact that probably isn't going to help us here," I said. "How many subs are missing?"

David began counting on his fingers. "The framer we were just discussing, the plumber, the electrician, the cement person, and who was that smelly man, Rick?"

"The heating and air conditioning sub, but we won't miss him," Rick said. "His body odor was atrocious."

"But he is missing?" I asked.

"Like the others," David said.

"Maybe there's a lot more than a possible story here," I said. "I wonder if someone is actually killing these guys."

77

"Where are my girls?" Eddie Wallace asked, as he walked into our entry hall.

Friday afternoon, Eddie flew into O'Hare using the frequent flyer miles he had acquired from paying his alimony with a United Airlines credit card. He used Uber to deliver him from the airport. He used the same credit card to pay for the ride.

Eddie is a few inches taller than I am, but he is about the same weight as he was when he played baseball at the University of Nebraska.

"Macy is doing what she does best, other than breastfeeding," I said.

"Sleeping?"

"She is."

"Where is my lover girl?"

"Kerry is presently in time out."

Attitude is something she has acquired since she began going to preschool. The tough-love mommy has to be the bad cop. Carter, not so much.

"How much longer?"

I looked at my cell phone. "Three more minutes."

"Ah, come on. I want to play with her."

"I said 'three minutes'."

"Whoa, okay, warden. I see you don't let the inmates run the prison."

"I don't, but it does give us time to talk. I have a problem."

"Is somebody trying to blow you up or shoot you?"

"Both."

His eyebrows elevated. "You have to be kidding me. Is this why you want to know more about the business of medicine?"

"Kind of. I think Diane Warren is behind this, and we need to stop her."

"You mean you're not going to shoot her?"

"Why does everyone keep saying that? It's not like I go around shooting up the neighborhood."

"Tina, look at me."

I stared at my hands. If I made eye contact, he would know I was lying.

"Don't tell me you shot somebody else," he said.

"I had to," I said to my hands. "The guy was going to use an RPG to blow us up."

"Is that a rocket?"

"A big one, which is why I had to shoot him."

"Tell me."

I did, and now I would have another sleepless night.

78

"I presume you didn't call the cops," Eddie said, when I finished.

"We didn't," I admitted.

"What did you do with the body?"

"Frankie says it's harder to get rid of a corpse than you would think," I said. "He suggested using new construction."

"You buried the guy you shot? Unbelievable."

"I didn't do it myself. Frankie's boys did it. They put the body in David and Rick's basement."

"I feel like I'm in the middle of a TV reality show."

"It is a little weird, but that's why we need your help. We want to stop Mrs. Warren before she can try something else."

"How do you know it was her guy?"

"I don't for sure. I know he used to be employed by her, but I can't be sure he was when I shot him."

He formed his hands into a T. "Time out. You knew this guy who tried to blow you up?"

"Not exactly by name, but he confronted me in the parking lot at Costco and threatened me to keep us from working on the story about Fertig."

"And how did that go?"

"He laughed at me."

"A seriously bad move on his part. Did you slug him?"

"No, I pointed my gun at him and he left, but he said he would keep watching me."

He shook his head. "All I do is pick noses. The real action is here in Chicago."

"Several days after that, he accosted Linda and me in the parking garage of the MidAmerica Hospital."

He sighed. "Let me guess. He laughed at you again."

"No, it was a little more than that."

I told him about the man and how he lost a few of his fingers.

"Is it possible he did this rocket thing on his own in retaliation for you blowing off his fingers?" he asked, when I finished.

"We discussed that, but David and Rick think otherwise."

"The hairstylists?"

"They are. Diane Warren hates the Irregulars, and they think she might have been responsible for this last attack."

"Sounds like you better get her first before you run out of bullets."

79

"When are we going to discuss all this medical business?" Eddie asked.

"Tomorrow night," I said. "Marcia Peebler, the newest Hamlin Park Irregular, is giving a dinner party so we can listen to what you have to say."

"Is Marcia a stay-at-home mother too?"

I laughed. "Hardly. I have no idea how old she is but I would guess in her late sixties."

He shrugged his shoulders. "A little long in the tooth for your group, isn't she?"

"Truthfully, she kind of invited herself to join, but her husband, Alan, is a doctor and I felt like he might help us on this story."

"What's his specialty?"

"Internal medicine, but he doesn't practice any more, at least not in the conventional sense."

"Did you say his name is Alan? Alan Peebler? You know Dr. Alan Peebler?"

"I had a strange interview with him two days ago."

"Do you have any idea who he is?"

"The husband of an extremely wealthy woman."

"I'll take your word on that, but Dr. Peebler is one of the most distinguished physicians in the United States. He's the editor of the most prestigious textbook on internal medicine. He's won every medical award there is except the Nobel Prize, and I read that he was being considered for that from his basic work on Alzheimer's."

"Boy, is that ironic."

"How so?"

"He has it, or at least a form of it. He calls it mad cow disease."

I told Eddie about the interview.

"I've heard other doctors talk about how eccentric he is. He never took the boards in internal medicine. He said there wasn't anyone smart enough to test him."

"There sure is now, at least when his brain is off-line. The weird part is that sometimes he seems totally normal and can carry on a sane conversation."

"Write down the details of what he says when he's like that. He still might be the smartest man you'll ever meet."

"Even smarter than you?"

"It doesn't take a Mensa IQ level to pick noses."

"But it pays well."

"Not like it used to, which we'll discuss tomorrow night."

80

Saturday night, Carter drove my van to Marcia and Alan's home. I was in the passenger seat. Eddie was in the third row of seats, since the second row held both kids' car seats. Most people might take the seats out, but they're so darn hard to put back in we always leave them in place.

"Dude, you think you brought enough wine?" Eddie asked Carter.

My husband's passion in life — other than the kids, work, and his lovely and talented wife — is wine. Downstairs we have a full climate and humidity-controlled wine cellar, which is okay with me even if there are two vintage Chicago White Sox bleacher seats in the middle of the room next to an empty wine barrel that has an infrequently used candle on its lid.

Carter's dream is for us to sit in candlelit bliss on those stupid seats and sip wine while classic opera plays in the background. Ain't no way a true Cubs fan is going to plop her still-large pregnancy butt down in those seats in a fifty-four degree temperature while she drinks wine, even if it is with her hubby.

"For our group, I usually bring six bottles," Carter said. "I don't know if Mrs. Peebler will consume any wine, but Tina assures me that Dr. Peebler won't drink, so I have enough."

Carter pulled into the large curved driveway. There were four cars stopped in front of us. The first one was a black Bentley. A man wearing a red parka with the name of a car parking company on the back opened the Bentley's driver's door and handed a claim check to the exiting man.

Another man, wearing a matching red parka, assisted a lady out of the passenger seat. She was about Marcia's age and wore a full-length, dark brown sable coat. After the two guests were clear of the car, another man in a red parka ran to the car and drove it away.

We watched as the well-choreographed process was repeated three more times before it was our turn. All the women wore expensive coats. So did the men.

"Tina?" Carter said.

"Yes, dear."

"How many people did you say are attending Marcia's party?"

"I thought it was the Irregulars and Marcia and Alan. I guess I was wrong."

A large black Mercedes pulled in behind us.

"I think it might be prudent if we left the wine in the car," he said. "I'll bring in the Fourth Estate pinot as a gift."

"Marcia won't care if you bring in your wine."

"I beg to differ. Unless I'm mistaken, that's the mayor's car behind us."

81

There was a receiving line to the left of the front door. Five couples stood in front of us. Amber, Marcia's maid, took our coats and handed them to another woman similarly attired in a maid's outfit.

"Tina, so nice to see you again," Amber said. "Do you have your invitation?"

"I didn't know we were supposed to bring it, sorry," I said.

Macy had spit up on it yesterday, but I never considered bringing it anyway, since it hadn't occurred to me that we would need it.

"Not a problem, I'll handle it."

She pulled out a stack of cards from her white apron and put on reading glasses. She shuffled through them until she found the one she wanted. "This would be your husband, Carter Thomas, is that correct?" she asked, nodding toward Carter.

"It is," I said.

Carter handed her his gift bottle of pinot.

"Thank you so much." She turned to Eddie. "And this would be Dr. Edward Wallace."

"It is," I said.

The line inched forward. Two more couples came in behind us. Amber handed our cards to Amanda, Marcia's secretary. She glanced at a card already in her hand and whispered in Marcia's ear as the next couple advanced to her. Marcia greeted them by name and said something personal. The couple smiled and laughed as she made them feel like they were her best friends.

Amanda then handed the same cards behind Marcia's back to Lori, Alan's nurse. She repeated the process in Alan's ear. His response wasn't as smooth as Marcia's. He shook hands and tried to smile, but it seemed more like a grimace.

Amanda glanced down at our cards and whispered to Marcia. It was our turn.

82

"Marcia, I had no idea there would be this many people here," I said, as I shook her hand.

She wore a black Chanel pantsuit with matching low-heeled shoes, and a patterned, red silk Chanel blouse.

"Don't worry. We'll eat in a separate area from the rest of the crowd so we can talk."

She extended her hand to Carter. "I enjoyed the article your reporters did on the iPad and its impact on newspapers. Well done."

Carter blinked a couple of times. "Thank you. I'm thrilled to meet anyone who still reads a newspaper."

"Newspapers have to survive for our nation to be strong," she said. "I can't begin the day without reading at least one." She squeezed my arm. "I love your wife. She is handy to have around."

Carter furrowed his brow, unsure as to what Marcia was talking about. I knew, so I leaned in and kissed her on the check, at the same time whispering in her ear. "He doesn't know about my gun."

"Got it," she whispered. She then leaned back and winked at me.

We moved forward, and Lori said something into Alan's ear. When he glanced up, his eyes quickly brightened. He wore a black tailcoat, a crisp, white, winged collar shirt, white vest, cargo pants, and black Converse tennis shoes. His bow tie was a white polar bear. The roll of toilet paper was attached to his suspenders.

"Welcome, Tina," he said. "How are your headaches?"

"Fine, Dr. Peebler," I said. "Your medicine is working beautifully."

"As I knew it would. Is Molly Miller one of your friends?"

"She is."

"Amazing breasts."

Alan might be cuckoo, but he was still a man.

"She gets that a lot."

"I presume they are implants."

"Her fourth set, I believe."

"She received her money's worth."

"I'll tell her."

"No need. I already did."

He studied Carter. His eyes dulled, and he stiffly stuck out his hand. "Welcome."

They shook, and we moved out of the line.

"Is there a problem with Dr. Peebler?" Carter asked.

"I forgot to tell you that he has what he calls mad cow disease. Marcia says his brains blew up."

"It must be a trying time for her."

I watched as Eddie stopped in front of Alan. His eyes brightened as Eddie leaned in and said something to him. Alan pulled a piece of toilet paper off of the roll and, with a flourish, wiped his nose. Eddie clapped his hands. Alan bowed and threw the used toilet over his head into a basket behind him. Eddie gave him a thumbs up and joined us.

A young man in a tuxedo came up with a tray full of drinks. "May I offer you a glass of champagne?" he asked. "It is a *Crystal* '01."

We each took a flute and sipped it.

"Amazing," Carter said.

"Looks like you owe Marcia and Alan a really nice dinner," Eddie said.

"I'm not sure that will happen, with Alan's problems, but I could be wrong," I said. "Let's find our group."

83

One of the waiters ushered the three of us into the West Gallery. The people behind us walked in a different direction.

The Irregulars and their husbands were already there. Marcia had declared the theme for her party would be "business casual," so we had all dressed in what we assumed that was.

Except for Molly, we wore our usual clothes of loose-fitting slacks, sweaters, and flats. Molly had on a tight black mini skirt, black tights, knee-high leather boots, and a black bustier that prominently displayed her implants.

Linda tipped her champagne flute to me. "Guess the rest of the guests have a different concept of business casual than I do," she said.

"I agree," Cas said. "I feel way underdressed." And this from a woman who thought dressing up was wearing an exercise top with long sleeves.

Linda put her hand on my arm. "Tony is here."

"David and Rick invited him," I said. "What's the big deal? I was through with him many, many years ago."

"I know, but he has a date."

"Linda, Tony has dated half the women in the greater Chicago area."

She lowered her head.

"What?" I asked.

She raised her head and we made eye contact. "He brought Brittany Simon."

Whoa.

Brittany is one of Carter's best young reporters. She is smart and aggressive and will do anything to write a compelling story, a mirror image of what I was before I was fired by the *Washington Post* for pursuing the abortion bomber — despite being told by the FBI not to — and had two kids. She has long, straight, blond-streaked brown hair, way too cute dimples, flawless skin, and a ballet dancer's lithe body and muscular legs.

And no cellulite.

Carter had previously assigned her to help me with a couple of stories. The way it turned out, she'd received the credit for them, and I'd gone home and changed diapers.

She is way too good a reporter to sit at dinner and listen to what we were going to talk about without becoming interested. Once again, I was going to be screwed out of a story.

Unless.

"Carter, Tony brought Brittany here tonight," I said.

He knew Tony and I were lovers in a past life, and he didn't like Tony. My hubby wouldn't hear anything but Tony's name and focus on that.

I smiled sweetly. "Do you think that she would want to help on the Zhukov story?"

His jaw muscles clenched. "She's consumed by two complex assignments. She won't have time. It's your story."

Yes!

"Good, but I've kind of become interested in Diane Warren again," I said. "Brittany worked on that story. Do you think she'll have time to help me on it, if I need her?"

He arched his eyebrow. "Is that what this party is all about? Diane Warren?"

"Not exactly, but her name might come up. Why would you ask that?"

"She's here."

What?!

Suddenly, it was hard for me to breathe. "Diane Warren… is… here?" I gasped.

"I saw her talking to the mayor."

I turned around. Marcia stood behind me listening to our conversation.

"Marcia, is this true?" I asked.

"It is," she said. "I invited Diane. I thought we might need a little entertainment. Conflict is so invigorating and makes for fabulous after-dinner conversation."

84

A long dining table had been placed in the Gallery. Marcia sat at the head next to David on one side and Rick on the other. Alan was at the other end. Lori, his nurse, was next to him. I was next to Alan on the other side. Carter was next to Lori. Eddie sat next to Carter. Alan stared straight ahead while we waited for the first course.

The rest of our group sat on the chairs in the middle of the table. There were two empty places until Tony and Brittany walked in as the waiters began serving. Marcia waved Tony over to her. She shook his hand as she eyed him up and down.

"David and Rick were right," she said to Tony. "You are yummy."

Most men would at least blush or be put off by a remark like that, but not Tony. He tugged at the hem of his black silk sport coat to smooth out any wrinkles, shot his French cuffs, and flashed his dazzling smile.

"Sorry, we're late because my pants," he raised his eyebrows and smirked, "got wrinkled. Had to go home to change."

Marcia studied Brittany, who always wears her skirts short to display her legs. Tonight it was a tight white one. It was wrinkled, as was her royal blue silk top.

"I think I know what happened," Marcia said. "You'll have to tell me about it later."

I saw Brittany glance around the table. When she saw Carter, she smiled widely and walked to our end of the table.

"If she calls me 'Mrs. Thomas' I'm gonna slug her," I whispered to Linda, who sat next to me.

"As short as her skirt is, if she bends down too far, Janet might have to arrest her for indecent exposure," Linda responded.

Brittany greeted Carter by shaking hands. At least she didn't try to hug him.

"Hi, Tina," Brittany said across the table.

"An unexpected surprise to see you here," I said.

"Tony called at the last minute to invite me," she said. "You probably remember how it is to be working on several great stories and have so little time to have fun, but since I knew Carter was going to be here I thought it would be okay."

"It hasn't been that long ago for me," I said. "And I do remember having deadlines for stories, but I never took time off for fun. I worked too hard to beat the male reporters."

"I'll work extra hard tomorrow, even though," she smiled at Tony, "I probably won't get much sleep tonight.

I'm sure you remember about those nights, even though it was a long time ago."

I felt my face flush. She turned around and went to her seat. Linda leaned close to me. "Where's your gun?"

"In the van. Maybe I can borrow Janet's. I'm sure she'll understand."

The waiters served the salads. Marcia signaled for quiet by tapping her crystal wine glass with her knife.

"Greetings to the members of the Hanscom Park Irregulars and their mates." David tugged at Marcia's sleeve. She leaned down and he whispered in her ear.

She straightened up. "I mean the Hamlin Park Irregulars, but I'm not sure why that even matters. We have a lot to discuss about how hospitals make money. Dr. Wallace, would you please begin?"

85

"Last week, Tina asked me to explain to you how hospitals make so much money," Eddie began. "A recent study was done in which a person called more than one hundred hospitals in each state seeking prices for a hip replacement for a sixty-two-year-old grandmother who was uninsured but had the means to pay out of her own pocket. Only about half of the hospitals, including several top-ranked orthopedic centers, could provide any price estimate. Those who did gave quotes that varied from eleven thousand one hundred dollars to one hundred twenty-five thousand seven hundred and ninety-eight dollars."

"That's ridiculous," Frankie said.

"Sadly, it isn't," Eddie said. "The lady was fictitious, created for a research project on health care costs, but the findings illustrate the unsustainable growth of American health care costs and an opaque medical system in which prices are often hidden from consumers. For example, I insert tubes into a little kid's ear drums. My charge for the surgery is two hundred dollars. The kid is under anesthesia for five minutes. My hospital's outpatient facility fee is five thousand dollars, but it could be twice that at another hospital in my same city."

"How is that even possible?" Janet asked.

"Transparency is all the rage these days in government and business, but there's been a minimal push for pricing transparency in health care, and there's virtually no information available to the patient," he said. "You can get the price to purchase a car, but health care? That's not easy."

"Are we missing something here?" David asked.

"They do it because they can," Eddie continued. The hospitals blame the insurance companies. The insurance companies blame the hospitals, and the costs keep rising."

"If one hospital can perform a hip replacement for eleven thousand dollars, then all hospitals should be able to do it for the same price," Rick said.

"But Rick, when there's one hundred percent variation in sticker price, there is no real price," David said. "It's obviously only about profit."

"No kidding," Molly's husband Greg said. "This is like paying one hundred twenty thousand dollars for a twelve thousand dollar Honda."

"I had a breast MRI not too long ago in Dr. Fertig's office," Janet said. "The bill came to twenty-eight hundred dollars for that test. The rest of the bill — including the ultrasound, lab, and consultation — totaled an additional seventeen hundred dollars. Did he overcharge me?"

"Let's examine the real cost of the MRI," Eddie said. "How many people were there to do the procedure?"

"One lady brought me in and put me in the machine," she said. "Another guy ran the machine. The first lady came back and took me out about an hour later."

"You never saw Dr. Fertig?"

"I don't think I did, unless he was hiding in the back."

"Two people. One hour. How much were you charged for their time?"

"Haven't a clue."

"And you'll never know unless you requested an itemized bill, and even then, you won't be able to figure it out. Assume the first woman makes eighteen dollars an hour. Pay her the full amount and give her boss a twenty percent profit. The total cost of her time, including the profit, would be twenty-one dollars and sixty cents. Do the same thing for each individual cost for the procedure. Electricity? Probably no more than ten dollars. The technician running the machine? Fifty dollars including the twenty percent profit."

"What about the cost of the MRI machine?" Howard, Linda's husband, asked. "It can run well over one million dollars. That's why the test is expensive."

"Howard, if they do twenty to thirty MRIs a week, the machine will be paid for in less than a year. And what if they bought that machine four years ago? They've already depreciated it out, allowing them to play with house money."

"Seems to me like we're getting screwed," Joe, Cas's husband, said.

86

"I'm just getting started," Eddie continued. "If you have a cardiac cath, they will charge three hundred dollars for anesthesia."

"Is that the procedure where they stick a needle in one of your blood vessels?" Greg asked.

"In your femoral artery," Cas said. "It's in your groin."

"Man, I'm paying whatever it costs for that anesthesia," Greg said. "If they shove a needle down there, I don't want to feel anything and I damn sure don't want to move."

"Guess what the anesthesia is?" Eddie asked.

"Two cc of Xylocaine, the same drug my dentist uses to work on my teeth," Cas said. "And he never charges me for it."

"And he won't, since the total cost, including the syringe, is less than a dollar. The hospital charges over three hundred dollars for the same drug."

"Tell them about Rocephin," Cas said.

"Is that an antibiotic shot?" Greg asked. "I had one of those in the butt, and it hurt like crazy. Limped for a week."

"It costs about sixty-five dollars wholesale, right?" Cas asked.

Eddie nodded. "That's what they charge my office, but the hospitals get a deep discount due to their volume."

"What do you charge for a shot in the office?" I asked.

"Seventy-eight to eighty-five dollars. Depends on the insurance company, but that same shot given in the ICU at my hospital costs four hundred and twenty dollars."

"Expensive elevator ride from the pharmacy to the ICU," Rick said.

"But is the owner of MidAmerica Hospital doing anything that other hospitals aren't doing too?" Marcia asked.

"That's why they're all so profitable and why it's hard to understand why her hospital is in financial trouble," Eddie said.

"Forget the MidAmerica Hospital for a minute," Alan said unexpectedly. His dark brown eyes now looked black.

This should be interesting.

"A twenty percent profit is great in any business," he continued. "Why not take the actual cost of each individual part of a procedure and tack on a twenty percent profit? Then add them together and you have a cost platform that will be significantly lower than it is presently. To solve the issue of skyrocketing medical costs, we need to standardize the costs and then control them from the inside out rather than the outside in."

"If you have a total hip procedure done, it should cost the same if it's performed in Omaha or Chicago," Rick said.

"Almost the same," Alan said. "There will always be regional differences due to the variations in cost of living, like rent in different parts of the country."

87

"I have a question," Brittany Simon said.

Marcia made an effort to raise her eyebrows, but her Botox precluded that. "Who are you again, dear?"

"Brittany Simon. I'm one of Carter's reporters."

"And an extremely talented one, I might add," Carter said.

I wanted to kick him, but he was across from me and he was right, so I didn't. She was that good.

"As most of you know, I covered Dr. Fertig's story," Brittany said. "As Eddie just said, there are rumors that the finances of MidAmerica Hospital are shaky. Until he died, Fertig brought in most of the profits to the hospital."

"He did," Linda said. "It was about seventy-eight percent."

"Do you think MidAmerica's financial problems are because he died?" Brittany asked.

No one responded.

"And you guys also thought that there was something possibly illegal about his treatment," she continued.

"That was our assumption because of his unbelievable breast cancer cure rates, but we never found out how he did it," Cas said.

"After Fertig died, have the doctors Diane Warren hired been able to reproduce his results?" Brittany asked.

"We don't know for sure," Cas said.

Alan stood up and leaned forward with his palms outstretched on the table. His now-black eyes were glistening. "*Nobody* knows what causes cancer. Many cancer therapies are as poisonous to healthy cells as they are to cancer cells."

His nose began dripping, and he pulled another piece of toilet paper from his roll and dabbed at his nostrils. "A treatment that is able to distinguish between healthy and cancerous cells would be less toxic and less difficult to endure for those with cancer."

Putting the soiled tissue in his pocket, he pounded his fist on the table. "*This* is the answer to your question."

He turned around and walked to the interior door to his house. Lori jumped up and punched in the code. She opened it for him and they left together.

"An interesting comment," Marcia said. "This soup certainly is delicious."

88

Dinner was over. Our group stood in the West Gallery sipping a succulent, cold Chateau d'Yquem. Most of the men were outside smoking cigars. Marcia was with them. David and Rick were with us. Brittany had departed with Tony without asking any more probing questions.

"What was Alan talking about?" Molly asked.

"I'm not sure," I said. I nodded toward David and Rick. "Any ideas?"

"Alan is brilliant, or at least he used to be," David said. "I think he has given us a clue."

"A clue?" Linda said. "I think it's the rambling of a man with dementia."

"But what if he is trying to tell us something?" Molly asked. "He might have the answer on how to bring down Diane Warren."

"Tell you what, Molly," I said. "You seem to have connected with him. Why don't you work on that, and the rest of us will attack Diane from a different angle."

"When I met him in the receiving line, he seemed to like my boobs, so that might work," Molly said. "I'll see if he wants to have lunch with me."

It was difficult to picture that encounter. I wasn't sure Alan was any more ready for Molly than she was for him.

"Maybe I can show him the recordings Cas gave me from Zhukov's office," Molly suggested. "He might like those."

"Molly, not now," I said with a vigorous shake of my head. "I don't think we should discuss this in Marcia and Alan's home."

"Oh, okay."

"Tina, come on," David said. "Let Molly and Cas tell us what they found. God knows we need a juicy tidbit after all that dreadfully dull medical talk."

I looked at Cas and nodded. "Okay, but don't say I didn't warn you."

"Zhukov had a couch in his office that folded out into a hide-a-bed, and he had a mirror on the ceiling above it," Cas began. "Above the mirror he had a hidden camera where he recorded what he did."

"How spicy!" Rick exclaimed. "I can't believe you didn't want her to tell us this. Please do keep talking, sweetie."

"Tina and I found the recordings of all his encounters," Cas said. "Since Molly's the expert on this type of behavior, I gave them to her to analyze. I haven't seen them."

They waited. I considered helping wash the dishes.

"It was the usual," Molly said.

"The usual *what,* for God's sake, Molly?" David asked.

"Zhukov was having sex, right?" Linda asked.

"Was it kinky sex?" Rick asked.

"It kind of was. The women were actually guys dressed up like women."

The group was silent.

"I obviously wasn't expecting that," I said.

"God, neither was I," Cas said.

"I guess we should have watched those recordings with you," I said. "We didn't know what we were missing."

"I can verify that Molly's report of what she saw on the recordings is correct," Janet said. "The lab guys tested the sheets you gave Tony from Zhukov's office bed. The DNA was from two men."

"Not a woman?" I asked.

"Nope."

"I guess it's possible that the killer I saw was a man dressed as a woman" I said.

"Sounds like Mr. Zhukov was a naughty boy," David said. "I am surprised we never met him."

"I don't understand," Linda said.

"Me either," I said.

"Well, dears, we know a little something about men who dress like women," Rick said.

There was more silence in the group.

"I think our group needs an education in this area, don't you, Rick?" David asked.

"I totally agree," Rick said. "How about we all meet up at The Max?"

"Isn't that the place in Northalsted that bills itself as the best LGBTQ dance club in the Midwest?" Molly asked.

"Sweetie, you are so with it, I can't believe what I'm hearing," David said. "We all have to go."

"Guys, we're getting off the track," I said. "Did you get any hits on the DNA from the two men, Janet?"

"We're working on it, but slowly," she said. "The Captain isn't too thrilled having us use expensive tests for what now appears to be either a missing person or, according to the FBI, a flight from justice."

"You and I know that isn't true," I said.

"The FBI never lies," she said.

"You know what I think about the FBI," I said.

"And I know what they think about you," she said. "Watch your back. They think you know where Zhukov is."

89

"Let's go have some fun," Marcia said, as she joined us. Her hair and clothes reeked from the stench of freshly smoked cigars and cigarettes.

"Fun?" I asked.

"I've waited all night for this," she said. "We have to hurry before she leaves."

"She?" Linda asked.

"Diane Warren. David, you and Rick stay here. If she sees you with Tina and the rest of the Irregulars, she'll never tell Leslie Van Horn anything we can use."

Our group moved into the library where Diane Warren stood with two men. She is slender and close to Molly's height, which is six feet not including her heels.

Tonight, Diane's heavily sprayed, blond hairdo was swept into a chignon. Professionally applied makeup covered her almost-translucent, wrinkle-free skin. The decrease in the size of her pot of gold hadn't affected how she dressed. The last time we encountered her she was all Chanel. This time it was couture, but I wasn't sure which designer.

"Molly?" I said, nodding toward Diane.

"Oscar de la Renta. The shoes are Manolo Blahniks. The bag is a Birkin from Hermes."

One of the men stood next to Diane. He was Peter Warren's brother, William. He's an attorney, and his main client is Diane and her hospital. He wore a black suit with a white pocket square, a starched white shirt with French cuffs, and a silk rep tie.

Crap!

Suddenly, I remembered more about him. He also invested and managed the money in the hospital's foundation for a sizable fee. That would be a significant incentive for him to cover up any illegal activities Diane might be doing with the foundation's funds. We would have to find another way to trap her.

She was engaged in a conversation with the other man, the mayor, and didn't see Marcia approach. We were a few steps behind her.

Marcia tapped the mayor on the shoulder. "Honey, let me borrow Diane. There are people here I want her to meet."

The mayor moved on. Diane turned around with a radiant smile on her face. It vanished when she saw the Irregulars standing about five steps behind our hostess.

Diane reconfigured her tight facial muscles into a snarling smile. "A lovely party, as always, Marcia," she said, through clenched teeth. "The food was delightful." She turned and began to move away. "I'm sorry William and I have to leave, but we have another event we must attend."

Marcia grabbed Diane's arm and yanked her to a standstill. "Not so fast, sweetie." She pulled Diane around to face us. "I want you to know that these are my new best friends, and I am now part of their group."

"I can't imagine why you would ever want to associate with people like this," Diane said.

I thought I heard Marcia growl, but it was difficult to tell with all the background noise of the party.

"Associating with vacuous, overdressed people like you is exactly why I want to hang around with them."

"Marcia, I cannot believe you said that," she replied.

"Believe it, and if you ever want me to support any of your idiotic charities again, you better remember that anything you do to them you do to me. Got it, sweetie?"

Diane whirled around on her Manolo Blahniks and stomped off.

"God, was that fun," Marcia said. "I've wanted to do that for a long time." She put her hand to her mouth and coughed heavily. "She will have to think twice before she comes after you. Now we have some time to kick her skinny little butt before she figures out how to pay you back. What do we do?"

90

Sunday morning, Carter and Eddie took Kerry to Ann Sather for breakfast. It's our favorite brunch restaurant in Chicago. Macy had a fussy night, so I volunteered to stay home with her. I also wanted to check my home for listening devices.

This had happened to me before. Then, I thought they were hidden by the FBI. I was wrong. It had been my neighbors who turned out to be bad guys. After they were disposed of, I thought the devices were no longer active.

But I was wrong again.

Dr. Mike Doyle was another criminal I wrote a story about, which resulted in him being sent to prison. When he got out, he had used an apartment behind our home to spy on me, and he had activated the devices again. Before he was killed, he watched and listened to all the events that happened to me and everyone who was in our home.

The devices had never been removed, and now I was afraid the FBI might have taken over the bugs and were using them to discover what I knew about Zhukov.

I had a scanning device to detect listening bugs. I found the small, oblong black box in a kitchen drawer. I took it out and flipped the switch. Nothing happened.

Several more clicks, and the green light still didn't come on. There was a small Phillips-head screw securing the battery box lid, but I couldn't find the right screwdriver.

After twenty minutes, I found it in my sewing kit. I unscrewed the back of the box and removed four AA batteries. Rummaging around in a different kitchen drawer, I found each type of battery but the ones I needed. Hokey Pokey Elmo came to the rescue. I stole four from him and put them in the device.

This time when I flipped the switch, the green light came on. I went around the house, but the light remained green. Linda knew how to check my computer for a keystroke logger, which I would have her do the next time she came over, but if there were no bugs, my bet was the machine was clean.

The FBI was interested in the Zhukov case, but they had a limited budget and they weren't going to use more expensive resources to continuously monitor my home. I would check my house daily for bugs. If I found any, then I would be certain that the feds were after me and the rest of the Hamlin Park Irregulars.

91

Eddie walked into the kitchen as I was putting the bug detector back in the kitchen drawer. Carter stuck his head in the door, waved, and went into the family room with Kerry.

"Ann Sather is great," Eddie said. "I wish we had one in Omaha."

"Maybe they'll sell you a franchise," I said.

"Another great doctor investment. I would totally screw it up. I don't know anything about restaurants."

"It seems easy enough."

"That's the problem and the reason doctors invest in crazy stuff like that. I'll stick to picking noses." He sat down at the kitchen table. "Before I pack, we need to discuss what Dr. Peebler said at the dinner party."

"He said several things, some of which I'm sure are accurate, but with him it's hard to tell. Why?"

"I've been puzzling over his statement about cancer therapies being as poisonous to healthy cells as they are to cancer cells."

"That isn't exactly a startling revelation. I know several people that became extremely sick on chemotherapy."

"He also said that a treatment that is able to distinguish between healthy and cancerous cells would be less toxic and less difficult to tolerate for those with cancer."

"I do remember him saying that."

"Put those statements in the context of the conversation we were having."

I sat down beside him. "We were discussing Diane Warren and the hospital losing money."

"But we were actually talking about Fertig."

"We were?"

"We were. You said he cured every breast cancer patient he operated on."

"Supposedly, but I was never convinced of it. Right after Fertig killed himself, I suggested to Carter that I needed to investigate the breast cancer cure issue further. It was a loose end, but I became pregnant and didn't pursue it."

"I think that's what Peebler was talking about, and that might have been a mistake for you to stop working on that story."

"It was?"

"You told me that, post-op, Fertig made each patient take supplements."

"After Janet was seen by Fertig, his nurse told her and me that he found herbs somewhere in the Amazon rain forest that natives ingested and lived to be well over one hundred years old."

"What if Fertig discovered those herbs were not a treatment for aging but, rather, a cure for breast cancer?"

What?!

"Do you think that's possible?"

"How else do you explain his cure rates?"

"I can't, but it sounds like a science fiction movie."

He laughed. "Have you ever heard of Sir Alexander Fleming?"

"No, who is he?"

"The researcher who discovered penicillin. He was in his lab doing experiments on staphylococci bacteria. He left a Petri dish containing the bacteria near an open window. Mold spores blew through the window onto the dish. He found the mold killed the bacteria."

"You're telling me Fleming discovered penicillin by accident?"

"I am, and I think maybe that's what Fertig did, too, only he took it one step further. He didn't share his discovery with anyone."

"Why would a doctor do such a heinous thing?"

"He had the cure for breast cancer, so everyone had to come to him. He became rich and famous. Why would he share it?"

"How about to keep millions of people from dying of breast cancer?"

"Maybe he would do that in the movies, or on TV, but not in real life. It was his discovery and not his surgical skills that led to him being considered the best of the best.

No one could match his results anywhere in the world. That would be the ultimate ego trip."

"Do you think he killed himself without sharing this?"

"I do, and it's easy to check. Find out if the surgeon who replaced him is obtaining the same results."

"You mean curing each new breast cancer patient."

"That and maintaining Fertig's cure rates with his existing patients. That's even more important. If I'm right, those patients will begin to have a recurrence of their cancers without the supplements."

"Then Diane Warren better find another batch from South America before that happens."

"If Fertig's nurse told their patients about his discovery in South America, Diane had to have known about it too. Bet me that she's already doing everything she can to find it."

Part 4

92

It was a snowy Monday morning. Kerry was in preschool. I felt compelled to finish these stories, so although reluctantly, I took Macy to Alicia's. The only good part was that at least most of my daughter's time there would be during her morning nap.

David Scott sat in the passenger seat of my van. "What time did Sullivan say he would be at your house?" I asked, as I pulled out of my driveway.

David glanced at his watch. "He should be there by now. Let's hope he's working."

Rick had to take care of Marcia and her standing hair appointment, so he was with her at their salon. The boys wanted me to question Sullivan to see if we could figure out what was going on with the missing subs.

There was one available parking place in front of their home when we arrived. I didn't see Sullivan's truck.

"Looks like he isn't here yet," I said.

"He usually parks in the alley behind the house, so hopefully he's already inside," David said.

The snow continued to fall as we walked up the planks to the front door. David opened the front door with his key to the lock box. Several *thunks* of what sounded like compressed air from a machine came from somewhere inside the house. The noise stopped when we stepped into the entryway and shut the door.

"What is that annoying sound?" David asked.

"I think it's a nail gun," I said. "Carter used one when he worked on our patio. Maybe Sullivan is here, after all, and he's working."

"I can only hope."

The only other sound was a flapping noise that came from the north wind blowing the protective plastic tarps covering the walls to our left. David took a step forward, and the flooring boards creaked under his foot.

"Charlie?" he called out.

We waited.

"Charlie, it's David," he said with more gusto. "I'm here with Tina Thomas."

Three more *thunk*s from the nail gun came from the back of the house. We walked toward the sound.

From the hallway we saw Sullivan sitting thirty feet away at the makeshift table in the great room. His back was toward us. His hands rested on architectural plans open in front of him.

"Charlie?" David said again.

Sullivan didn't move.

David began to step forward. I stopped him with my hand.

"Something doesn't seem right," I whispered to him.

David raised his eyebrows.

"I don't see a nail gun," I said.

I reached for my backpack, but I'd left it in the van along with my gun. Clearing my throat, I took a step into the great room. David remained in the hallway. He wrapped his arms across his chest and hugged himself.

"Charlie?" I asked. "It's Tina Thomas and David Scott. We're here for our meeting."

He didn't move. His hands remained on the house plans in front of him.

Walking forward, I didn't see a McDonald's wrapper on the floor. When I stepped on it, the unexpected crunching noise made me jump.

I tapped Sullivan on the shoulder. He didn't move. I walked around to face him. There were three nails in his face, one in each eye and one in the middle of his forehead.

93

I knew I should run and take David with me, but as scared as I was, this was turning into a terrific story. I was going to stay.

Fresh blood trickled out of his eyes and ran down his cheeks like he was crying red tears. I sniffed and detected a copper odor. A watery, pink fluid oozed out of the nail between his eyes and dripped off the end of his nose.

I looked down. His hands were nailed to the plywood in front of him and his feet were nailed to the floor. As I stooped down for a better look, I heard a *thunk*. A nail whistled over my head and stuck in the wall behind me.

Uh-oh!

"David, run!" I screamed. "Get out of here!"

He sprinted down the hall. He was shrieking when he yanked open the door and disappeared outside.

Crouching down behind Sullivan's body, my heart began racing as I tried to figure out what to do. My immediate problem was that I had to traverse about thirty feet of open space before I could get to the front door.

I should have run when I had the chance.

Two more *thunk*s and two more nails slammed into the wall behind me.

Call 911!

A great idea but my phone was in my backpack with my gun.

Thunk, thunk, thunk, thunk. I felt Sullivan's body jerk as the nails hit his torso. The floors creaked in the kitchen area to my right, which was followed by a metallic sound, like the killer was reloading the nail gun.

My only chance!

I sprinted in a zigzag fashion toward the hallway. Rapid-fire *thunk* sounds preceded several nails that flew around me, but I made it to the hallway without being hit. As I ducked to my left, three more nails hit the wall behind me.

Running out the front door, I jumped off the stoop, and landed awkwardly in the ice and snow in the front yard. I tried to maintain my balance but couldn't get any traction and did a frontal, four-point landing in the snow.

The front yard is on an incline, and I slid on my chest and stomach all the way to the sidewalk before I skidded to a stop. I tried to get up, but I slipped and fell again, this time on my back.

After rolling over, I crawled to the van and got behind it. I peeked over the fender. No one followed me out of the house. I checked in the van's windows, but David was missing too. The only sound came from the north wind blowing against the plastic tarps.

Keeping the van between me and the house, I opened the driver's door. David was bent over, cowering in the passenger seat, his hands over his head.

Expecting another round of flying nails at any second, I hunched over the steering wheel and started the van. I tromped on the accelerator, but the front wheels spun in the snow before they gained traction and we finally roared away.

Four blocks later, I pulled into my driveway and slammed on the brakes. I had misevaluated this entire story. I pounded my hands on the steering wheel. How could I have been so stupid? The subs were disappearing right and left, and I had thought it was kind of funny. I was wrong.

I felt a tug on the sleeve of my ski jacket.

"Thank you for saving me," David said.

He hugged me. I hugged him back.

"I should have had my gun with me," I said. "But I'm an idiot and left my backpack in the van. I'm so sorry."

"How could you know?" he said. "I mean to tell you, we never took a gun to a meeting with Sullivan before. Why would this time be any different?"

"The subs have been disappearing. I should have realized something serious was going on." I leaned back and took out my cell phone to call Janet. "At least this time I have a body." I pictured Sullivan nailed to the table and floor. "And he isn't going anywhere."

94

Fifteen minutes later, Janet and Tony met David and me in my driveway. They followed as I drove back to David and Rick's house. This time, there were no parking places on either side of the street. Tony double-parked their Ford Police Utility SUV in front of the house and put on his blinking blue cop lights. I double-parked in front of them.

The falling snow had partially filled the imprints I'd made in the front yard, but it was still obvious that a person had slid all the way from the front door to the sidewalk.

David remained in the van. We got out and stood staring at the house. They pulled out their guns. I had my backpack but didn't take out my Glock.

Tony pointed to the disrupted snow. "Makin' snow angels?" he asked.

"No, Tony, I wasn't making snow angels," I said. "I ran out of the house and fell on my ass. Happy now?"

He smiled. "Typical skirt. Runnin' instead of fightin'."

I clenched my fists, but he was right. I ran and never considered any other course of action.

"Let's get on with this," Janet said. "It's cold out here." She turned to me. "Take us through it."

We moved forward. "David and I walked up these planks," I said. "After we entered and closed the front door, I heard a noise which sounded like compressed air coming out of a machine."

"Nail gun?" Tony asked.

"It was, but I didn't know it for sure at the time."

Tony and Janet held their guns in front of them. Janet nodded at my backpack. "You might need to protect yourself if this goes upside down."

Pulling out my gun, I made sure I had a round in the chamber as we walked through the still-open front door and stepped inside. We stopped but I left the door open.

"What happened next?" she asked.

"David called out, but Sullivan didn't answer. David remained here in the hallway, and I walked in and found Sullivan's body."

"Stay here," Janet said. "Do not leave this spot."

They walked down the hall into the great room. I waited for the sound of gunfire. Instead, I heard laughter.

"Did it again, sweets," Tony said, from the great room.

"Did what?"

"Lost another body."

95

No freaking way!

I ran into the great room. Janet and Tony stood in the middle of the space where Sullivan's body had been.

It was gone. So were the plywood desk, the folding chair, and the house plans.

"This is impossible!" I fumed.

Janet holstered her gun. "For most people, I would agree with that statement. But not with you. You seem to be good at this. Tell us exactly what happened in here."

I walked over to the spot where Sullivan had been nailed to the floor and table.

"Sullivan was right here," I said, as I pointed at the spot where he'd sat. "His feet were nailed to the floor and his hands were nailed to the makeshift desk."

Tony looked around. "Seems to be missing, along with the body."

"You guys know I'm not making this up."

Janet walked around the perimeter of the room and then peered out the back windows. "It's hard to figure how this went down."

"What happened is that someone killed Sullivan and removed his body, cleaned up the evidence, and took everything out into the alley," I said. That's why we didn't see anyone when we drove up." I pointed toward the detached garage. "They parked back there."

"Two vehicles, Sullivan's and the killer's," he said. "Where are the tracks?"

"What tracks?" I asked.

"Should be foot tracks in the snow if the perp removed the body with all the evidence and tire tracks when he drove away," he said. "Don't see either one or Sullivan's truck."

The backyard was a morass of cement chunks and overturned dirt where footings had been dug for the patio. A tarp partially covered a stack of boards. A larger tarp had been thrown over another area in the yard that seemed like it was waiting for cement, but the fresh snow covering it had not been disturbed. I didn't see any footprints or tracks in the snow indicating that anything had been dragged away from the house.

I turned to Janet. "Sullivan's body has to still be in here."

"If you're right, maybe the killer is here, too," she said.

She took out her gun again. So did Tony. The two detectives left the great room to search the house. I remained, looking for clues to prove my case.

There were several nail holes in the floor, but I couldn't be sure if any of them matched up to where Sullivan was sitting. I checked for blood spatter on the floor or nails stuck in the wall where the killer had fired at me.

I hadn't found any by the time they returned.

"Anything?" I asked.

Janet gave me a small shake of her head. "A big goose egg."

Tony came in from the backyard. He stomped his feet to clean the snow off his Hunter boots. "No cars. No trucks. No tracks. Nothin' to prove anybody drove a vehicle in or away. Nothin' out there."

"I can't believe this," I said. "The guy killed Sullivan and tried to kill me. I know what happened."

"How do you explain this?" he asked.

I leaned against the wall. "I can't."

They waited. I glanced around and noticed something.

"The McDonald's wrapper. It's gone."

"Too bad," he smirked. "Clue we coulda' worked with."

"It proves the killer cleaned up this area before he left," I said. "He didn't want to leave anything behind. Talk to David. He'll verify what I saw."

"I already did while Tony walked around in the back," Janet said. "David's in shock and not sure what he saw."

"Call Sullivan's house," I said. "See if he's there."

"It's where we're headed next," she said. "If he answers the front door, you might want to rethink this whole deal."

96

Midmorning on Tuesday, the core Irregulars were in the locker room of XSport Fitness having completed a forty-five minute spinning class. Our kids were either in school or XSport's child care center.

Rick was doing Marcia's hair. David was in their condo having a post-traumatic stress attack after what happened to us. I needed a workout to release the tension for the same reason.

I told my friends about Sullivan and the disappearance of his body.

"What did Janet and Tony find when they went to Sullivan's house?" Cas asked.

"He wasn't there," I said.

"Then he's dead, like you told them," Molly said.

"I agree," Linda said. "That would seem to confirm your story."

"Janet said that his neighbors told them he likes to gamble, and he's been known to hit the casinos for days at a time without telling anyone where he's going," I said.

"What does his wife say?" Linda asked.

"He's divorced," I said. "They visited his ex-wife, and she told them she didn't like his gambling away all their money. She said she would let Janet know if he doesn't send his alimony check to her; otherwise she admitted she could care less about him."

"Maybe she did it," Cas said. "I might kill Joe if he blew our money at a casino."

"I think it's the same woman who killed the Russian guy," Molly said.

"Why on earth would you even suggest that?" Linda asked.

"Gosh, it's pretty obvious. She removed his body after she killed him. Now she's done it again, and we need to do what we did at Zhukov's office."

"Which was what, Molly?" I asked.

"We go back to David and Rick's new house and hunt for clues."

97

Tuesday night, Carter took care of the girls. I was back at David and Rick's home to search for clues. I had helpers with me.

"Be careful, Alan," I said, using the beam from my flashlight to guide him. I turned to Molly, who also had a flashlight. "If he slips and breaks a bone, I'll never forgive you."

"Don't worry, Tina," Alan said. "I might have mad cow disease, but my physical skills are still intact."

He followed that statement by slipping off the board leading into David and Rick's house and falling on his back into the snow.

I jumped down to help him up and shined my flashlight on his face. He blushed.

"I guess I'm not as agile as I used to be," he admitted.

"I can't believe Marcia said you could come with us," I said.

He didn't say anything.

I turned the flashlight on Molly. "Marcia does know about this, doesn't she?"

"Not exactly," she said.

I waited.

"I stopped to see Alan tonight and we began playing Super Mario on his Wii. I remembered what we talked about after spinning this morning, so after Marcia left to go to some party thingy for the opera, I called you to meet us here."

"What about Lori, his nurse?"

"She showed me how to make sure he was safe in his part of the house before she left."

"And you decided to take a little detour without telling Marcia or Lori."

"I thought it would be fun. He gets bored staying inside all the time, isn't that right, Alan?"

He stared straight ahead.

"I think he's having a moment," I said. "Once I get the door open, you help him into the house to get him out of the wind. I'll be as fast as I can."

Taking out my lock pick gun and torque wrench, I opened the lock box. The chatter from the gun made Alan blink several times, and he leaned closer to me to see what I was doing.

"This is a lock pick gun, Alan," I said. "It comes in handy for situations like this."

His eyes remained dull, and he didn't say anything. Once the door was open, Molly helped him into the hallway. I went into the great room and began spraying luminol on the spot where I thought the desk had been. I turned off my flashlight but no blue colors appeared.

"Damn," I said to myself.

"Luminol," Alan said from behind me, causing me to jump in the dark.

I turned the flashlight back on. "It is. Have you heard of it?"

His eyes brightened. "$C_8H_7N_3O_2$, or what you know as luminol, exhibits a blue chemiluminescence when mixed with an appropriate oxidizing agent. It reacts with the iron stores found in hemoglobin. It is used by forensic investigators to detect, among other elements, trace amounts of blood left at crime scenes."

He blinked and stared into the darkness. I flashed the light around the room, but Molly was gone.

"Molly, where are you?" I asked.

"Checking for clues," she answered from the basement.

"And?"

"It's weird. Part of the floor is cement but the rest is dirt."

I walked to the head of the temporary basement stairs and glanced back to make sure Alan's brain was still in the off mode. "Ah, Molly?" I whispered. "Better leave this alone. The cement part is where Frankie's guys buried the guy I shot."

Her flashlight moved back and forth. "If you say so, but I think it's a clue."

"It is, but it's to a crime I committed. I think we should forget about it."

98

I followed Molly and Alan back to his home. She punched in the security code on his front door, which was located on the side of the house. We took him inside.

"Do you need any help, Alan?" Molly asked.

"Help?" he asked.

"Getting ready for bed," she said.

His eyes narrowed. "I am not that far gone that I cannot properly prepare for bed."

"Before we leave, I have a question," I said. "Do you know much about vitamins and supplements?"

His eyes brightened. "Ah, yes, complementary and alternative medicine. Seventy percent of the health care in the world is levied by nonmedical personnel. We can posit these formulations are efficacious in many clinical settings."

"So, like Sir Alexander Fleming accidentally found penicillin, could other substances be found in nature that might cure cancer?" I asked.

"They might and probably will be in the future." He peered into my eyes. "Does this have to do with Fertig and Diane Warren?"

"It does."

He smiled. "You finally figured it out from what I told you at the dinner party."

"Fertig's supplements cured the breast cancer, not his surgery."

"That's it?!" he shouted. "That's what you deduced? Unbelievable. Did you not listen to one word I said?"

"I did, and I thought that's what you meant."

He stomped his foot. "Do I constantly have to be exposed to small minds? Is there no one who can comprehend what I am saying?"

I hung my head. "If it's not good enough, I apologize."

He raised his voice. "Can you not see it? The solution is right before your myopic eyes. Expand your view, and you will have Diane Warren in your clutches. She is in an indefensible position. You will win if you simply listen to what I told you."

He whirled around and left the room.

"He sounded kind of upset," Molly said.

"No kidding," I said. "I wish I knew what the heck he was talking about."

99

Wednesday morning, the core Irregulars were in the locker room after having finished a strictly strength class at XSport Fitness.

"Yesterday I forgot to tell you guys that before Eddie left he presented an interesting idea to me," I began.

I told them what he said about Fertig and Diane Warren. I didn't say anything concerning Alan's rant about my inability to understand the ramifications of Fertig's supplements.

Linda disagreed. "All Eddie has is a theory based on words a crazy man uttered. In my opinion, that's extremely meager evidence."

"And like Eddie told you, there's a problem investigating this," Cas said. "New patients who have a breast cancer operation done by Diane's current surgeon will be given conventional post-op breast cancer treatment. It'll be at least five years before anyone discovers the cure rates have changed."

"Yes, but that's for the new patients," I said. "What about the existing ones? If they were cured on Fertig's supplements and now no longer can get them, won't they risk getting a breast cancer recurrence?"

"It's possible, but again, it might take several years for this to occur," Cas suggested.

"If Fertig's nurse told us about his discovery of herbs in the South American rain forest, Diane obviously knows about them too," I said.

"And she has at least five years to find them," Linda said.

"I wonder if her breast cancer doctor is still selling supplements to his post-op patients?" Cas asked.

Huh?

"If he is, and she knows he's not selling Fertig's South American supplements that cure breast cancer, that might be the real story here," I said.

"That's a great legal point," Linda said. "She and her employee would be willfully and knowingly committing fraud and potentially allowing patients to die of breast cancer who think they are receiving Fertig's treatment regimen."

"But they wouldn't be," Cas said.

Molly looked up. "Yeah, so she would be killing those poor ladies."

"It is possible a prosecutor might file murder charges too," Linda added.

"If we can prove this, we can put her out of business," I said.

"And when they slap her in jail, she won't be able to blow us up," Molly said.

"Okay, but how do we prove Diane's doctor is selling different supplements than Fertig used?" Cas asked.

I thought back to the visit Janet and I made to Fertig's office when we were told about the South American supplements.

"Frankie," I said to myself.

"What did you say?" Cas asked.

"Sorry, I was thinking about when Janet and I went to Fertig's office. His nurse tried to sell us his supplements, but we didn't buy them. Later, Frankie had one of his guys complain about Fertig's charges. The result was Fertig's office manager sent Janet a one-month supply of the supplements for free."

"That was a year and a half ago," Linda reminded me. "How is that going to help us now?"

"Janet gave those supplements to Frankie to have them analyzed by another one of his guys. If we can compare those supplements to the ones her doctor is selling now and prove they're not the same, we'll have her."

"Did Janet ever tell you what Frankie's guy found out about those supplements?" Linda asked.

Whoopsie.

"No, and honestly, I was busy having Macy and forgot about it," I said.

"Why don't you call Janet and find out the results?" Cas asked.

I did and put her on speaker. I told her what we needed.

"Sorry to disappoint you, but Frankie's guy told me these were high grade vitamins, nothing more, nothing less," Janet said.

Darn it!

"They weren't some exotic new herb from South America?" I asked.

"No, they were made in a lab in California, which is why I never followed up on the results with you."

"But you don't have breast cancer, and neither do I," I said. "There was no reason for Fertig to sell us the real goods that would cure breast cancer. He could peddle anything to us, and we wouldn't know the difference."

"And it will not do us any good to try and obtain what Diane's surgeon is using now, because if they're giving supplements, they're probably the same ones Fertig's nurse tried to sell you when you were in his office," Linda said.

"Which Diane has a ready supply of because she can buy them in California," Janet reminded us.

"It sure couldn't be what Fertig sold to his breast cancer patients, because he was the only one who knew where to get them," Cas said.

"And he's dead," Molly said.

Now what?

100

Thursday morning, Carter was at work and I was busy being a mommy. Macy had finished breastfeeding and was down for her nap. Kerry was in preschool.

I sat in front of my computer and reviewed my files on Zhukov.

Huh?

I called Linda. "Something is screwy," I said.

"Something is always screwy in your life," she responded.

I wanted to disagree, but after losing two bodies, it was hard to do.

"Did you go over Zhukov's computer files again?" I began.

"I did, and then I asked a forensic accountant in Howard's firm to repeat my work. He emailed me the report yesterday." She paused. "Why are you calling about this right now?"

"I was going over my Zhukov files and saw I hadn't received a follow-up report from you."

"It must be hard keeping track of all these stories."

"Tell me." It was my turn to pause. "Give it to me."

"Remember that I guessed the Russian Mafia was one of Zhukov's clients."

"You did, and you thought he was stealing from them."

"We were spot on. Zhukov's final theft tally was one hundred fifty million dollars."

Whoa.

"One hundred million was Russian Mafia money," she continued. "The rest came from his other investors."

"Where did Zhukov hide the funds he embezzled?"

"In a secret off-shore account in a Cayman Islands bank, but I missed one item, and it was so simple I'm embarrassed to admit it."

"What was it?"

"I didn't notice when Zhukov stole the money."

"I assume he did it before he was killed."

"He did, but it was stolen a second time, the morning of the night you copied his files."

What?

"Wait, I'm confused. Are you telling me that Zhukov didn't steal all the money?"

"No, I'm telling you he did steal it all, but that was three days before he left on Tuesday."

"He didn't leave. He was shot and killed Monday night."

"Whatever. He hid the money in the Cayman off-shore bank, which was where Howard's guy found the paper trail."

My pulse rate accelerated. All I could see were dollar signs. "Is the money still there?" I asked, thinking I did have a story.

"No, Howard's guy discovered all the funds were withdrawn from the bank a second time."

The dollar signs disappeared, and my pulse returned to normal. "Where is all that money? Who has it?"

"You said the killer came back and downloaded the files on Tuesday night when you were there with Molly."

"I did."

"And on Wednesday night you returned with Cas and downloaded the files yourself."

"Yep, but I don't see where you're going with this."

"The money disappeared from the off-shore account on Wednesday morning."

Uh-oh.

"If the killer works for the Russian Mafia, they now have their money back, Zhukov is dead, and I don't have a story," I said. "And don't say he isn't dead. He is, the end."

"But that's the problem."

"I don't understand."

"What if the killer doesn't work for the Russian Mafia? Suppose one of the other angry investors hired her to kill Zhukov and steal his computer files."

Uh-oh.

"The killer tells Zhukov she won't kill his family if she gets the password to his computer, and he tells her where the money is hidden," I said.

"And the angry investor pays off the killer, opens Zhukov's off-shore files, and transfers all the stolen money to his own account," she said.

"If that's true, the Russian Mafia will be extremely unhappy and they'll be hunting for that investor."

"They know that one hundred million of their dollars are missing, even if it is illegal money. They could go after Zhukov, but according to you, he's dead and the FBI now has his computer hard drive."

"But why is the FBI even interested in me?" I asked. "I don't know anything about the stupid money."

"They don't know the killer downloaded Zhukov's computer's information," she said. "They think you know what happened to Zhukov and, more importantly, what happened to the money."

101

Damn.

"They don't care about Zhukov, but recovering that much illegal money would be front page news — and you know how much the FBI loves positive publicity," I said.

"They're sitting back and waiting for you to lead them to the money or Zhukov or both," Linda said.

"It doesn't take much effort on their part. They let me do all the work and then they sweep in and take all the credit."

"And maybe convict you of something illegal in the process. Good thing you have me for your lawyer." She paused. "Remember, the last time the FBI was after you about a story, they tapped your phones and computer."

Uh-oh.

I stared at my cell phone. "Jana," I said.

"Who?" she asked.

"FBI Agent Jana. She said they would be watching me."

"But be realistic. You know they have a limited budget. Would they spend a lot of money monitoring what you do?"

"No way, but they might do it electronically, which wouldn't require much staffing."

"Do you think they are using a keystroke logger on your computer?"

The FBI has developed a keystroke logging software called Magic Lantern. It can be installed remotely via an email attachment, so the person doesn't even know her computer has been compromised. It had been done to my computer before, and when I last had my computer checked, it was gone. Or had the feds reinstalled it?

Stomach acid bubbled up into my throat.

"Remember, we downloaded all of Zhukov's files on your computer," she reminded me. "You saw the FBI take Zhukov's hard drive, and they have all his files. If they're now using a keystroke logger on your computer, they know you do too."

Crap!

"They have to believe I stole the information the Monday night I was there to interview him because they don't know I came back on Tuesday and Wednesday nights."

"I'll come by tonight and check your computer to make sure we're right about the keystroke logger."

"Deal."

Hanging up, I sat down at my computer. If it were compromised, the FBI agents would immediately know what I typed on the keyboard.

On the other hand, I could use this and play with them a little. I was going to proceed like I normally would in working a story, except they wouldn't know I was on to them.

I called up Zhukov's files. The list of investors was my starting point. There were two hundred thirty-two names. Linda had referred to Zhukov's killer as a female, but the sex tapes seemed to indicate otherwise. I scanned the list for female names. There were seventy-two. There were also twenty-one investment funds, including the Sturgeon Corporation.

One of the most boring aspects of investigative journalism is to do background checks, and this was a big list. I typed in the names that I would typically investigate, but then I stopped. Trying to figure out what I was doing would make a long day for an FBI agent. I was going wake up Macy and play with my daughter.

Let an FBI agent try and figure out what I was doing.

102

Friday morning, Janet and Frankie were in our family room. Macy was upstairs taking her nap. Her Nanit was on. Kerry was in preschool.

I told them about Zhukov's money and how Linda discovered a keystroke logger on my computer last night.

"It couldn't have been the Russians who killed Zhukov and got the money," Janet said. "If they did, the FBI would have given up by now. The keystroke logger Linda found on your computer proves the feds are working this hard, and that means there's a lot of missing money still out there."

"The FBI might be thinking you're the one who stole the one hundred and fifty large," Frankie said to me.

"Or they think I know who did," I said.

"This is amazing," she said. "The Russian Mafia and FBI searching for the same money."

"Which I don't have. I wish I did. I would gladly give it up."

Frankie furrowed his eyebrows. "Whoa. Finders keepers, babe. Let's not be giving the freaking farm away unless you have to."

"What do we do?" I asked.

"How about finding the stiff," he asked, "since he's the dude that started all this?"

"I disagree," Janet said. "You have to find the money."

"I think the best way is to do both, find the body and the money," I said. "But how do we do that?"

"By finally having our Chicago PD lab guys go over the crime scene," she said.

"We don't have Zhukov's body, so it's still not a crime scene" I reminded her. "Will your boss be okay with that?"

"He will when he finds out we're trying to screw the feds on a case. He hates them more than I do." She paused. "I'll have the computer techs go over the files you downloaded."

"Be right back."

I rushed down to the computer room and pulled a flash drive copy of Zhukov's hard drive out of my desk drawer. I brought it back to the family room and handed it to Janet.

"Last night, since Linda discovered a keystroke logger had been installed on my computer," I said, "I used Carter's office computer after he went to bed so I could go over Zhukov's list of investors again. There were a lot of Russian Jews, mostly lawyers and doctors, but no names jumped out at me. Maybe your techs can help me out."

"Done," she said.

"Might have my computer guy do a little sniffing too," Frankie said.

"Can't have too much help." I paused. "Not to change the subject, but what about Sullivan?"

Frankie turned to Janet. "That the builder guy?"

"Yeah, but I told you what happened," she said to him. "Tina lost another body."

"I did not," I said. "Sullivan was killed with a nail gun. The killer shot him in both eyes and his forehead and nailed his hands and feet to the table and floor. I saw his corpse."

"And then the corpse pulled the nails out of his eyes, head, hands, and feet and drove home without leaving any foot or tire prints in the fresh snow," she said.

"Tough to do," Frankie teased. "Love to have seen that one."

"This isn't funny," I said. "Has anyone notified the police that he's missing?"

"No one, and his mail delivery is being held at the post office," she said. "He notified them he's on vacation. He did the same thing with his newspaper."

"The killer did that," I said.

"Why bother?" she said. "Most killers don't go to that much trouble."

"Gotta agree with Janet," he said. "You off a guy, that's it — bada bing, bada boom. No need to jack around with all this other stuff."

"I know what I saw. Someone is doing this, and I'm going to prove it to you guys."

103

"Frankie, one last thing," I said. "We need your help in bringing down Diane Warren before she tries to harm the Irregulars."

"Whaddya need?" Frankie asked.

"Janet, on Wednesday I called you about Fertig's supplements, and you said the ones he gave to you were ordinary vitamins from California."

"I did," Janet said.

"Eddie thinks Fertig might have discovered herbs in the Amazon rain forest that actually cure breast cancer."

"Why does he think that?" she asked.

"My research on Fertig showed that he frequently flew to the Amazon rain forest, and his nurse confirmed that to us," I said.

"That was part of her pitch to sell us his supplements, but she was talking about aging."

"It was for us, but Eddie thinks Fertig sold actual South American supplements to his cancer patients."

"Be worth a lot of money if that's true," Frankie said. "Guy shoulda' sold it worldwide on the Internet."

"You didn't meet him, Frankie," Janet said. "Fertig would be the kind of guy that would keep the secret to himself so he would become world famous."

"If he shared it with anyone, including Diane, the world would know it was the supplements that cured the women and not his surgical skill," I said.

"You think Diane figured it out?" he asked.

"Eddie thinks she did, but only after some of the women who were operated on by Fertig and took the supplements developed a recurrence of their cancers since they can no longer get them."

"Why doesn't Diane go to South America and buy more of the stuff?" he asked.

"Eddie and I think Fertig killed himself without telling her exactly where he got them. Diane might now be faced with the possibility that the new breast cancer surgeon she hired isn't any better than the rest of the breast cancer doctors in the world."

"She would lose all those new breast cancer patients, and that would cost her serious dough," Janet said.

"Rick and David said they were told she went all in financially to save the hospital and the clinic," I said. "If her business evaporates, she'll owe the foundation all the money she stole from it and any personal funds she invested, and except for a couple of million dollars, she'll be broke. But worse, when the word gets out, the world will know she's a fraud as the CEO and owner of the most profitable hospital in the world."

"She's a woman with a big ego who needs to buy some new supplements from South America to fix her cash flow problems," he said. "Maybe we can be her supplier instead."

After Janet and Frankie left, I made a conference call with the rest of the Irregulars and told them what we'd discussed. We needed to devise a plan to sink Diane.

104

After I finished talking to the Irregulars, there was one other thing I had to do, and I needed to do myself. I wasn't crazy. I was positive Sullivan had been murdered.

I breastfed Macy and took her to Alicia's. Once again, all I would miss would be her nap.

Using the Internet, I found out Sullivan lived in an apartment on West Deming Place in Lincoln Park. The first fifteen minutes of my investigation was wasted searching for a parking place. I found one two blocks away and walked to the front door of his brownstone building, which was the third one from the corner. It was midmorning, so there almost no activity in his neighborhood.

This was not a place that had a doorman or security cameras, and the front door wasn't locked, so I stepped into the entryway where the mailboxes were located. According to the addresses on the boxes, Sullivan lived in 1-A.

Glancing around, I slipped on latex gloves and took out the lock pick gun and torque wrench from my backpack. I had his mailbox open in ten seconds. It was empty, as was the slot below it for his newspaper.

The lock into the building itself was flimsy. I had the second door open almost as quickly as the mailbox. The stairs going to the upper floors were to my left. 1-A was to my right. I knocked on the door, and there was no response. I used my equipment to open the lock and sneak inside.

The air was cold and musty. I checked the thermostat on the wall to my right. It was set at sixty-two degrees.

The living room was to my left. The fireplace was cold. A newspaper was on a side table next to a reclining chair. It was dated the day before I discovered his body.

I walked down the hall and found a small kitchen. There were a few old items in the freezer but no fresh foods in the refrigerator. There were no dishes in the dishwasher.

The bedroom and bathroom were in the back. The bed was made, and the curtains were pulled down. There were empty hangers in the closet. There were no shoes on the closet floor. I hunted around for a suitcase but didn't find one. His underwear and sock drawers were empty.

Opening the cabinets in his bathroom, I found his toiletries were missing. I turned on the faucet, and it took a few jerks of the old pipes before any water appeared. It was rust-colored before it cleared.

Was Sullivan dead? Or was he out of town? Or was I completely crazy? I was positive I saw a dead man, and now I was in his apartment and it looked like he'd gone on a trip.

Walking out the front door, I realized I was making myself nuts and I didn't need to. No story was worth screwing up my mental health, and I never did think the builder story was all that interesting or challenging to begin with.

Zhukov? Let the feds and the Russian Mafia fight it out. It could be dangerous and I didn't need that.

The Warren story was worth pursuing. Diane might have hired the missing-fingered man to kill all the Hamlin Park Irregulars, and we had to stop her.

But right now, all I wanted was to go home and play with Macy.

Part 5

105

Saturday morning, the Irregulars were in the locker room at XSport Fitness after finishing Cas's core class. I sat in front of a locker with my head down. Sweat dripped off my forehead into my eyes, off the tip of my nose, and onto the floor. I draped a towel over my head and face to absorb the moisture.

"Alan thinks you don't get it, Tina," Molly said.

"Get what?" I asked through the towel.

"I can't understand you," she said. "You're mumbling."

I wiped my face and ran the towel through my hair. "Sorry. What did Alan mean?"

"Yesterday, we were at his house playing Wii Guitar Hero, and he asked me how the story with Diane was coming. I told him about your cool plan to trick her into buying fake supplements, and that's when the trouble started."

"Trouble?"

"He started talking about sick cars at MidAmerica Hospital, and he said you didn't understand anything."

"Cars?"

"Uh-huh. Sick ones."

I dropped the towel on the floor and used my foot to wipe up the puddle of sweat. I grabbed another fresh towel off the counter.

"What a minute," I said. "Did he use the term 'auto'?"

"Yeah, cars."

"Did he say anything about autoimmune diseases?"

"I think so, but then it got confusing."

"What exactly did he say?"

"That's what I don't know."

"Try this. Tell me what you remember."

"I can't."

"Did he write it down?"

Molly has a reading disability. If Alan wrote anything down, there was no hope that she would comprehend what he was talking about.

"No. He wasn't speaking in English, and I couldn't understand him."

"What language was he speaking?"

"I don't know. He sounded like one of those foreign spy guys in the movies. The more he talked about you and the car stuff, the worse it got. He began yelling in that foreign language and then shut off the Wii and went to his room." She paused. "And it was too bad."

"Too bad?"

"I was winning."

106

I pushed a bundled-up Macy in the stroller as I walked home from XSport Fitness. The issue of autoimmune diseases kept surfacing and it bugged me, so I called Eddie.

"Remember when I wrote the article about Dr. Mike Doyle?" I asked.

"The Fat Doctor?" Eddie said.

"That's the guy."

"I remember that you called me during my freshman year in med school and said one of your sorority sisters took his supplements trying to lose weight before your spring break trip to Cabo, and she almost died of kidney failure."

"You helped me figure out what happened by talking to the professors at your medical school."

"But they were never able to prove his formulation caused her renal disease. His product was considered a supplement, which wasn't under the FDA's jurisdiction, and thus, no one tested it before it was released to be sold."

"Her family sued Doyle, but he was arrested and his company went bankrupt. There wasn't any money left, and the suit was dropped."

"Stuff like that happens all the time with over-the-counter supplements. No agency regulates the potential side effects of the products unsuspecting people buy."

"Do you think Fertig's cancer-curing supplements might be doing something like that?"

"Like what?"

"Maybe causing autoimmune diseases."

"That's a mighty big jump from a supplement contributing to kidney failure to them causing an autoimmune disorder."

"Why? I don't understand the difference."

"An autoimmune disease is caused by an overactive immune response which makes the body attack its own cells."

"Why does this happen?"

"No one knows, but I've never read that it might be caused by ingesting a plant product from South America."

"I've been thinking about this a lot since Peebler talked about cancer therapy when we had dinner at their house. If Fertig did discover that supplements from South America did cure breast cancer, how did they do it?"

He laughed. "If I knew that, I would win the Nobel Prize for Medicine."

"Sorry. I guess what I mean is, would his supplements change how the body's immune system works and the result would be that the patient's own body could kill the breast cancer cells?"

He didn't say anything.

"Eddie?" I said. "Are you still there?"

"Sorry, I was thinking about what you said."

"And?"

"Maybe Fertig's supplements did reset the body's immune system to recognize the abnormal breast cancer cells and destroy them. The result was a cure of the cancer, not from his surgery but from the supplements."

"Then what happens when the supplements are stopped?"

"Well, it might not be a clear-cut and obvious response as a recurrence of the cancer. Maybe the immune system is damaged or permanently altered and begins seeking other cells to kill. It begins attacking normal cells in multiple organs. The result would be an autoimmune disorder like Graves's Disease, Systemic Lupus Erythematosus, or Sjögren's Syndrome."

"How do you treat diseases like that?"

"With immunosuppressive drugs to slow the progress of the disease, but these are chronic and basically incurable."

"How would I prove his supplements did this?"

"Check all the recent admissions to MidAmerica Hospital who have an autoimmune diagnosis. If they had breast cancer and were on Fertig's supplements but then stopped it before they became ill, that would be strongly suggestive of a cause and effect."

107

Saturday afternoon, I was in the Creative Hair Salon to talk to David and Rick. Carter watched the girls. Marcia was having her hair colored by Rick. In the next chair, David cut Frankie's hair.

I sat on a stool at David's station.

"We have to assume Diane is spending a fortune to find the source of Fertig's supplements which he discovered in the South American rain forest," I began. "At this point, Diane is playing with these patient's lives — duping them — and the patients are getting sick and dying because of her deception. My fear is that if she's successful in bringing Fertig's supplements back to Chicago, no one will ever know what she's done because I won't have any proof and there'll be no story."

"If one of her guys finds Fertig's stash down there, she'll knows it's the real deal," Frankie said. "All we have to do is stop her delivery guy and steal the product. Then, when we approach her, she'll have to deal with us and we nail her."

"How are we going to know if and when she finds it?" Rick asked.

Frankie leaned forward and examined David's progress with his hair. "Plant listening devices in her home."

"I can do that," I said. "It's about time I bugged somebody else for a change. I have enough in my house that I can use a few of those. The FBI will never miss them."

David turned to me. "The FBI is listening to the details of what you say? My, that is kinky. Why on earth are they doing that?"

"I checked last night, and they still aren't monitoring me, but they have compromised my computer."

"How?" Rick asked.

I told them.

"Why?" David asked.

"It's about Zhukov. They want to know what happened to the money he stole, and they seem to think I know where it is."

"If you find it, please let Alan know," Marcia said. "He was devastated when he lost everything."

Everything? Huh?

"That's too bad," I said.

"You have no idea how bad it is," she said. "He had saved what to him was a large sum of money from his medical practice. He wanted to endow an academic chair at his medical school. It meant a great deal to him, and when the money disappeared, he was crushed."

"I feel so sorry for him," I said.

"And it happened at a most inopportune time," she said. "First, his brain blew up, and then recently, Zhukov lost all Alan's money."

"At least he still has your money," Rick said. "You could endow the chair in his name. No one would know which one of you gave the money."

"The old fool won't let me help him," Marcia said. "He wanted to do it on his own."

108

A tear trickled down Marcia's cheek. Rick handed her a Kleenex, and she dabbed at her eyes.

"Wouldn't it be easier if we had someone on the inside?" David asked. "A person Diane trusts and won't realize is being a spy for us?"

"Any suggestions?" I asked.

"What about Leslie Van Horn, her hairstylist?" Marcia asked. "She would never suspect him of anything. I certainly wouldn't."

"Has he recently said anything about Diane to you guys?" Frankie asked.

"We were with Leslie Van Horn last night at The Max, and he said Diane seems to be increasingly volatile emotionally," David said.

"Two days ago, she was completely undone when she was in his salon and she yelled at her own precious doggy," Rick said.

"Doggy?" Frankie asked.

"Bear, her Tibetan Mastiff," David said. "She wanted to bring that monster here when she first bought him, but we wouldn't let her, which is why she fired us and hired Leslie."

"But to answer your question, Leslie said she was in such a snit about events at the hospital that she snapped at her poor pooch," Rick said. "He was positively devastated and peed on the floor."

"A terrible mess," David said. "Thank God it wasn't here. I can't imagine how much a beast that size can urinate, can you, Rick?"

"Gallons, I would imagine."

"Enough with the freakin' dog story," Frankie said. "Will Leslie help us?"

"I'm sure he will," Rick said. "The employees in his shop positively hate Diane."

"Does he ever go to her home to do her hair?" Frankie asked.

"He does," David said. "She used to summon us there on a moment's notice when she found a stray hair out of place."

"Maybe Leslie could plant the bugs for us," Frankie said.

"Is this installing business difficult?" David asked. "I mean to tell you, Leslie is a whiz with hair, but I'm not sure how mechanical he is otherwise."

"Why don't we break into Diane's house and plant the bugs ourselves?" I asked.

"The boys and I have been watching her house and office, and she has serious security around her," Frankie said. "It would be risky but it's doable. If she suspects we're making a move on her by installing listening devices, she'll figure out something's going down and she'll be suspicious of anything that happens."

"Maybe we want her to know we're interested in Fertig's supplements, then she won't realize what I'm actually going to write about her," I said.

"Which is?" Rick asked.

"Autoimmune diseases."

"Tell us," David said.

109

I told them about my conversation with Eddie concerning autoimmune diseases.

"Eddie thinks the lack of Fertig's supplements might be making the breast cancer patients sick, right?" Frankie asked, when I finished.

"He does," I said.

"Then we don't need to be planting any bugs at Diane's," Frankie said. "Like Eddie said, check out the hospital admissions. Be a slam dunk."

"How would Tina go about getting this information from the hospital?" Rick asked. "The security forces there will be on the lookout for her big time."

"That's why I think we should try and plant the bugs," I said.

Frankie shrugged his shoulders. "Lost me, babe."

"Diane knows I'm trying to write a story about her. She's waiting for us to do something. If we plant listening devices at her home or office, or even in her car, she'll think that we're behind it and wonder why we're doing it. Leslie will give her the clue."

"I must be dense, but I don't understand any of this," Marcia said, punctuating her remark with another loose cough.

"I have to admit I'm a little confused myself," David said.

"Same here," Rick said.

"We have Leslie tell her that he heard from a client about Fertig's supplements, not his surgery, curing breast cancer," I said. "Diane will be puzzled about where Leslie heard this, but she won't want him to know she's interested and she'll be afraid to ask. Then you two," I nodded to David and Rick, "arrange to have her see you with Leslie, maybe out to dinner. She'll put it together and know why he is asking her about the supplements."

David raised his carefully plucked eyebrows. "Delightfully Machiavellian, sweetie. Congratulations."

"We plant listening devices in places where she or her security minions will find them," Rick said. "She wonders who is doing this and why, and then she remembers that Leslie asked her about the supplements."

"She guesses that you installed the bugs and your story is going to be about the supplements and curing breast cancer, not about the supplements making people sick," David continued.

"If her people do find the supplements in South America before you write the story, you'll have no evidence of anything evil that she's doing, so she'll think she's in the clear," Rick said.

"But if her people do find them, Frankie can steal the whole supply," David said, "and then she's in real trouble."

"And if her guys don't find the supplements, Frankie calls offering to sell a supply to her," Rick said. "She'll think we're behind it and are trying to trap her."

"But she's desperate and can't take the chance that our supplements are fakes so she meets with Frankie," David said.

"While all this is going on, we'll be scouring the hospital records for the details Tina alluded to about autoimmune diseases," Rick said, "and then we can bring dear Diane down for making Fertig's breast cancer patients sick from selling them the *faux* supplements."

"If there is a meeting to buy the fake product, she might have her guys try and eliminate the seller, knowing it's one of us," David warned.

"Will that be a problem, Frankie?" I asked.

"Only for her guys," he said.

110

Monday at noon, I had lunch at Paradise Bakery with David and Rick. They had news for me.

Macy was asleep in her stroller. Kerry didn't get out of preschool until two.

"Mission accomplished," David said. "I called Leslie Van Horn right after you left our salon on Saturday."

"Later that afternoon, while Leslie was doing her hair, he mentioned to Diane that he heard a rumor that Fertig's supplements and not his surgery cured his breast cancer patients," Rick said. "She told him she didn't know anything about it."

"As she was leaving, he overheard her talking on her cell phone about an eight o'clock dinner engagement at Prime & Provisions," David said.

"I bet I know where you ate Saturday night," I said, as I munched on a chocolate chip cookie.

"You got it," Rick said. "We arrived there at seven thirty, before Diane sat down with her party thirty minutes later."

"She ignored us," David said.

"But not for long," Rick said.

"Leslie and his partner, Larry Carlson, arrived at eight-fifteen," David said. "And I mean to tell you they swished right up to our table."

"It was all kissy-kissy and huggy-huggy," Rick said. "We managed to make a minor scene."

"Poor Diane's eyes almost popped out of her head," David said.

"She stormed out," Rick added.

"Now she knows you and Leslie are friends," I said.

"Oh, she most certainly does, honey," Rick said.

"Close friends," David said.

"We did our part," Rick said. "Now what"

"Remember at your salon I suggested we plant listening devices in her home to find out what she's going to do?" I asked.

"We do," David said.

"Frankie texted me an hour ago and said he knew a guy who would sell us the listening devices we need, but I told him we should use a few of the ones my terrorist neighbors installed in my house and which have never been removed."

"Are they active now?" Rick asked.

Whoops.

"I've been checking them every morning, but, honestly, I got busy and forgot to do it the last couple of days."

"Why don't we drop by and check to see if they're on?" Rick suggested. "Do you have the equipment to do that?"

"I do," I said.

"If they are active, is there a safe room in your home?" Rick asked.

"The wine room."

"I suggest we adjourn, and we'll meet you there in, say, an hour," Rick said.

"Great that will give me a chance to feed Macy and put her down for her nap."

111

An hour later, David and Rick joined me in our wine room. I'd already breast-fed Macy and put her down for her nap.

"What do these bugs look like?" David asked. "Are they wiggly and hairy?"

"I don't know," I said. "I've never seen one."

Rick put his hands on his hips. "Kids, please. In the day, this was part of my life."

"The sneaky phase?" David wondered.

"It blended in with, 'don't ask, don't tell.' As long as I did my job, my military bosses didn't say anything. How many do we need?"

"You're the expert," I said. "You decide."

I handed him my black box. He knew what it was. He flipped on the switch. The green light flashed on.

He walked around the computer room. The light turned from green to red and began blinking.

Damn!

He pointed it at the landline on my computer desk. He unscrewed the back of the phone and pointed at what appeared to be a tiny hearing aid battery.

He left it in place and moved around the room, finding one device hidden under the couch, another one in the ceiling light, and a final one that looked like a straight pin stuck in the top of the window drapes.

After an hour of searching each room in our house, Rick was finished. We were back in the wine room. He had a small pile of the listening devices in his hand.

He held one up. "I never saw one like this before. Must be new since I was planting them." He held up another one. "Same with this one."

"Do you think Frankie's guy can make them work for us?" I asked.

"I thought the idea was for her to find them."

"It is, but if they do work for a while, so much the better," I said. "We'll know what she's planning for us before they're discovered."

"What's the range for these devices?" David asked.

"A few hundred yards," Rick said. "Frankie can find a spot for his boys to park near her home, so they can record what's going on."

"You'll have to show me how to plant these," I said.

"Us, honey," he said. "You can't do this alone."

112

It was 11:30 a.m. on Tuesday. Macy was with Alicia. Frankie, Rick, and I were in a Cox Communications truck parked one block away from Diane Warren's Gold Coast mansion. We wore Cox uniforms and carried equipment boxes with the Cox logo. One of Frankie's guys provided the truck and uniforms. The devices we were going to plant were hidden in Frankie's box.

Early that morning, his computer guy corrupted Diane's entire Cox system. He also diverted the call her secretary made to the real Cox office to one of Frankie's dedicated cell phones. When the secretary called about the malfunction, Frankie arranged the appointment for us.

We waited for a call from Enzo. He had been following Diane. Frankie's phone dinged.

Frankie looked at the screen. He turned to us.

"Enzo said she just arrived at the Four Seasons Hotel. He followed her in and saw her going into a charity luncheon. Her name is listed on a poster out in front as a major donor to the charity."

"She'll be there at least an hour," Rick said. "Let's saddle up and get this show on the road."

"Enzo'll let us know if she leaves early," Frankie said, as he started the van.

He pulled into her circular driveway. We jumped out and walked up to the front door. Rick rang the doorbell.

A burly man with a buzz cut, wearing a poorly fitting cheap blue blazer, answered the door. Frankie nodded toward the man's hip. The loose coat could not hide the bulge from the gun he carried. Rick stepped forward and handed the man a business card that Frankie had another one of his guys make up.

"I am Richard Dick, a supervisor for Cox Communications," Rick said. "We were notified that Mrs. Warren is having a problem with our equipment. Since she is such a valued customer, I came with two," he pointed toward us, "instead of our usual one repair person."

The guard took his time reading the card. "Your name really Richard Dick?"

"It is," Rick said. "Is that a problem?"

He checked Rick up and down. "Nah, I guess not."

We stood in the entry hall. The man didn't move.

"Sir?" Rick said. "We need to get to work."

"Dick Dick," he said. "Musta' had fun at school with that name." He laughed. "Ricky Dick. Dickie Dick. Lotta' ways you could go with that."

This was the reason Rick had selected the name. He wanted the man to lose his concentration.

"And I've heard them all, believe me," Rick said. "Now can we hurry this up? My employees have other calls to make, and I have to get back to the office."

"Follow me... Dickie," he said.

113

The guard led us into a bare-bones office off of the main hallway. There was a metal detector, a chair, and a desk. My stomach began to feel queasy when I saw that a camera was attached to a laptop computer on the desk.

"Take all the crap outta your pockets and step through here," he said pointing to the metal detector, "one at a time."

Frankie anticipated this might happen, and we'd left our guns in the van. We each passed through without any issues.

"Now I need to look at your equipment boxes," he said.

Rick stepped forward. "Please be careful. If you damage any of the tools, we will have to come back."

He stared at Rick. "If it happens, it happens. I gotta job to do."

I handed him my metal box. He opened it and took each item out, one piece at a time. When he finished, he left the mess on the desk, forcing me to reload my gear.

He turned to Frankie. "You're next, pal."

The guard began unloading Frankie's tools. He stopped when he came to a magazine Frankie had hidden in the bottom of the box. It was full of pictures of naked women doing unusual things with other naked women. As the guard turned the pages, Frankie began reloading his box.

The man flipped through the last few pages and closed the magazine. "I'm gonna keep this for a while," the man said as he stepped closer to Frankie. "You guys got work to do."

Frankie's face turned red and a vein popped out on his forehead.

The man noticed. "We're not gonna have a problem here, are we, sport?" the man said to Frankie.

"Whatever trips your trigger, *sport*," Frankie said through clenched teeth. "We gotta fix your boss's system."

"Before you do, there's something else," he said. "We need a picture of each one of you."

Crap!

We hadn't planned on this. We had discussed wearing disguises like wigs and glasses, but I didn't think we would need them. I was wrong.

"You first," he said, pointing at me.

It was hard for me to breathe, and my knees began shaking, making it difficult to stand completely still as he snapped the picture. He walked over to the computer and punched a few buttons on the keyboard. I put my knees together to stifle the urge to pee in my pants when my picture came up on the screen.

He waited a few seconds and then punched more buttons. "Fuck," he said to himself. He turned to me. "I gotta take another picture. This one didn't turn out."

"Small wonder, pal," Frankie said. "Every computer in this house is as fucked up as you are. You can screw around with that system all afternoon and it ain't gonna work."

The man unbuttoned his coat, giving him easy access to his gun. Before he could do anything, a woman walked into the room. She wore a black suit with a knee-length skirt and low-heeled shoes.

"That's enough, Charles," she said. "I'm Rochelle Horrigan, Mrs. Warren's secretary. We need to get the system up and running before she returns. Please follow me."

114

One hour later, we climbed into the van and Frankie drove away from Diane's mansion. One block to the north I saw a black Jetta with darkened windows parked on the street. Frankie slowed down and double-parked across from it. He powered down his window.

The driver's window slid down, and Luca peeked out. He wore a set of earphones. I could see the top of a boxy machine next to him on the passenger seat.

Frankie nodded. Luca flipped a switch on the machine and several lights came on. He adjusted a knob and listened. He rotated the knob and continued to listen. He turned to Frankie and said something in Italian.

Frankie powered up his window and drove away. "Good to go. Bugs are live and working."

"Let's hope Diane says something useful before the security guy finds the devices," Rick said. "Do you think they sweep the place every day?"

"You saw that guard," Frankie said. "Think he does any more than necessary?"

"I hope not," I said. "If he does, we might have another problem."

"It's that picture the guard took of you," Frankie said.

"Yep. If he runs the facial recognition program once the computers come back on line, Diane will know we were there, and then they will for sure scan the house for bugs."

"You better get to work on finding out about the autoimmune stuff before that happens," Frankie said. "Hard telling what she might do when she finds out we were in her home. You don't want another guy with an RPG visiting your house."

Rick sat in the passenger seat fiddling with one of the listening devices we hadn't planted. "Remember when I said I hadn't seen anything like it before?" he asked.

"You told us it was new since the time you did this kind of thing," I said.

"I was wrong about that," he said. "It wasn't made in the U.S."

"China?" Frankie asked.

"No, Russia," he said.

"Are you sure?" I asked.

"After I saw it at your house, I called a guy I was in the service with, and he checked it out," Rick said. "Weird that our side is using their technology, but maybe their stuff is better. Or the Russians, and not the FBI, planted that device in your house."

Words I did not want to hear. Acid began bubbling up into the back of my throat. The thought of the Russians doing that terrified me.

115

On Wednesday, Janet met me at Dinkel's before the rest of the Irregulars arrived to discuss the Diane Warren story. We sat in the side room.

Before I talked to her, I'd swept the space with my bug detector and found it clean. At least here we could talk without the world knowing what we discussed.

"Frankie told me about the Russian-made bugs," she said, as she sipped her black coffee. "First the FBI, and now the Russians. It's kind of like the U.N. is listening in on what you say."

"Carter has been busy at work, and he hasn't asked me about the Zhukov story. If he did, I would have to fess up about these recent events." I swallowed a bite from my plain glazed donut. "Did you run the names of the investors in Zhukov's fund?"

"I did, and Tony did too." She watched my face. "Don't frown like that. He's better at computer research stuff than I am."

Never would have guessed that.

"Did either of you find anything?"

"The same facts Linda did. Somebody took off with one hundred and fifty million dollars."

"And no names stuck out?"

"None. Peebler lost all of his investment. Everyone else did too."

"Now what?"

"I'm going to run the list again. I'll go back to when Zhukov started his fund and see if there are any anomalies among the investors before they began giving Zhukov their money."

The rest of the Hamlin Park Irregulars joined us. They sat down with their coffees and donuts.

"We have to access the MidAmerica Hospital's medical records and look for recent admissions of patients with autoimmune diseases," I began. "We need to know how many of them were treated by Fertig for breast cancer, then took his supplements post-op and, finally, got sick when they stopped them."

"Gee, that sounds easy enough," Molly said. "All we do is have someone hack into their computers and download what we need."

"How about Frankie's guy?" Rick asked. "His skill in taking down Diane's home computers was amazing."

"Frankie talked to him this morning," I said. "He checked MidAmerica's computer system and found multiple new firewalls and other security devices built into its system to prevent us from doing what we need to do. He would have to sit down and work on one of their computers to complete the hack."

"It's too bad Alan is off his rocker," Marcia said. "He would be perfect for this since he's one of their doctors."

What?!

"I didn't know he worked at MidAmerica," I said.

"He and his partners had so many referrals there that he reluctantly joined the staff," she said. "He quickly became disenchanted with Diane Warren's method of administration, and he stopped going there with any frequency."

"Did he resign from the staff?" Cas asked.

"Knowing Alan, he is probably still on the staffs of most of the Chicago area hospitals," Marcia said. "It's not like him to quit anything, even if his brains have blown up."

"Where are you going with this, Cas?" I asked.

"When a doctor comes to the desk in a busy hospital ICU, most nurses don't even bother to look up. The doctor could examine each chart at the nurse's station and no one would ask him why he was doing it."

"Marcia, how many doctors know Alan is sick?" I asked.

"Only Dr. Richard Murphy, the internist who takes care of him. They are — or better, were — partners in the medical group founded by Alan. Dr. Murphy and I decided it would be best to keep Alan's problem secret. When the time comes, I want all of his patients to remember him for the brilliant physician he was, not the demented old man he's become. As far as I know, the hospital staff thinks he is able to practice but is now semi-retired."

116

It was Thursday afternoon. Linda and I had joined Cas and Lori at Alan's home office. For the past two hours, we had taken turns attempting to prepare him for our visit to MidAmerica Hospital's ICU. He hadn't given us any positive indication that he understood what we needed him to do for us.

Cas was dressed in a white nurse's pantsuit, which she had worn when she worked as an RN. Over it, she wore a long white lab coat with a stethoscope draped over her shoulders. She had on a blond wig, black-rimmed glasses, and a heavy application of makeup, something she rarely uses.

Alan had on a black pinstripe suit, a starched white shirt with French cuffs, and a red and black bow tie. His eyes had been dull since we arrived, not a good sign with what we needed him to do. He stared at the wall and didn't say anything.

Lori was dressed in her usual nurse's outfit. She was also going with us to the ICU. The idea was for Cas and Lori to follow Alan who, as a staff doctor, would appear to be making rounds on his patients with his own two nurses.

Molly wasn't with us. None of us could come up with a way to disguise her figure enough that she wouldn't stick out like a Bears fan at a game in Green Bay's Lambeau Field. Instead, she was babysitting our kids at her home.

Our plan was based on MidAmerica Hospital's continued use of both computer hospital charts and conventional paper medical records. They did it because that was the way Fertig had wanted it to be, and Diane Warren had never bothered to change the system.

Lori would sift through the paper charts at the nurse's station while the nurses worked on their computers. If any patient had an autoimmune disease, she would grab the chart and lead Alan into the patient's room.

She would discuss the patient with him loudly enough that anyone walking in the hall past the room would think it was hospital business as usual. Cas would check through the chart and take pictures of any information helpful to us.

Linda and I were unisex from head to toe. I wore padding under a shapeless, brown exercise outfit and men's leather shoes. David was an expert with makeup and had made my nose wider and had added size to my cheeks. My hair was tucked up under a black, short wig, and I wore heavy brown glasses and blue contact lenses. My own mother wouldn't have known me.

Linda opted for a short, curly, gray wig and wire-rimmed glasses. She had on a flannel shirt and bib overalls with work boots.

David had made her nose as big as her husband's, and she had deep wrinkles on her forehead and cheeks.

Rick would place a small smoke bomb in the men's bathroom. I would do the same thing in the women's bathroom. If it all went to hell, we would use remote controls to start what appeared to be fires in both restrooms.

Linda would then pull the fire alarm, and David would call 911 to report the disaster. We hoped to escape in the ensuing chaos. Frankie would be in the lobby with Enzo and Luca. If guns became the final option, they would be there to save us.

"Alan, we are looking for patients with autoimmune disorders," I said. "We need your help."

He turned to me, and for the first time since we had arrived, his eyes lit up. "And you shall have it." He turned to Lori. "We need to leave. I hate to keep my patients waiting."

Cas drove her Hummer. We climbed in.

Show time!

117

When our group arrived at MidAmerica Hospital, Cas, Lori, and Alan continued on to the nurse's station in the ICU. I stopped in the woman's bathroom and placed the smoke bomb in a trash can. The remote control was in my backpack. Linda waited for me and then we proceeded to the ICU waiting room.

David and Rick were already there posing as family members of a sick patient. David wore a black suit with a white shirt and narrow black tie. He had on sunglasses and a back fedora. Rick was dressed in a similar outfit. Apparently they had chosen to channel the Blues Brothers.

I noticed a bulge at Rick's right hip, so I knew he was armed. When he made eye contact with me, he nodded. He had placed his device in the men's bathroom.

Locked and loaded.

We watched Alan and his nurses through the windows of the waiting room. When they arrived at the nurse's station, I opened the door so we could hear what was being said.

"Nurse, we need to see the charts of Dr. Peebler's partners' patients," Lori said.

"Are you making rounds for them?" the nurse asked.

"Yes, we are," Lori said.

"I heard you were retired, Dr. Peebler," the nurse said.

"Do I *look* retired, young lady?" he asked loudly.

"No, doctor, I guess you don't."

"There is *no place* in medicine for *guessing*. It is how patients get killed. Now *let's get cracking* and see if I can prevent that."

118

We had planned our visit to coincide with the shift change. The on-duty nurses had to finish their computer charting before they went home. The nurses coming in had to read about any new patients or medication changes during the previous twelve hours.

They were too busy to notice Lori shifting through the paper charts. She picked up one of them and led Alan and Cas into the patient's room. They were in there about five minutes, and then they repeated the process in another room.

Forty-six minutes later, Alan stomped out of a room and went to the nurse's station. Lori tried to grab his arm to stop him but she wasn't quick enough.

"What *idiot* wrote this order?" Alan demanded, waving the patient's chart in the air.

Lori stood next to him and hung her head. Cas came out of the same room, turned the opposite direction, and went into another room. She glanced around as she took that chart with her.

"I did," a tall, dark-skinned doctor said. He had a British accent.

Alan peered over the top of his glasses. "And *who* might you be?"

"I am Dr. Qamar, the hospitalist."

"Do you routinely attempt to *kill* your patients, *Doctor*?"

"I am sorry?"

Lori put her arm on Alan's shoulder. "Dr. Peebler, I think it's time to leave."

He pulled away from her and got in the doctor's face. "*Doctor*, what are you treating this lady for?"

The doctor checked the name on the chart. "She has Lupus with end-stage renal disease."

"When was the last time you examined this unfortunate creature?"

"I am not sure."

"Did you *examine* her at all today?"

"I looked at her chart."

"I have a new concept for you. Try examining the patient instead of checking the chart. This lady is having an evolving stroke and *you missed it*. I strongly suggest you go into her room and do what you were trained to do, save her life. You might want to stop the medicines that are at this moment destroying her brain with *an intracranial hemorrhage*."

He didn't exactly yell, but he made his point. The doctor ran into the patient's room followed by three nurses. I heard shouting followed by a "Code Blue" blaring over the loudspeaker system.

Lori grabbed Alan's arm and headed for the elevator. Cas came out of a room and joined them. The elevator doors opened and four security guards stepped off. Diane Warren was with them.

119

"Dr. Peebler, I have to say I was surprised when the head of hospital security called me and said their cameras showed that you were in our ICU," Diane said.

Alan didn't say anything. Since his back was turned to me, I couldn't see his eyes, but his lack of a response could only mean that he was in la-la land again.

Diane turned to the security guard to her left. "Dr. Peebler was alleged to be one of the top internists in the United States, but for the life of me, I never saw it. I felt it mostly hype since he was married to Marcia Peebler. He certainly never produced any significant revenue for this hospital."

Alan remained silent.

"Please take these people to my office. I have no idea who these two women are, but from what I've recently heard about Dr. Peebler, they are most like here to make sure he doesn't get confused or wander off. Oh, and you need to be careful. People with dementia can be combative and belligerent."

Standing up, I reached into my backpack and took out the remote control to set off the smoke bomb in the woman's bathroom. I held it up for Rick to see.

"Ready," he said, holding his control up, his thumb on the button. He pushed his button. I did too.

"Linda, run out to that fire alarm box on the wall," I said. "I'll let you know when to pull the lever."

"Where are you going?" she asked, as she stood up.

"I have an idea," I said, as I pulled out my gun.

The security guards ushered Alan, Cas, and Lori on to the elevator. Diane followed. I ran toward them, but their backs were turned and they didn't see me approaching.

When they were all on, they turned around, and the guard to my left pushed the button for the first floor. I reached the elevator door and stopped it from closing with my foot. I raised the Glock and pointed it at Diane. I kept my finger on the trigger guard.

"Change of plan," I said, as I turned to Cas. "Get off the elevator. Take Lori and Alan down the exit stairs to Frankie."

I shifted to my left to let them leave but kept my foot against the elevator door. The trio moved past me into the hall and toward the stairs. Smoke began to pour out of the bathrooms into the hall.

Moving my gun up, I pointed it directly at Diane's face. The guard to my right twitched slightly.

I put my finger on the trigger. "I wouldn't do that if I were you," I said. "I don't think blood will look good on your boss's designer dress."

Out of the corner of my eye I saw Linda standing by the fire alarm box. "Do it!" I shouted over my shoulder.

She broke it open and pulled the switch. "Done!" she yelled. The fire alarm began shrieking and red and white lights on the ceiling began flashing. "Code Red, ICU! Code Red, ICU!" blared from the loud speakers on the wall.

I moved my foot and the elevator door slid closed. The noise from the machine meant it was moving.

Linda ran to me. "Why'd you want me to do that?"

"When the fire alarm goes off, the elevators stop running. It'll take a minute or two for the machines to recycle, and then they'll head to the floor closest to an emergency exit, which is the basement. Diane and her guards will be trapped and then taken to the wrong floor."

Rick held the door to the exit stairs. David had gone through it. Linda and I followed as smoke continued to roll into the hallway. The "Code Red" call was now continuous.

The ICU was on the fourth floor. By the time we hit the landing on the second floor, firefighters were racing up the stairs. They stopped when they saw us.

"What's going on?" one of them asked.

"Fires in the bathrooms on the fourth floor," I said.

The man in the lead was a captain. "Robbie, get these people out of here."

A fireman turned to us. "Follow me. I'll escort you to safety."

120

We returned to Alan's home and gathered in the West Gallery.

"Guys, I am so sorry," I said. "I didn't anticipate that they would react like that when they saw Alan's face on the security cameras."

"You saved us," Cas said. "That's all that counts."

"I guess, but it's still embarrassing. Did you get anything?"

"Did we ever," she said. "Every patient in the ICU who has an autoimmune disease has a history of breast cancer."

"Did it say who treated their cancer?" Linda asked.

"No, it didn't, but I think that was done on purpose," she said. "Several different doctors dictated the H and Ps, but in each case, the wording about the patient's breast cancer history was exactly the same and the treating doctor wasn't named."

"That can't be a coincidence," I said.

I turned to Alan to see if he had any ideas, but from the blank look on his face, that wasn't going to happen.

"Does that mean we have Diane in our clutches?" David asked.

"I would certainly hope so," Rick said.

Frankie walked into the room. "If you have anything on her, you better hurry."

We waited.

"Alberto, another one of my boys, is monitoring the bugs in her house. Since Diane came home, she hasn't stopped screaming about you guys."

"That's no surprise," David said.

"Tina, you had most of her story, but we all missed the most important part," Frankie continued. "It's the lawsuits that are gonna break her."

"The criminal system will have a difficult time proving a case against Diane," Linda began. "But Frankie is right. In the civil courts she could get decimated if she doesn't have the right kind of insurance to cover her liability."

"I don't understand," I said.

"The breast cancer patients started getting sick after the supplements Fertig sold them ran out and were changed without their knowledge," Linda continued. "He's dead, so they can only sue his estate, and that is difficult to do."

"But can they sue the hospital corporation where Fertig worked and where he was employed?" Cas asked.

"They can, and the hospital does have insurance for that," Linda said. "But Diane isn't a doctor so she doesn't practice medicine; therefore, she can't get medical malpractice insurance."

"Where does that leave her?" Rick asked.

"She owns the hospital. Her wealth will entice the lawyers to go after her as the sole owner," Linda answered.

"That could be big dollars," Cas said.

"That would be true, and any personal insurance coverage she might have won't cover the size and number of these medical lawsuits," Linda said. "As each new one is filed, it will attract more publicity and more patients will think they might have been damaged by the supplements, even if they weren't."

"It will be a feeding frenzy," David said.

Linda smiled.

Gotta love lawyers.

121

Frankie's cell phone rang. He answered, responded in Italian, and disconnected.

He turned to us. "Alberto. He says Diane's guys found the listening devices. He heard her freaking out before they shut us down. He heard her say she's gonna leave."

Uh-oh.

"Where is she going?" I asked.

"They found the bugs before she said anything about that," Frankie said.

"I obviously don't know her destination," I said, "but the hospital foundation owns a private jet that she has access to. Fertig used to fly in it to South America. It was parked at the Chicago Executive Airport in Wheeling and probably still is."

"With her money, she can afford multiple travel options," Linda countered.

"She can, but if she's in a hurry, I think she'll access the easiest and quickest one. Hang on and I'll prove it."

From my previous trip to the Chicago Executive Airport in Wheeling while working on a story, I had their phone number in my contacts. I called the main desk.

"John speaking."

"This is Diane Warren," I said. "Is my plane ready?"

"Ms. Horrigan, your secretary, called," he said. "Your plane will be on the flight line ready for your departure in two hours."

"That is unacceptable. I am on my way. Do you want me to waste my time sitting with strangers while I have to wait for your people to do what should only take one hour?"

"We will clear out the executive lounge, and no one will disturb you while you wait. I hope that's acceptable."

"Hardly, but it seems I don't have a choice. Have a chilled bottle of Dom ready when I get there."

I disconnected before he could reply.

"Well done," David said. "You make a wonderful diva."

"She can fly away and that's it?" Rick said. "This can't be happening."

"She'll probably fly to a country that doesn't have extradition," Linda said.

"What about the civil cases?" I asked. "What about the people the *faux* supplements made sick?"

"Once she leaves, they're screwed," Linda said. "They'll never collect a dime."

122

I had a terrific story to write, but it was slipping through my fingers.

"You're not gonna let this one go, are you?" Frankie asked.

"I can't," I said. "People have been intentionally harmed. The public needs to know what Diane did, and I'm going to tell them. That may be Fertig's patients' only chance for survival."

"You need to confront her to get her side of it — if she'll give it to you before you write the story," Linda said.

"You're right, and hopefully I will write it."

"How you gonna do this?" Frankie asked.

"I went through this before, when we guessed that Fertig was going to flee the country in his big jet. It can fly several thousand miles without needing to refuel. Like the guy at the desk told me, it'll take them at least an hour to preflight a plane that size and another hour to file the flight plans and get a takeoff slot. I'm going home to take off this makeup and wash my face. Then I'm going to change into my power suit to interview her."

"Might need backup," Frankie said. "Me and the boys'll tag along bein's we've been in this from the get go."

"Count David and me in," Rick said.

"I hate to miss this, but my nanny is off today," Linda said. "Molly is watching my kids, and she's probably nuts by now so I have to pick them up. Call me when it's over."

"I'm in the same boat," Cas said. "Sorry."

"Tell Molly I'll pick up Macy and Kerry when this is over," I said.

Alan stared at the wall and then turned around and walked over to the door into his house. Lori punched in the code and opened the door for him. He entered and she closed the door behind him. He had done his job.

Now I have to do mine.

123

Frankie drove his black Mercedes. I was in the passenger seat. David and Rick were in the back. We were on our way to Wheeling.

"Gosh, this car is beautiful," I said. "I noticed it says BRABUS on the front logo. What's that all about?"

"A German company modifies the Mercedes AMG GT 63S. They get a little more speed out of it."

He stepped on the accelerator to emphasize his point. My head snapped back in the seat as we rocketed forward.

"It'll do zero to sixty in 2.9," he continued.

Comparing my mommy van to this howling monster reminded me of the tortoise and the hare.

"I probably wouldn't drive it to Whole Foods," I said.

He laughed and slowed down. We were going over 120 mph, and I couldn't tell we were traveling that fast.

I glanced out the rear window. A black Escalade was catching up to us.

"Luca and Enzo?" I asked.

"And Alberto. He's good at close-up work. Figured we might need him if her bodyguards crowd you."

"Comforting to know," I said, as I leaned back into the soft black leather seats.

Twenty minutes later, we parked in the front lot of Chicago Executive Aviation and waited. On the tarmac was a white Gulfstream G550. A gas truck parked next to the plane. Several people wearing baggy gray coveralls with a logo on the front left chest pocket bustled around the plane. We were too far away for me to read the logo.

"There's Fertig's plane," I said, pointing at it as they attached the gas hoses.

"You sure?" Frankie asked.

"The tail number is 915 RF. It's Fertig's."

"God, I wish I had a tail number," David said. "But I would pick a more exotic number and certainly not in block letters."

A black Tahoe SUV followed by a black Mercedes-Maybach sedan pulled up to the front door. Four men wearing cheap blue blazers, white shirts with blue ties, and gray pants simultaneously hopped out of the four doors of the SUV. They had ear buds in their ears. They slammed the doors and then circled the Maybach.

A man wearing a similar cheap blue blazer got out of the passenger side and opened the back door. He leaned inside and assisted Diane Warren out. The driver jumped out and joined the other five men. They spread out with three on each side of her, and they bracketed her as she walked inside.

She wore a designer dress at the hospital. Now she was in a designer pantsuit covered by a stroller-length, black mink coat with a sable collar. Her version of casual is different from mine.

124

Five minutes later, two of Diane's men came out and drove the SUV and Maybach into the reserved parking area. They parked and walked to the front door of the building. They stood on each side of the front door, their coats open and guns easily visible on their hips.

"Waitin' for us," Frankie said.

"It sure seems like it," I said.

"I make six guys, those two outside and four more inside," he said.

"Diane won't allow any of them to be in the executive lounge with her," Rick said.

"I agree," Frankie said. "It's not the way she rolls."

"Tina, did you say you've been here before?" Rick asked.

"I was here with Janet and Tony when we were chasing Fertig."

"You been inside?" Frankie asked.

"We met the Wheeling police in the executive lounge."

"Any other ways in or out?" Rick asked.

"One door on the north side that goes out to the tarmac."

Frankie put the Mercedes in gear and pulled toward the other end of the building where we could see that door. Two more security guards flanked it.

"Two men at this back entrance," Rick said. "Two more at the front and the last two at the door to the lounge where Diane will be sipping champagne."

"All we need to do is cull the herd," David said.

"Cowboy talk?" I asked.

"David grew up on a ranch in Montana," Rick said.

"I still have a pair of darling cowboy boots, which I wear when my parents visit," David said.

"Hat, too?" Frankie asked.

"Oh, for sure," he said. "One has a divine magenta ostrich plume. It's to die for."

A short woman wearing the same baggy, gray coveralls as the other workers descended down the stairs from the Gulfstream. She walked toward the building. She was close enough that I could read "Chicago Executive Aviation" stenciled on the left chest pocket of the coveralls. The guards at the back door let her enter without stopping her.

"We had more time, my boys coulda' made up suits like that for us," Frankie said. "Make it easier to get inside."

He turned around and parked in our original location in front of the building. He made a call on his cell phone. He spoke in Italian for a couple of minutes and then closed the phone.

"Alberto will deal with the guys in front first so they don't alert the other four. Then Luca and Enzo gonna take care of the two goons at the entrance on the north side."

A short man got out of the Escalade.

"Alberto?" I asked.

"Gonna talk to the guys at the door," he said.

"He's kind of tiny."

"That's why he works up close. You ready to roll?"

"I am."

"Rick?"

"Semper Fi, dude," he said, as he pulled out a Glock 22.

"David? You in?"

"He'll stay with the car," Rick said, remembering David's trauma with Sullivan's murder.

"Okay, when we go in, get in the driver's seat and keep the engine running," Frankie said to David. "If we need to blow outta here in a hurry, you drive."

"Exciting," David said, bravely. "My heart is going pitter-pat."

Frankie pulled out a .44 magnum and screwed on a silencer. He tossed one to Rick who attached it to his Glock.

"As soon as Alberto does his thing, be ready to roll," Frankie said.

He turned toward me. "Tina, you wait out here until one of us signals for you to come in. Then do what you gotta do with Diane and we'll split when you're done."

125

Alberto walked toward the two men. They reached into their coats and pulled out their guns. They held them at their sides as he approached. They dwarfed him when he stood directly in front of them.

Frankie powered the windows down, enabling us to hear what was being said.

"You work here?" the man on the left side of the front door said.

"They can't afford me," Alberto said.

"Then beat it, shorty," the other man said. "This place is closed until the boss takes off."

"Sorry," Alberto said. "She can't take off until we talk to her."

"That ain't happening," the first man said.

"Then we have a fundamental problem here," Alberto said.

"Hit the bricks, pal," the second man said, as he raised his gun and pointed it at Alberto's chest.

Alberto grabbed the man's wrist with his right hand and twisted it counterclockwise, levering his left arm under the guy's elbow. The bone-snapping sound of the guard's elbow breaking was accompanied by the clunk of his gun hitting the cement.

The other guard raised his gun, but Alberto destroyed the man's left knee with a vicious sidekick to the outside of the joint. He collapsed, screaming and holding his knee. The first man remained standing, staring down in disbelief at his newly deformed arm.

Alberto hit him in the throat with a quick strike of his open palm and then followed it with a roundhouse kick to his groin. The second man struggled to get up, but Alberto hit him on the side of the head with a closed fist. The man went down and began twitching.

Alberto waved us forward.

126

Frankie and Rick jumped out of the Mercedes. They raced to the front door of the building and went in. Enzo and Luca hopped out of their vehicle and ran around the building to the door on the north side. Enzo had an Uzi and Luca his lupara. The sawed-off shotgun was a perfect weapon for close work in tight spaces.

My hands were sweating as I got out and stood next to Frankie's car. I watched as Alberto used plastic ties to bind up the two men. He stood up, assessed his work, and went inside.

He came out five minutes later and beckoned to me.

"Come in," he said, as he opened the door. "It's all good."

He was calm, but my pulse was racing. I recognized the woman behind the desk from my previous visit. Rick stood in front of her with his gun at his side. Frankie walked down the hall toward us with the last two guards. Their hands were secured behind their backs with plastic ties.

"These are the two who were guarding the door to the lounge," Frankie said. "My boys disabled the other two at the north end. You're good to go."

"Any problems?" I asked.

"Not so far," he said, as he pushed the guards forward, "and there won't be, right guys?"

The guards didn't say anything.

Something didn't seem right, but with my heart pounding in my chest and adrenaline pumping through my system, it was hard to concentrate.

I walked down the hall, turned to my left, and went another twenty feet to the executive lounge. My hand was shaking as I reached for the door handle. I decided not to knock.

Diane's back was toward me. She sat on a tan, cloth-covered couch staring out at her plane through the floor-to-ceiling glass windows in front of her. There was a glass of champagne on the table next to her. The room air was stale, and I smelled furniture polish.

I cleared my throat. She didn't respond.

"Diane, I want to give you an opportunity to tell your side of this story before it goes to print," I said.

She didn't say anything.

I walked forward. "I am going to write this story whether you comment or not."

I felt heat creeping up my neck.

Damnit.

Stepping around the couch, I confronted her. Her makeup was perfect as always, and her eyes were open but she wasn't blinking. Her lips were compressed into a thin line and her nostrils appeared deformed.

"Diane?" I said, as I nudged her shoulder. "Are you okay?"

She didn't move.

"What happened to your nose?" I asked.

Her nostrils were pinched together. I held my hand under them but there wasn't any airflow. With my right index finger I pulled on her left cheek, trying to bring her nostril back into normal position. It didn't move. Neither did the right one. I used both hands but her nostrils were firmly stuck together.

Her skin temperature felt the same as the fish in the coolers at the Paulina Meat Market. I tried to pry her mouth open, but her lips were stuck to each other and I couldn't move them. I checked her neck for a pulse, but there wasn't one.

I stood up and studied her face. Her mouth and nose had been glued shut, making it impossible for her to breathe.

Something cold touched my neck. A jolt of electricity made my head explode in a shower of multicolored lights. I felt all the muscles in my body spasm and then the lights went out.

127

"What happened?" I asked when I came to.

"I'm thinkin' a Taser," Frankie said. "Couple of red marks on your neck."

I struggled to push myself up off the carpet, but I couldn't support my body weight with my arms. Rick and Frankie lifted me up. I had trouble standing, so they helped me to the couch where Diane had been sitting.

I shook my head. "I don't understand any of this."

"We gave you fifteen minutes, and when you didn't come out, we came in and found you on the floor," Rick said.

"Where is Diane's body?" I asked.

No one said anything.

"Guys, where is she?"

"No one was in here when we came in," Frankie said.

"Diane was sitting on this couch and she wasn't breathing. Someone had glued her nose and mouth shut."

"Probably superglue," Frankie said.

"Hard to believe she would let a person do that to her without resisting," Rick said.

"I'm thinkin' the killer used the Taser on her, then applied the superglue while she was out," Frankie said.

"He probably did the lips first," Rick said. "When she came around enough to realize something was wrong with her mouth, he glued her nostrils shut as he stared in her eyes while she slowly suffocated."

"A terrible way for Diane to die," I said.

"If she is dead," Frankie said.

"I did *not* make this up, and before either of you say anything, I did *not* lose another body," I said.

"All I'm saying is that she isn't here now, so unless she's walking around with her face all glued together, somebody removed her body," Frankie said.

"Other than the woman at the desk and Diane's guards, there wasn't anyone else in this building who could remove her body," Rick said.

I remembered what was bothering me. "What about the female employee we all saw come into the building?" I asked. "Where did she go?"

"Luca said she walked out of the north door and went out to the plane," Frankie said. "They didn't think nothin' of it since she works here."

"Diane's body has to be here," I said. "Help me up so we can hunt for it."

No one moved.

"Okay, I'll do it myself." I staggered over to the glass window and glanced out. What I saw made it difficult for me to breathe. Diane's plane was gone.

128

That night, Carter and I sat in the family room. The kids were in bed. He sipped a Pride cabernet. I drank a neat single malt scotch. The ice bag I had on my neck helped the pain from where I was hit by the Taser, but the scotch was more effective. I told Carter I'd hurt my neck doing one of Cas's exercise classes. If I told him the truth, the Warren story was dead.

"Tell me more about this evidence concerning Diane Warren," he said.

I knew the feds and the Russians were listening, but this didn't have anything to do with them. After what had happened to Diane, I didn't care about them.

"Cas took these pictures of the charts at MidAmerica Hospital," I said.

He pointed at the papers on the coffee table. "And the way I read this is the patients with autoimmune diseases in the ICU have all been treated for breast cancer."

"They have."

"But Fertig is not mentioned in any of these charts as the breast cancer surgeon."

"He isn't, but notice that in each patient's breast cancer history, the wording is exactly the same even though different doctors dictated the history and physical examinations."

"You assume that the information has been altered."

"I do."

"I know how you obtained the pictures of the charts, and it was a creative way to push the story forward, but it was illegal, a fact the hospital's lawyers will point out."

I sipped my scotch. It burned a little as it went down my throat, but the resulting buzz felt good.

"And then there's the sample size," he said. "Were there only five patients?"

"There might have been more, but we ran into a time issue."

Not exactly a lie, but I didn't want to tell him Diane and her security guards arrived and stopped Alan, Cas, and Lori.

"That's my problem with this story. You need to give me more proof before I can publish the story. Can you get it?"

"I'll try."

"May I help? I think this is potentially a terrific story, and I want you to get the credit."

"Thank you for saying that, but I've run into a little problem that I'm trying to solve."

"Maybe I can help with that too."

"I'm not sure if anyone can help me with this one."

He finished his wine and put down his glass. "What about Zhukov? Anything happening with that story? You haven't mentioned it. Maybe I can help with that one."

"All I know is that one hundred and fifty million dollars is missing, and I don't have a clue where it went."

Let the Russians and FBI digest that information. Let them figure it out.

Part 6

129

For the next three days, I spent my free time researching where Diane's plane could have landed. It had taken off during the time I was knocked out from being zapped by the Taser. I discovered the flight plan that had been filed proved to be phony. The real destination of the plane was as yet unknown.

The lack of success in both stopping Diane and finishing a story I wanted to write was depressing. I had been a successful investigative journalist, and then I wasn't — because I got blown up and fired. Now I had a chance to do a compelling story again, and then I didn't.

On Monday morning, at David's suggestion, I was having a manicure at their salon. He said having my nails done was a cure for my melancholy. Macy was asleep in her stroller.

But it wasn't working.

I sat in the waiting room waiting for the polish to dry. David and Rick had taken a break to sit with me. They drank Starbucks coffee from the store one block away. Rick bought a Grande hot green tea for me.

"You poor dear girl," David said.

"You appear miserable," Rick said.

"I am," I said. "I had three stories and now I'm down to the one about Zhukov, since Sullivan is missing and Diane's feature is in the dumper. I know her body is on that stupid plane, but I can't find it to prove I'm right about her being dead."

As far as the world knew, she had left the country. I knew better. She was dead, and someone had put her body on the plane before it flew away.

"Sweetie, there's one tiny problem," David said. "Who killed her?"

Great question.

I didn't have an answer for that. The most logical suspect was the person sitting with David and Rick waiting for her nails dry. If the police knew that I had killed the man I assumed Diane had hired to blow us up, that would put me at the top of the list of those who had it in for Diane.

"We — Rick and I — think you might need to stop pursuing this," David said.

"Indeed we do," Rick said. "I would hate to have the police begin doing a diggy-dig in our basement, especially if Diane did hire that disgusting man who is buried there."

"And we are positive everyone knew she hated you and you felt the same way about her," David said.

"I didn't exactly hate her," I said. "I just didn't like her very much."

"Let's find a different project," Rick suggested. "Do you ever write about social events?"

"I covered all kinds of stories when I was a cub reporter, but I haven't done anything like that in years. Why?"

"We are in charge of a charity fundraising event called the Imperial Windy City Court of the Prairie State," David said. "It will be held at the O'Hare International Westin Hotel in three weeks, and we would love to have some fabulous publicity."

"Guys, I need background first."

"Let's meet at The Max," Rick said. "We are having a run-through of the show we are producing for that fund-raising evening."

"It'll be fun, and sweetie, you look like you could use a few laughs right now," David said.

"And don't forget to call Marcia about that Russian person," David said. "You have to finish the story, then you can devote full time to our project."

My journalistic juices slowed to a trickle. Their story wouldn't be boring, but I didn't see a nomination for a Pulitzer Prize in my future.

"I need to check with Carter. I'm pretty sure the *Tribune* will publish it, but you have to realize that it won't be on the front page."

"Oh, poo," Rick said. "But if they must, we understand."

"Before I text Carter about it, let me call Janet first," I said. "She might have new information for us."

I did. "Anything new on the names of the investors?"

"One thing I haven't figured out yet," Janet said. "Dr. Alan Peebler didn't exist before he entered Harvard Medical School."

"What the heck does that mean?"

"I'm not sure. I'm hoping you can tell me."

"I'll let you know what I find."

130

Alan was my primary lead to the Zhukov story, so I called Lori to make an appointment to see him. She didn't sound too optimistic but she told me to come over to his office at one p.m.

I dropped off Macy at Alicia's and drove to Alan and Marcia's. I parked the car in front of his side of their home. When Marcia and Alan joined the two houses together, Marcia said their architect suggested the entry door to Alan's home be removed and replaced with windows.

His new front door was on the side of the house next to the garage doors. It was the one Molly and I used the night we brought Alan home after hunting for clues at David and Rick's house.

Lori answered that door. She led me down a hallway into the waiting room of his office. She offered me coffee or tea, but I declined.

"I'm sorry I'm late, but I had to drop Macy off at Alicia's," I said. "Did you talk to Alan?"

"I tried to, but things aren't good. He's gone downhill since our trip to the hospital."

"What do you mean?" I asked.

"He isn't talking."

"Not at all?"

"Not one word. Each morning, I put his clothes out and he gets dressed. He then sits in his office all day. He eats breakfast and lunch alone and then has dinner with Marcia if she's not out at a fundraiser."

"What about working out?"

"He doesn't do that either."

Now what do I do?

"Is he in there?" I asked, pointing at his examining room.

"He is. He sits at his desk and looks at medical articles on his computer."

"Can he operate his computer?"

"No. I sign in for him and log on to one of his medical journals."

"Which he reads?"

"I'm not sure he does. When I sign off before I leave, the screen is always at the same place I started."

"He stares his computer all day long?"

She shrugged her shoulders. "I guess."

"And that's it?"

"Like I said, it's been that way since the confrontation with Diane Warren. It's as if the vile things she said put him into a tailspin. She's an evil woman."

"I don't think we have to worry about her anymore."

She arched an eyebrow. "Finally, some good news."

131

I studied the plaques and diplomas on Alan's wall again. "Maybe you can answer a question for me since Alan is indisposed."

"I'll try," Lori said. "What do you need?"

"Did Alan ever change his name?" I asked.

Her eyes widened. "I, ah, I don't know if I should answer that."

"Why?"

"I'm not sure I'm supposed to know any of this," she said, as she began picking at the skin around her nails.

I need this.

"Given the deterioration of Alan's mental health, I don't think it'll matter now, do you?" I asked.

She nodded in agreement. "Okay, so rumor has it that before Alan and Marcia were married, he changed his last name to Peebler."

Didn't expect that.

"As you know, Marcia has lots of inherited money," she continued. "She used to drink excessively, and her parents were furious with her for her wild ways. After her last divorce, they sent her to rehab and insisted she marry a man with substance and stability."

"Like a doctor."

"But not just any doctor. They wanted a physician who was one of the best, if not the best, in his field."

"Alan."

"Exactly, and as part of the marriage arrangement, they insisted he change his last name."

Weird.

"Why would they do that?"

She squirmed around in her chair. "Alan is Jewish, and they didn't want Marcia to have a Jewish last name."

"That's reprehensible."

"You might think so, but I met her parents before they died and I can easily understand it. They were huge donors to the Catholic church and extremely conservative."

"Hard to reconcile that with Marcia's two divorces."

"Her first two husbands lived off of her money and drank and used drugs. Her parents blamed Marcia's substance abuse on them."

"Which was why they wanted her to marry a man who worked for a living."

"Exactly. Her father had a rare disease that no one could figure out. He was dying and finally had an appointment with Alan, who made a the proper diagnosis and saved his life. When he learned that Alan was single, he made a large donation to fund a research project Alan was doing. The Peeblers had dinner with him and were so impressed that they decided he was the perfect choice for Marcia."

"As long as he didn't have a Jewish last name. What was it before he changed?"

"I don't know, but Marcia could tell you." She paused. "But if you want to remain a friend of hers, it might be better if you figure out another way to find it. Since she stopped drinking, she has become a totally private person about family matters."

132

After I picked up Macy from Alicia's house, I played with her, fed her, and put her down for her afternoon nap. Kerry had a birthday party at preschool until four so I had some free time.

I logged on to my computer and brought up "Dr. Alan Peebler."

From the dates on the screen, that name didn't exist until thirty-seven years ago, one year before he matriculated at Harvard Medical School. I entered Marcia's name in my research engine to check her background. Most of her early years were the fluff that sells tabloids at the supermarket.

She did it all and sometimes more than once. There were two documented divorces and possibly one earlier marriage that was annulled. One society reporter quoted Marcia as calling it a "whoopsie."

I finally found a one-line notification of a marriage license issued to Marcia and Alan thirty-seven years ago. A week later, "Alan Peebler" appeared for the first time on a credit card issued in his name. The address listed for him was in Boston. There was no coverage of their wedding in the society pages.

I went back to Marcia's story. At the same time Alan entered Harvard, her address was listed as being the one where she and Alan now lived. Her address remained the same, but Alan's changed several times in the Boston area, and then he lived two years in Baltimore when he was at Hopkins.

"Wait a minute," I said to myself.

The first time I visited Alan's office, I checked out the diplomas on his wall and wrote down what I felt was the relevant information, including the dates. I saw this again when I was there talking to Lori. According to his Harvard diploma, he graduated from medical school five years after Marcia and he took out their marriage license.

These dates weren't adding up.

They were married thirty-seven years ago. Lori said that Marcia's parents wanted her to marry a doctor, especially one that was the best in his specialty. How could that be possible when Alan didn't become a doctor until five years after they were married?

I opened my Zhukov files to the list of investors. Alan was one of the first, and his address was listed as being in Chicago. The date he sent Zhukov his first investment check was one year after he had finished his fellowship programs and had gone into private practice in Chicago.

What the heck?

I made a list:

1.   *Marcia marries Alan and he changes his name.*

2.   *One year later, Alan enters Harvard Medical School and graduates in four years.*

3.   *Four years after that, he finishes his residency training at Harvard and then completes two more years of a fellowship at Hopkins.*

4.   *He moves to Chicago and begins investing his money with Zhukov.*

I sat back and read my list. Marcia's parents selected Alan to marry her after he saw Mr. Peebler as a patient. He should have married her after he finished his training and entered private practice, not a year before he entered medical school.

The year Alan went into practice was the first time they were mentioned in the society news. There was one report that Marcia M. Peebler had married Alan Peebler at an undisclosed place and time. No one mentioned, or seemed to care, that Peebler was Marcia's maiden name. And it wasn't mentioned that Alan Peebler appeared on the planet the year before he entered medical school.

Alan told me he had known Zhukov for a long time. He knew that Zhukov had been a dentist in Russia and that Zhukov couldn't pass the certification test to practice his profession in the United States. My research into Zhukov had confirmed this.

When I queried Alan about investing his money with Zhukov, he lost his focus and I didn't learn anything else. Alan seemed to know a lot about Zhukov, but he could have known this since he was a long-time investor.

Or could Alan have known Zhukov before he became Alan Peebler? If he did, maybe he could help me understand the hazy back-story about Zhukov and the Russian Mafia. If I had that, I might finally understand what was going on.

133

On Tuesday, the Irregulars and their kids visited Hamlin Park for the first time since late last fall. It was April 2nd, and Chicago was having an unseasonably warm day. We wanted to take advantage of it since a thunderstorm was in the forecast for Wednesday.

The park is at North Damen and West Barry Avenue in Roscoe Village. It is almost eight acres, with activities for every member of the family. There are softball fields where Carter and his reporters play twice a week in the summertime, a large, free swimming pool, and a good-sized playground. It's where I first met the moms who have become the Hamlin Park Irregulars.

We congregated in the playground. I told them about my inability to find out Alan's last name before he morphed into Dr. Alan Peebler.

"Does it matter?" Cas asked. "What if you find out his last name? How is that going to help you?"

"For once, I have to agree with Cas," Linda said. "Poor Alan is off his rocker. It was long ago, and he probably doesn't even remember who he was."

I pushed Macy in a swing. She was happy. I was bummed. "I guess you're right, but he's my only hope to figure this story out."

"What, in essence, is this story anyway?" Linda asked. "Zhukov has disappeared."

"He was killed," I said.

"Whatever," she said. "He is no longer around. Someone made off with a lot of money that allegedly belonged to the Russian Mafia. They want it back. The FBI is interested, and I'm sure by now so is the IRS, but is this a compelling enough story to write? Will the average reader want to know anything about this?"

"I would," Molly said. "Gosh, when I worked for the farmers they had me work on stuff like this all the time. It was fun."

"Okay then, how would you proceed?" I asked.

"I'll talk to Alan," Molly said.

"How?" Cas said. "Tina said he's not talking to anyone."

"He has been a little off since that deal at the hospital, but before that we talked a lot," Molly said.

"What about?" I asked.

"Stuff. He's fascinated by my breasts."

"Most men are," Linda said.

"But Alan?" I said. "He doesn't seem like that."

"Alan is different," Molly said. "He loves to talk about clothes and fashion."

"How come you never told us about this?" Cas asked.

"Gosh, you never asked."

134

My stomach began to churn. "Molly, did he ever tell you his real last name?"

"Uh-huh," Molly said.

We waited. She threw a ball to her oldest son, Chase.

"Molly, what is it?" I asked.

"Some kind of animal."

Linda hung her head. "Unbelievable."

"Do you know which animal it is?" I asked.

"Don't have a clue, but it's definitely an animal, maybe a furry one now that I think about it."

"Any ideas, Linda?" I asked. "You're the only one of the Irregulars who would know which Jewish last names might be animals."

"Furry animals," Cas reminded us.

"Right, ones with hair," I said.

"Wulf," Linda said and spelled it for us.

We turned to Molly. She kept playing catch with Chase.

"Lamm," Linda suggested.

"A stretch," I said.

"They are sort of furry," she argued.

Molly didn't react.

"Gozman."

"What the heck is that?" Cas asked.

"A rabbit."

"That's a good one," I said, but Molly didn't respond.

"Loew or Loeb. It means lion."

Molly yawned.

"Perkin is a bear," Linda said.

Nothing.

"Stier is a bull or an ox."

Still nothing.

"Molly, are any of these Alan's last name?" I asked.

She looked up. "What?"

"Linda gave us a few possibilities for Alan's real last name. Do you recognize any of them?"

"Uh-huh."

We waited.

"It's a bear."

"I thought that was Perkin," Cas said.

"Wait a minute," Linda said. "Maybe it's Berman. I forgot that one."

"Molly, is it Berman?"

"For sure."

"Alan Berman," I said. "Let's hope that's who we're hunting for."

135

With someone listening into my conversations at home, I had also purchased a burner phone. I needed to narrow down my search for Dr. Alan Berman. From the wine room, I used the phone to call Lori, his nurse.

"Sorry to bother you, but when I first came in to see Alan, you mentioned that he is fluent in several languages," I said.

"I did, but as the mad cow disease has taken more control, he increasingly reverts back to only one, especially when he plays his concert grand piano," Lori said. "But he doesn't do either one anymore. All he does is sit at his computer."

I remembered hearing Chopin being played on a piano before I first met Alan. "Was that him I heard playing the first time I came in here?"

"Yes, but he didn't realize either one of us could hear him."

"I don't understand."

"Among his other talents, Dr. Peebler is a concert-level pianist, but he never plays in front of anyone."

"Not even Marcia?"

"Especially her, but he writes and records a new song for her each day."

"Where are the recordings?"

"He locks them in one of the bedrooms above his office."

Alan's weirdness.

"I'm curious. What language does he speak?"

"Russian. It's the language of his youth."

My heart began racing. "Are you sure?"

"Positive. God knows I've heard it often enough."

"Did he ever mention the name Berman?"

"I don't think so."

"Did he ever talk about Russia?"

"Only once. He mentioned Leningrad, or I think he might have called it St. Petersburg. I guessed he lived there at some time in his life."

With this new background information on Alan, I needed computer help, but my keyboard was compromised. I called Linda and told her what Lori said to me.

It didn't take long for Linda to find Alan L. Berman on her search engines.

"He was born in what was then called Leningrad and graduated from the Saint Petersburg Pavlov Medical University at age twenty-two," Linda began. "After further training, he quickly became a world expert in neurodegenerative diseases."

"That's probably when he began seeing Marcia's father as a patient, but it wasn't here, it was in Russia," I said. "Look at Alan and Marcia's timeline. What does that tell us?"

"Two years before they were married, Alan moved to the United States. One year later, Dr. Alan Berman ceased to exist. He was replaced a year later by Dr. Alan Peebler."

Bingo.

"Look at Zhukov's file," I said. "See if you can find Alan's connection with him."

It took seven minutes.

"Got it," she said. "They were in training at the school in St. Petersburg for the same period of time."

"It's not much of a stretch to assume they knew each other there and then reconnected after Alan went back to medical school again, finished his residency and fellowship, and then again when they both moved to Chicago. After that, Alan invested money with Zhukov, his friend from the old country."

"Who then lost all of Alan's money, but did he know all this about the Russian Mafia?"

"What Russian wouldn't? If he still had any of his marbles, he might be able to help me fill in the details."

"But he can't, and I don't know what else to do to help you. There are no more viable leads."

I disconnected and shut down my computer. The only story left was doing PR for David and Rick's charity event.

Part 7

136

On Wednesday, the melancholy about my stories disappearing along with the three bodies wasn't going away, so I went in for a pedicure at David and Rick's salon. Usually I never schedule one until it's officially summertime and I'll be wearing sandals or flip-flops, but I needed to relax and pamper myself.

While my feet soaked in the warm water, I scooted down in the soft chair and closed my eyes. Kerry and Macy's faces bobbed up into my subconscious. This was one reason I didn't do this more frequently; with working on stories and being a mom and a wife, I never had time.

I smelled coffee before I opened my eyes. David stood beside me sipping a Venti Starbucks.

"Daydreaming?" he asked.

"This feels so good," I said. "I was wondering why I don't do this more often."

"Mommy, you don't have time. You need to finish up on the Russian story, then you can do the publicity for our event."

"You're right," I said as I wiggled my toes in the water, "but this is amazing."

I sat up when the woman approached to begin scrubbing the dead skin off my feet.

"I'm putting a hold on the Zhukov story," I said.

"You found the money? I hope you saved some for us."

"Writing a story is all about uncovering solid facts that I can document and prove. After spending a considerable amount of my time on this, the only documentation I have is Alan's background." I didn't want to add that investigating the Russian Mafia scared the crap out of me.

"Tell me, tell me."

I did.

David shook his head when I finished. "I knew Alan had secrets in his closet, but I never dreamed being a Russian was one of them."

"Are there other secrets about him I need to know?" I asked. "Maybe his story isn't dead."

"Sweetie, there are so many things about Alan that I can't even begin to tell you, but some of them are best kept between us boys."

Huh?

I made a mental note to find out more about that at a later date. David went back to work. I watched as the woman began to cut and file my toenails. This was getting frustrating. Would learning any more about Alan make a difference in my being able to write the Zhukov story? David knew something, but I doubted that it had to do with Zhukov.

Before I decided what to do next, I had to face the pedicure moment of truth. I needed to select a color. Rick came over to the pedicure station as I was going blind trying to pick the perfect hue.

"Honey, it's not springtime yet, but it's close." He thumbed through the bottles. "I'm thinking this one." He handed it to me. "Hot Pink."

Whoa.

"Don't you think it's too bright for early April?"

"Think Chicago. Think no sun. We need color here!" He took the bottle out of my hand. "Slap it on, Cheri. The shade will blast her out of her funk."

He turned to me. "David told me about Alan. The little stinker never said he was Russian. Maybe he's a spy. That would make a fabulous story."

"Yeah, right, I can see that headline. Chicago doctor with dementia spies for the Russians. Maybe they can make it into a twelve-part story for cable TV."

137

Thursday night, the Irregulars walked onto the Main Dance Floor of The Max, a dance club that bills itself as the best LGBTQ dance club in the Midwest. It's in the River North area on North Clark, one block away from The Baton Show Lounge, a Chicago institution in the LGBTQ community.

The first floor is 12,000 square feet and almost two stories high. There were multicolored flashing lights, three wrecking ball-sized rotating disco balls, and a pounding beat blaring out of the speakers that surrounded us.

"Wow," I said.

"Unreal," Cas said.

"It's changed since I was here last," Molly said. "They've added another disco ball."

"Why are we here?" Linda asked.

"David and Rick invited me to see a rehearsal of a show they're directing for a fundraiser," I said.

"What charity?" Linda asked.

"The Imperial Windy City Court of the Prairie State," I responded.

"I went to that last year," Molly said. "It's really cool."

None of us were going to ask her why she attended.

"They want me to write a story about it and also thought I needed to have some fun since all of my stories suck," I said. "I called you guys to come here and see it with me."

"It appears they want us to observe another part of their lives," Linda said, as a familiar-looking, tall, slender brunette walked toward us. She wore a red, floor-length ball gown slit up to her right thigh. Her hair was piled high on her head with ringlets framing her face. Her heavy makeup was flawless.

"I love her hair," Cas said, as she came closer.

"I love her shoes," Molly said, pointing at the red, five-inch heels she wore.

"I love her style," I said.

She stood in front of us and did a runway pose.

"Well you should, honey," she said.

That voice!

"David?" I asked.

"Not David," he said. "When I'm at events like this, I am Salza."

"I, ah, I..." I stuttered. "I'm speechless."

"Obviously." He did a slow spin with his arms outspread. "Well, kids, what do you think?"

"I'm impressed with how fit your body is," Cas said.

"I had to take a diuretic to get into this tight dress, otherwise my tummy would poochie-poo."

"The dress is spectacular," Molly said. "And I love your shoes."

"Jimmy Choos. They fit me perfectly."

Linda held up her hand to stop us. "Would someone please tell me what is going on here?"

"This is the way, as Frankie says, I roll," he said.

"What about Rick?" I asked.

"Do you mean Czar Rick?" he asked.

"Let me guess," I said. "That would make you Czarina David."

"Close, sweetie, but no tiara," he said. "It's Czarina Salza."

"Oh, for sure. How could I be so stupid?"

"Guys!" Linda said. "*What the hell is happening here?*"

"I am a female impersonator," David said.

"What does that even mean?" Cas asked.

"That he's a man who dresses and acts like a woman," Molly said. "When I was modeling, a lot of them were my buddies. We used to share shoes, since I'm so tall and have bigger feet than most women."

"And why do you do this?" Linda asked.

"We do it to perform, but I also act as the emcee."

"Like for the Imperial Windy City Court," Molly said.

"Exactly, but Rick and I are the official hosts and in charge of the entertainment, which is one reason you're here, to see our show rehearsal." He turned and walked toward a spiral staircase to our left. "Follow me, kiddies, we are going to have some serious fun."

138

"This is the Arena," David said, as we entered the room. "The owners have been kind enough to close it down for tonight so we can block out our staging."

The room was as big as the one downstairs, but there was a full stage at the far end where several women in ball gowns were walking back and forth. Rick was dressed in a black jump suit. He had a headset on and was talking to a group of women and men off to our left.

He said something to them and walked over to us.

"Salza, you need to get up on stage," Rick said. "We need to run though the entire show without stopping this time."

Rick turned to us. "So glad you could be here, but let me tell you, it would be easier to work with all men. There's always way too much drama with this group."

"Rick, aren't they all men?" Linda asked.

"They are, but when they're in character, some of them become such divas, I can't begin to tell you."

He checked his watch and clapped his hands at the group by the stage. "Everyone in position." He rotated the microphone from the headset down to his mouth and spoke into it. "Clarence, cue the music. Howie, ready the lights."

The lights came down, and the music began playing. Salza strutted out to center stage and stood with a mike in her hand. Rick waved the music down and Salza began the introductions.

The stage technicians blew several of their cues or didn't get the music started on time so there were multiple starts and stops, especially with the performers who lip-synched their lyrics. The show was entertaining, but the constant interruptions were beginning to bug me.

The last production number ended, and the lights came up. Rick walked over to us. "What did you think of the show?"

"Fabulous," I said.

"It still needs work before we go up for real."

"Now what?" I asked.

"We have to run through it again."

He must have seen the strained look on my face. "You don't have to stay if you don't want to."

"How about arranging a few interviews for me with the cast members, maybe next week?"

"Then you'll write an article for the show?"

"I'm happy to do it. It's not as if I have anything else to do right now."

I felt a tug on my sleeve.

"Check out the lady over there by the bar," Molly said.

She was short and wore a tight-fitting, slinky black dress with dark hose and high heels. Her black hair was piled high on her head, displaying her long, dangling diamond earrings. She had on heavy eye makeup. She chattered animatedly with several performers.

One of the performers spoke to her and pointed at the piano a band member had been using. The lady sat on the unoccupied stool and began to play, softly at first and then with more gusto. A few people stopped to listen. Most kept talking. The piano player seemed happy to be playing.

"I love that song," Cas said.

"It's Rachmaninoff's 'Rhapsody on a Theme of Paganini'," Linda said.

"Do you play the piano?" Cas asked.

"I used to be in a band in high school, but we didn't play music like that," she said. "I tried to play that same song in college, but it was hard because my hands aren't big enough."

The lady continued to play. Several performers moved closer to the piano. She switched to songs from *Phantom of the Opera*. A few of them sang along.

"She seems to know a lot of people here," I said.

"Small wonder," Molly said.

"You know her?" Linda asked.

"Kind of. I've seen her before."

"Here at The Max?" I asked.

"No, I've never seen her here."

"Then where have you seen her?" Cas asked.

"On a DVD."

"Did she make a movie or something?" Linda asked.

"Did she ever," Molly said.

"Have I seen it?" I asked.

"I tried to show it to you, but you said you didn't want to see it," Molly answered.

"I'm lost," I said. "What are you talking about?"

"She was in that Russian guy's DVD!" Molly exclaimed.

139

Adrenaline slammed through my system. This was the break I needed. The lady finished playing. The performers standing around the piano applauded. She stood up and did a curtsy. A young lady handed her a drink.

"I have to get to her," I said. "She's the key to my story."

"Which story are we talking about now?" Linda asked.

"Zhukov's," I said. "I think she's the one who killed him."

Instinctively, I looked for my backpack but realized I'd left it in my mommy van, which was in the parking lot. "Cas, do you have your Taser or spray?" I asked.

"No, I left them at home," she said. "Does she know what you look like? Maybe you can sneak up on her."

"Probably won't work. I think she was there the night I discovered Zhukov's body. She had to have seen me."

The lady glanced around the room. Her gaze stopped when she saw us. Her eyebrows shot up. She turned around and moved quickly behind the curtain on the stage.

Pushing my way through the mass of performers milling around the area, I stood on my toes and looked left and right, but the lady was gone. I turned to a tall woman with white-blond hair. She wore a black ball gown.

"Excuse me," I said. "Is there a back way out of here?"

"There's an elevator at the end of the hall. It's the one we use to bring up our props."

"Where does it stop?"

"In the alley behind the building."

I reversed my course, ran back into the main room and down the stairs to the first level. I sped out the front entrance of The Max. A door slammed in the alley, which was to my right, around the corner of the building. I heard running footsteps.

Following the sound, I rounded the corner of the building into the alley and saw the woman sprinting away from me. She turned the far corner and disappeared from my view.

I rushed to that end of the alley and turned right into the parking lot. I saw her speeding toward North Clark Street. The cement was wet from the recent rain, and my flats should have given me better traction than her high heels, but she was going faster than I was.

Following her toward North Clark, I saw the reason she was pulling away from me. Her heels were laying in the gutter next to a dumpster. They looked familiar. I slid to a stop and bent down to examine them at exactly the same time I heard a shot being fired and a bullet pinging on the building's wall behind my head.

The heels were my black Rolando Hidden-Platform Christian Louboutin pumps. They had saved my life.

140

Two more shots hit the same wall as I dove behind the smelly dumpster. I gasped for breath, both from the sprint and the terror of having a killer try to blow several holes in my head.

Rolling to my left, I picked up my heels and hid behind an SUV. The blaring sound of hard rock music was audible each time a patron went in or out of The Max, but that was the only noise I heard other than the cars whizzing back and forth on North Clark Street.

What was missing was the noise of an engine starting up. The piano player hadn't left by car, at least not one that was close. She was on a busy street. I hoped she wouldn't begin blasting away with her gun if I followed her.

Abandoning the safety of the dumpster, I ran to my mommy van, threw the shoes inside, and grabbed my backpack. I pulled out the Glock and racked a round into the chamber. If she continued to shoot at me, I could now defend myself and, if necessary, fire back.

I put the gun into the backpack and slung it over my shoulders. Loping forward to North Clark, I turned left. The sidewalk was full of people walking in both directions. I didn't see the woman.

Two young men brushed by me. I held up my hand to stop them. "Did you see a woman come running out of this alley?" I asked

"A short lady with a darling black dress?" the taller one asked.

"Yeah, and she didn't have on any shoes."

"Are you a cop?" the other one asked. "If you are, then we do not want to be involved."

"I'm not a cop. That bitch stole my Louboutin pumps and I want to have a serious talk with her."

"That is so trashy," the first one said.

The second one pointed over his shoulder. "She went that way, and I think she turned to the left at the next cross street."

Following his instructions, I ran to the end of the block and turned left. There were several brick condo buildings on both sides of the street. I spotted a large drop of blood about twelve feet directly in front of me. I sprinted to it. She'd cut her feet running away from me.

It was now almost ten o'clock, and it was hard to see any blood spatter on the sidewalk, even with the streetlights. I pulled out the flashlight from my backpack. I shined the bright beam on the sidewalk, and about every three or four yards I saw what appeared to be another drop or two of blood.

It's her.

People walked past me going both ways, and dodging them didn't make it any easier. One guy riding a bicycle almost hit me when I didn't look up as I followed the beam of my flashlight. My total focus was on the trail of blood.

The bloody drops went for one more block and increased in size, making it easier to follow. One more block and the smears turned left into a three-story condo building. A bloody footprint was visible through the locked front door. It led down the hall toward the back of the building.

Glancing around to make sure no one was watching, I removed my backpack and took out my lock pick gun and torque wrench. I opened the lock and stepped inside.

I closed the front door behind me and put my equipment and flashlight away. After pulling out the Glock, I slung my backpack over my shoulders. I checked the gun to make sure I still had a bullet in the chamber. I held the gun in front of me and followed the blood trail to 1-D, the last door on the left.

A puddle of clotting blood was smeared on the carpet in front of the door. There was a back exit to my right, but I didn't see any blood there.

Taking in a deep breath to control my rapid breathing, I tried the doorknob. It was unlocked.

Zhukov's killer was inside.

141

Carter won't be happy.

This was stupidly dangerous and I knew it. But this was my story, and the woman inside had all the answers. Slipping off my backpack, I squatted down and reached up to push open the door.

There were no lights on inside, and I didn't sense any movement. Not knowing the layout of the condo was a major problem. She could be hiding anywhere, and she had a gun.

"I know you're in there," I said. "I've already called Detective Janet Corritore of the Chicago PD. If you were still there after you killed Zhukov, you might have seen her. She's on the way."

No sounds.

"I have a gun, so you're trapped," I continued.

I took in another deep breath. My pulse rate slowed down.

"Be smart," I said. "There's no reason to do any more shooting."

There was no sound from the darkened room. Reaching into my backpack, I took out my flashlight. I turned it on and quickly lobbed it into the room, hoping the woman would shoot at it.

Nothing happened.

Standing up, I reached around the corner of the doorjamb and felt for a light switch. I found one, flipped it up, and quickly returned to the hall. I squatted down with my gun in front of me.

Peeking through the open door, I saw that the overhead lights provided ample illumination. I looked around the doorjamb and didn't see any movement. To my left was a stuffed chair, a table and lamp, and a couch.

"Okay, I'm going to wait right here until the cops come."

But I did the opposite. Pushing the lamp off the table on my left, I dove into the room, rolling to my right. I came to a stop behind another stuffed chair. The pounding in my ears from my hammering pulse made it hard to hear, but I didn't detect any sounds.

I jumped up and swept the Glock back and forth as I scanned the room. It was small, with an efficiency kitchen to my right. There was an open door across the room. I knelt down and picked up my flashlight. Keeping the gun in front of me, I advanced toward that door.

I hid behind the safety of the doorjamb and held the flashlight up as high as I could and shined the intense beam into the room. There was a bed and chest of drawers, but otherwise it was empty.

Flipping on a wall switch, I made a more thorough search of the bedroom and bathroom. Both were empty. I went back into the main room and hunted around again, but Zhukov's killer was gone.

142

I picked up the lamp I'd knocked over and shut and locked the front door to the condo. The decorating scheme was generic rental, with a blue couch, two green stuffed chairs, and a small kitchen table with two metal chairs.

The bedroom wasn't much fancier. There was a bed, a nightstand with a lamp, and a chest of drawers. The small closet was filled with a woman's clothes. I checked out the labels. The dresses were the same size and from all the major couture designers. So were the shoes and purses. She'd spent a ton of money on getting dressed up but nothing on furnishings.

Opening the medicine cabinet in the bathroom, I found high-end cosmetics and multiple pricy lotions for skin care and rejuvenation. Expensive soaps and shampoos were in the tub/shower combination, but there were no towels.

I went back to the front door. There were dried blood smears on the carpet. They led into the bathroom and then disappeared.

"How did you get out of here?" I wondered to myself.

The wastebasket in the bathroom was empty, as was the one in the kitchen. The kitchen cabinets were also empty. The refrigerator held four bottles of Crystal champagne. There were two bottles of Boodle's gin and one of Absolute vodka in the freezer, along with ice cubes, but no frozen foods.

She was a party girl who liked to dress up and drink with her visitors but never ate here.

What am I missing?

I went back into the bedroom and began going through the chest of drawers. La Perla seemed to be her choice in panties. The bras were a different matter. They were all heavily padded.

The answer was in the next drawer down. There was one men's shirt, three pairs of men's underwear, one pair of men's socks and one pair of jeans. There was a bike rider's multicolored jersey.

The biker!

The woman from the club had run into the condo and gone into the bathroom, where she applied Band-Aids to her feet after wiping them off with towels. She rinsed off the makeup with a face towel. She went into the bedroom and changed into men's clothes and shoes. She took the towels and Band-Aids with her and walked out the back exit door, which is why I didn't find any blood there.

My killer was a man. Now all I had to do was find out who he was.

143

The Hamlin Park Irregulars were waiting for me at the table when I returned to The Max. David and Rick stood at the bar with their friends. They had their backs to me.

"Did you catch her?" Linda asked, when I sat down.

"Him," I said.

"Him?" Cas said. "I saw a woman run out of here."

I pointed at David, who was still Salza. "He was dressed like David. The killer ran, and I followed. He changed into men's clothes in a condo near here, probably walked, or more likely rode a bike, past me on the street, and I didn't recognize who it was."

"Wow," Linda said. "This is a weird case."

"Easy to solve," Molly said.

We stared at her.

"I think David and Rick know who he is," she said.

"Then let's find out," I said.

We walked over to the bar.

"Gotta' sec', guys?" I asked.

They didn't seem happy to see me.

"Is everything okay?" David asked.

"No, it isn't," I said. "He got away."

David glanced at Rick but didn't say anything about my choice of gender identification.

"And we think you two know who he is," I continued.

"We do, but we never dreamed he was Zhukov's killer," Rick said. "You have to believe us. If we had known, we would have told you immediately."

"Even though it violates his trust in us," David said.

"His trust?" Linda asked. "You need to explain that."

"Not all of the ladies here tonight are lucky enough to have loving partners of the same sex," Rick said.

"You mean some are married to women?" Cas asked.

David nodded. "More than you would guess. People trust Rick and I to keep their identities a secret so their spouses don't find out."

"You're saying this man is married and you are covering up for him," Linda said.

"We are," Rick said. "He's a late bloomer, as it were."

"He began coming in about four years ago," David said. "He was shy at first, but he quickly adjusted."

"He became Genieva," Rick said. "He played the piano in our show three years ago, but we haven't seen him for a long while."

"We were stunned to see him tonight," David said.

"He was radiantly happy the last time we saw him, which is why we kept his identity secret," Rick said.

"Why?" I asked. "Do we know him?"

"You sure do, sweetie," David said. "It's Dr. Alan Peebler."

144

When I arrived home, I banged through the back door and headed for the computer room.

"And hello to you," Carter said, as I blew past him. He was seated on the couch editing articles written by his staff.

I paused at the head of the stairs. "Sorry about that, but I'm so excited," I said. "I think I finally have the Zhukov story figured out."

"Do you know who killed him?" he asked.

"I do. I need to go on the computer and go through my files to make sure I'm right."

I sat down in front of my computer and began checking my Zhukov files. This time, I didn't care who found out what I was going to type on my keyboard. This story was going to be finished before the feds or the Russians could react to what I was going to type.

Zhukov had lost all of Alan's money. Alan had a motive to kill him. But if he killed Zhukov, what did Alan do with the money?

I found it in Marcia's file. She told me Alan wanted to donate money to his medical school. I thought it was Harvard, since that was what the diploma on his office wall said, but that wasn't his first medical school. That was the Saint Petersburg Pavlov Medical University.

It was recent news, so it only took six minutes to find the answer. The day after the killer downloaded the files from Zhukov's computer, a total of one hundred fifty million dollars was donated to the Saint Petersburg Pavlov Medical University by an unnamed person. There were several endowed chairs included in the donation. I recognized one name. A chair in neurodiagnostic medicine was named for Dr. Alan L. Berman.

But what about Zhukov's body? Where was it? I sped through my notes again until I found the answer in Alan's file.

Got it.

I knew where Zhukov's body was buried.

145

The permutations of Zhukov's story whirled through my head as I drove in my van. David and Rick's house was close, and it didn't take me long to drive there.

There were no empty parking slots on the street, so I went around into the alley and parked behind their home. When I saw a bike leaning against the wall of their detached garage, I knew I was in the right place.

Holding the Glock in my hand, I wore the backpack with my equipment but didn't think I would need it. When I turned the doorknob and found the back door open, I knew I was right.

I walked in. He stood on his head in the far corner of the great room.

"Appropriate, don't you think?" Alan asked.

"It is, since that's the position you were in when I first met you," I said.

I held the Glock at my side. He rolled out of his headstand and stood up. "It took you longer to get here than I anticipated, but I am so glad you finally made it."

"I had to come. It's a terrific story."

"I was counting on you feeling that way."

"You were?"

"You wanted to write Zhukov's story, and now you will be able to."

"I have a few questions."

"I would be disappointed if you didn't."

"Do you have Alzheimer's?"

"Four years ago, I made a breakthrough with my Alzheimer's research," Alan began. "I discovered an intravenous isotope to be used with a PET scan that would identify the beta amyloid deposition before the onset of dementia symptoms. It would be the first step in developing a treatment paradigm before the plaques destroyed function. As part of the trials, we needed normal volunteers. Who better to do this than the primary researcher?"

"You?"

"Me."

"But the test came back abnormal."

"It was the only abnormal result from all the controls we tested. There was only one possibility. I had Alzheimer's."

"Why did you fake the symptoms?"

"The pivotal question in this story. I am told that a fiction writer begins a book with a 'what if' question."

"They do."

"What if you were asymptomatic when you learned you had Alzheimer's? What would you do?"

"No symptoms at all?"

"None."

"I would get a second opinion."

He smiled. "You would have made a good doctor. And if the second — and even third — opinion confirmed the first one, what would you do?"

"Cry a lot."

"No, no, no, you cannot do that. What would you do? Travel before your cognitive skills eroded? Write a book? Go to plays and movies? What would you do?"

"Spend my time with my two kids and my husband."

"But then they would see you deteriorate. Would you want that to happen?"

"Probably not."

"Why not right the wrongs that had been done to you before you deteriorated into a vegetative state?"

"You decided to kill Zhukov."

He nodded. "I had only one financial goal in my life. I wanted to make the medical school from which I graduated better so those young people could come to the United States and not be second-class doctors."

"It's hard to picture you being a second-class doctor."

"But that's what they thought of me in the United States. I had to go back to school here so I would no longer be stigmatized as an FMG."

"Which you hated."

"Wouldn't you? I graduated from Harvard and became famous in my field, but that *putz* Zhukov absconded with all my money."

"You shot him so you could take back the money he stole from you."

"That money and, as it turns out, so much more that he had taken from his Russian friends, but you came along and made me alter my plans. I had to come back the second night to download the contents from his computer, which you already knew since you were hiding in the kitchen with Molly."

"Molly told you we were there?"

"She did. We have become great friends. She even showed me the DVDs that Zhukov recorded when I was previously there with him and which she found."

"Did you know Zhukov was recording your encounters together?"

"I did not. Quite titillating, I must say. I immediately went on a diet because I looked so fat."

"A video recording does add a few pounds."

146

Alan checked his watch. "I hate to end this but you might want to leave before they get here."

"They?" I asked.

"Members of the Russian Mafia. When you told Marcia they had planted listening devices in your home, I checked your van and found a Russian GPS tracker under your left rear fender. That gave me the perfect denouement to this story."

"You used me."

"I did. I hadn't been to The Max for a good long time to validate to David and Rick my descent into my dementia. I knew you would be there to work on the story about their event. You knew what Zhukov's killer looked like. I went to The Max so you would see that killer."

"You?"

"It was."

"And when I recognized his killer, I would chase her to your condo."

"Yes, and once you arrived there and figured it out, I knew you would come here. I counted on the Russians following you."

"But why do this?"

"It's the only way I can keep them from harming Marcia."

"Suicide by Russian Mafia. They kill you and leave her alone, and you don't have to deteriorate into dementia since you'll be dead."

"Exactly."

"Does Marcia know about your plan?"

"I left her a note that explains that I am going to disappear forever and not to search for me. She knows how I feel about this dreadful disease, and she'll think I killed myself."

"I can't let you do this."

"Oh, I think you can and will. If you prevent this from happening, the Russians will come after everyone involved, including you and your family and the rest of the Hamlin Park Irregulars. It won't be pretty."

I elevated the Glock and pointed it in his direction. "I'll take that chance. I can't let them murder you."

"What would you be willing to do to write the other stories?"

"Which ones?"

"Sullivan and Diane Warren."

I heard car doors slam in front of the house.

"They're here." He pulled out a folder. "I'll give this to you if you leave right now. It explains everything."

147

I didn't hesitate to leave. I was terrified of the Russians. I'm a mom and a wife. No story is worth that risk.

But I wanted to know what happened, so I sprinted to my van, immediately found the GPS tracker Alan mentioned and threw it as far away as I could. I roared out of the alley and double-parked a block away where I felt safe and could still see David and Rick's house.

I was too far away to hear any gunfire if that was the method the Russians used to kill Alan. I did see four men walk out of the house and look up and down the block before they drove away.

It didn't take long to find out what they did with his body. Five minutes after they departed, there was an explosion followed by flames leaping from the roof. As I watched the fire burn out of control, I opened the file Alan had given me and found the answers to the details I had missed.

He obviously knew how to impersonate Alzheimer's patients since, as part of his practice, he saw them on a regular basis. With his mad cow disease, no one would suspect him of being capable of committing a murder. It was easy for him to shoot Zhukov in the forehead, but only after immobilizing him with a Taser and forcing him to tell Alan the password to his computer and his escape plans.

Initially, Alan buried Zhukov in his own backyard, but I gave him a better solution when I told him about how Frankie's guys had buried the missing-fingered man in David and Rick's basement. That night, he dug up Zhukov's body and put it next to the RPG man.

Alan didn't stop with Zhukov. Marcia had suggested that everyone wanted to kill his or her builder. Alan agreed with her, but he took it one step further. He began killing the subcontractors who had angered him too. They were buried in the basement close to Zhukov.

David and Rick had mentioned they were going to have a meeting with Sullivan, and thus, Alan knew Sullivan would be at the house. Alan took an Uber to the house and found Sullivan inside. Alan killed him with a nail gun.

Alan's first move was to immediately go outside and park Sullivan's truck a block away to avoid leaving any tire tracks near the house. He walked back in the middle of the street to avoid leaving any footprints and then used a broom he'd taken from the house to sweep snow over his and Sullivan's footprints into the house. The rapidly falling snow provided a much-needed assist, as did a neighbor who parked in the space Sullivan had used.

Alan fired the nail gun at David and me to frighten us off. This gave him time to bury Sullivan's body and all the evidence in the basement before I returned with Janet and Tony.

He walked out the front door, carefully stepping in the tracks I'd made in the snow after I sprinted from the house fearing that I would be killed. This time he didn't need the broom to sweep away his tracks.

Running to Sullivan's truck, he then drove it away and left it on the South Side with the keys in it, where it would be stolen — another trick he learned from me when I told him about Luca and Enzo leaving the RPG man's van in a neighborhood where it was sure to be stolen. He took an Uber home.

Molly saw the freshly turned dirt in the basement when we went back to David and Rick's home with Alan to hunt for clues, but I ignored her request to go down there and check it out. Alan wrote that was the only time he feared we could catch him.

His final murder made him the happiest. He killed Diane Warren using superglue. After he knocked me out with the Taser, he wrapped her body in a tarp and dropped it out the same window I had looked out of when I first walked into the room. He boarded the plane and paid the pilots to fly to Chile, telling them it was at Diane's request. He paid them to keep the plane there for the next six months.

He disembarked from the plane before it flew away and waited until we left before he removed her body. He buried her in the basement next to Sullivan.

He knew what the Russians would do to him, but they didn't start the fire. He did. Before the Russians arrived, he buried packets of accelerant with each body in the basement. Included in the packets were special chemicals he'd invented that would turn the bodies to mush making them impossible to be tested for DNA.

The bodies would be totally destroyed beyond all recognition by the fire. When the Russians walked in, he triggered a timer. They killed him and left.

When the timer went off, Alan burned down David and Rick's home. His body would be found in what remained of the house, but he didn't care because he had no DNA in any file in the United States and no one would know it was him.

The police report would say an unknown man, possible a homeless person seeking shelter in the partially constructed house, might have started the fire.

Alan covered all his bases.

148

Part of the story Alan had given me was missing, but I had already figured out on my own. He did one other thing when he found out he had Alzheimer's. He came out of the closet. It must have been scary for him at first, until he realized David and Rick would keep Marcia from finding out.

That was why he bought a condo close to The Max. He could sneak out at night and ride his bicycle down there. On bad weather days he took an Uber. He changed clothes and transformed into Genieva. If he had a visitor over to his condo, no one would find out.

In a way, despite the tragic aspects of the events, this was a terrific love story. Alan kept his other life secret from Marcia so her high society friends wouldn't find out about him and she wouldn't be humiliated. He willingly gave up his life to protect her from the Russians.

I closed the folder with Alan's "what if" question buzzing around in my brain. What would I do if I still had all my marbles but I knew for certain that I had Alzheimer's and there was no cure? What would I do?

What would anyone do?

Carter was still up when I returned home. "Did you figure it out?" he asked.

"Some of it," I said, "but I had help with the rest. But I have to confess something to you. I told you there was no living person in Zhukov's office when I arrived for the interview. What I left out was that he had been killed by a single gunshot wound to his forehead."

Carter jumped up. "What?! Why wasn't it reported?"

I held up my hand. "Relax and let me explain."

He sat down and I did.

"Who killed Zhukov?" he asked.

"Dr. Alan Peebler."

"Wow. Can you prove it?"

"Maybe, but I'm not sure I want to."

"A problem with your source?"

"He is the only one, and he has disappeared."

"Where is Zhukov's body?"

"I know where it is, but all it'll prove is that he's dead."

He stood up and hugged me.

"I know how much you wanted to write this article," he said. I'm so sorry. You did your best, but without Dr. Peebler as a source, you don't have a story."

His hug tightened.

"And next time, please tell me the whole truth about your investigations."

I wanted to say that in the future I would tell him the whole truth, but will there even be any more stories? How important is writing a front page story after being there when Alan was killed by angry Russians?

149

Friday morning, Janet and Frankie sat across from me at Starbucks. He drank a triple espresso. I had my usual green iced tea. She had a Venti black coffee. Laughing Larry sat in the corner with four other men about his retirement age. Larry is a regular who bellows out an annoying laugh in response to anything. As they talked, he bellowed so loudly it was hard for us to carry on a conversation.

"A good story," Janet said, after I finished telling them about Alan.

"Too bad you can't write it," Frankie said. "If the cops ever find out about the dude with the missing fingers and Diane Warren being buried side-by-side in that basement, it might be a problem because you would be the primo suspect for offing both of them."

"Thank God Alan took care of all that DNA, or I might be the detective who slaps the cuffs on you," she said.

"You'll need a new story, Tina," he said. "Any ideas?"

"Honestly, last night when I told Carter what happened, I was ready to hang it up and stop writing. But just now after I told you what happened to Alan, I realized I'll never stop. It's in my DNA."

From *forgotten-BOOM!* due out in the spring of 2020

1

"The last name on the Vietnam Veterans Memorial Wall is Second Lieutenant Richard Vandergeer," Greg Garland said.

It was Saturday afternoon. My husband, Carter Thomas, was at home with our two daughters, Kerry and Macy. Garland and I sat at a back table in our neighborhood Starbucks. The strong and familiar aroma of brewing coffee competed with Garland's Old Spice aftershave. Like many people his age, he'd liberally applied the classic scent, too much so in my opinion.

His lanky six five frame was folded into one of the wood chairs. I turned on my cell phone and put it on the table. As a former investigative journalist, I would record what he was going to tell me in case I decided to work on this new story.

"Six months ago I was in D.C. for a legal seminar," he continued. "On the last night, after a few too many after-dinner drinks, I decided to make my first visit to the Vietnam Memorial. I stumbled around in a downpour checking out the sections from my time in-country with the Air Force in 1975. I discovered Vandergeer's name at the bottom of Panel 01W."

I sipped on an unsweetened Grande green iced tea. Garland had a Venti black coffee in front of him, but he wasn't drinking it.

"At the time, his name didn't mean anything to me but it kept bugging me. At the hotel, I went online and did a background check on him."

"Ha, ha, ha, ha, ha," Laughing Larry Albert bellowed out. He sat with a group of four retired male friends in the corner opposite from where we were. The annoying noise made it difficult for me to concentrate on what Greg said as he told me the story of the *Mayaguez* attack, which happened in 1975 in the Gulf of Siam shortly after the fall of Saigon.

"I discovered that Vandergeer had been listed as killed in action. His remains were recovered in 2000 and buried the same year in Arlington, which is why he's the last name on the wall."

I tapped my fingers on the tabletop. "Why is this so important to you now after all this time?"

"I left Vietnam the day before the incident. Shortly after that, I was discharged from the Air Force. Until that night six months ago, I didn't know Vandergeer was dead."

I waited.

He stared at the tabletop. "It was my battle plan and orders that resulted in him being killed."

~

Author's Note

In my first book, *boom-BOOM!*, I included the article: "Lonely Stay-at-Home Mothers Are Now Wooing Each Other." It was written by my daughter Christina Duff, now Tina Duff Taylor, and was the background story for that book and the Hamlin Park Irregulars series.

My son-in-law, Jeffrey Taylor (Carter in all the books), also penned a book, *The Pru-Bache Murder,* which had a strong background influence on *brainy-BOOM!*

Here is a portion of a review of his book from the *Chicago Tribune.* I think you will see why it had a major impact on my book:

Anyone who has been taken in by a financial markets hustler will feel a reflexive jolt of fear and loathing on reading Jeffrey Taylor's tale of a high-pressure stockbroker who blazed briefly and then was snuffed out by one of his victimized clients.

Some might even feel that the retribution exacted, which included hacking the stockbroker's body apart and strewing the pieces about the landscape, was all too richly deserved.

The story of the broker, Michael Prozumenshikov, goes beyond the life and grim death of a lone con artist. It also delves into the changes in the business culture of brokerages in the 1980s and the sociology of the Russian Jewish immigrant community in America.

Even more, it offers a wealth of detail on how investors can get dragged into ventures beyond their means or control, and it is especially perceptive about the psychology of one investor whose losses tipped him over the edge.

Prozumenshikov was a Russian immigrant fascinated by American capitalism. He became a broker in the early 1980s and worked for Minneapolis-area offices of Merrill Lynch, Drexel Burnham Lambert and Prudential-Bache (now Prudential Securities.)

He grew up in the harsh, deprived environment of Leningrad in the 1950s and 1960s, living in a decaying apartment where 31 residents cohabited in space meant for one family.

His father was a factory supervisor. Prozumenshikov, showed athletic prowess in throwing the hammer and was helped by his sports connections in getting into a prestigious dental school and then attaining a prized place in a Leningrad clinic despite doing poorly in his studies.

He left the Soviet Union during a wave of Jewish immigration in the 1970s and went to Minneapolis, where a colony of Russian Jews had begun to settle. Despite dogged efforts, he failed his U.S. dental exams and was floundering until a stockbroker friend in the immigrant community helped him to learn the business and get a job.

He quickly showed prodigious talent, absorbing information and pursuing clients inexhaustibly. He also showed a ruthless ambition, greed for wealth and utter disdain for rules and ethics.

Acknowledgements

Does art imitate life? With the Marcia and Alan characters in this book, it does. Sadly, they are gone now, but their unique personalities and quirky ways will never be forgotten.

I could never begin to conceive of scenes like Alan standing on his head the first time I met him. Or the roll of toilet paper on his belt to solve his dripping nose problem. They actually happened.

And Marcia? Everything I wrote about her is based on her life, and what a life it was!

We miss them both.

But David Scott and Rick Carey are still with us! They have been kind enough to allow me to include them as characters in my books. I love writing about them, and I think it shows. I love you guys and hope you are with us for a long, long time.

My core production group has pretty much remained the same for all my books. Nancy Cohen is my trusted editor, and I doubt I could get any of my books printed without her fabulous help.

Ana Magno continues to amaze me. I suggest the concept of the cover to her in an email and, in short order, she has it done.

Abby Anderson does my Facebook entries, and Jen Maher is my website guru. Thanks to both of you.

Joy Larsen continues to be the voice of the first three books in the Hamlin Park Irregulars series, which are now on Audible (www.Amazon.com). She is the best.

A special shout-out to my daughter, Tina, who is the model for the protagonist Tina in all the books. As always, she read the almost-finished version of this book, and I finally got her: this time, she didn't figure out who the killer was.

And thanks to Tina's husband, Jeff, and their kids and our grandkids, Kerry, 20, Macy, 18, and Nick, 16, and their dog, Ruby.

Thanks to my son, James E. Duff, and his wife, Julia. They are in the final stages of finishing their next feature movie, *Sugaring Season*. Look for it.

To Brittany Haynie (Brittany Simon in the books) and her husband (and my golfing partner), Luke, and their son, Jetter, who will be three in December, and their dog, Dexter.

And to Mo, who continues to be Denny Crane to my Alan Shore and the reason I'm late coming home from the office.

And finally, to my wife Mindy. She is always there for me, except when she is doing one of her many other projects: check out AllCore360 to see her latest one. The concept works, and look for it if there is one in your area.

I can't forget to mention Bentley, our Bichon Frisé. He is my partner on our nightly walks as I try to help him lose the pounds we've added during our weekend trips to Starbucks where he "orders" a Puppaccino.

I enjoyed writing the next book, *forgotten-BOOM!* (book five in the Hamlin Park Irregulars series, which is scheduled to be published in spring 2020), because it deals with the forgotten Vietnam War. I was in the Air Force during that time (1973-75), stationed in San Antonio, Texas, at Wilford Hall USAF Medical Center.

The next book after that, *love-BOOM!*, will feature Tina's brother, Jimmy Edwards, a pitcher for the San Diego Padres. It is Mindy's favorite of all the books and was the first book I wrote.

I continue to have a full-time ENT practice in Omaha, along with my other non-nosepicker activities of being a husband, father, grandfather, magician for birthday parties, exercise nut, and golfer. Speaking of which, look for Rotary Swing Golf and instructor Chuck Quinton (rotaryswing.com) if you want to improve your golf game. It really helped me.

And finally, thank you for joining Tina and her friends for more Irregular adventures. As always, if you want to discuss this book, or anything about the books in the Hamlin Park Irregulars series, please contact me at hamlinparkirregulars@gmail.com or on my website: wallyduff.com or hamlinparkirregulars.com. You can also check out Tina's neighborhood on YouTube: boom-BOOM! by Dr. Wally Duff, the video book trailer.